Murder
on a
Stick

Murder
on a
Stick

THE THIRD PETE CULNANE MYSTERY

S.L. SMITH

SIGHTLINE PRESS

Alachua, Florida

SIGHTLINE PRESS

Sightline Press,
Alachua, Florida, 32615
www.sightlinepress.com

ISBN 978-0-9964640-7-9

For my sisters, Deb and Pam, and my brother, Dale. The road hasn't always been smooth, but I'd be hard pressed to find a better group to travel alongside.

ONE

"Can't believe we snagged this much loot. Unfortunately, now I regret it. I'm about to collapse. I can't make it all the way to the car. Let's stop here, Debbie. I only need a minute or two. I've got to put this stuff down. My arms are breaking." Cynthia could have saved the energy required to announce that. Her grimace, the cords standing out on her neck, her shuffling gate, and her labored breathing painted a clear picture. Obviously, the bags were too much for Debbie's friend.

"I know, Cynthia. My arms are breaking, too, but we can't stop. We have to hurry. Can't let those creeps catch up. What if they see us?"

Debbie thought about speeding the pace by carrying one of Cynthia's bags. Survival instincts took over, and she abandoned the idea. Like her friend, Debbie suffered under the weight of her load. She, however, suffered in silence. The bags weren't really that heavy, were they? She was fine last year. Surely the weight was comparable to last year. *Am I going downhill that fast? I'm only sixty-six. It has to be the heat. Right?*

After hearing the forecast last night, she'd conferred with Cynthia. Both wore baggy, pastel, cotton shorts. Despite self-consciousness about their middle-aged upper arms, they topped it off with tank tops. Cynthia's snow-white hair was too short to be a problem. To avoid the discomfort added by hair on her neck, Debbie tied her gray sprinkled chestnut hair in a top knot. Despite these efforts, both felt taxed by the heat—and the loads they carried.

True to form, Debbie's mother took advantage of this opportunity, invading her daughter's thoughts. *It's your own fault, Debbie. Do you know how to spell greed?*

That's grossly unfair! Debbie countered, squaring off in a nonverbal skirmish with her mother, her long-deceased mother—the woman who relished these face-offs. Besides, Debbie didn't have a corner on the market. Lots of people took every State Fair freebie they could get their hands on. The items ran the gamut, from shirts to pens, from key chain flashlights to Post-it notes, from reusable bags to backpacks, from water bottles to salad holders, from state maps to sunglasses. Almost every advertising specialty known to man was handed out at the fair. But, unlike many fair goers, Debbie didn't grab everything in sight. *I discriminated, didn't I?*

Anyway, the stuff was right there, begging to be taken. She couldn't resist. For nearly thirteen hours, she'd rarely resisted. Debbie had a friend who did this all twelve days of the fair every single year. Once a year was enough for her.

It had been a long day. Exhausted, she couldn't wait for it to end, to reach the car, to sit down. If they escaped detection by the unappealing men who'd glommed onto them, who ignored all polite hints, who wouldn't be brushed off, in a few minutes it would all be behind her. She'd relax and catch her breath in air-conditioned comfort. Or so she thought.

A few minutes before eight on this warm summer evening, the sun flirted with the western horizon. For most of the day, the cloud-free sky permitted the sun to hammer down mercilessly on those choosing or forced to be outside. Now, with the sun too low to continue the beating, thin swatches of white began forming in the western sky, above the trees and the Minneapolis skyline. Splashes of pink and a rosy-orange looked like they were added by a master of watercolor, creating a photo op for anyone intent on documenting their life in digital or print media.

Neither Debbie nor Cynthia fit in that group of picture-takers, and those sorts of things factored into their compatibility. Even so, either captured by the beauty or searching for any reason to pause, Cynthia poked Debbie with an elbow, tilted her head to the right, and said, "Oh, look. Isn't it gorgeous?"

Debbie glanced over her left shoulder, before stopping alongside her friend. "Wow, it is. Now c'mon. Gotta hurry. I know they're back there. They've got to be closing in on us. We're moving too slow."

After redistributing her load, Debbie began digging for her keys. "I hate this purse!" she announced. "Everything winds up at the bottom. It's impossible to find anything in here."

"No problem. Your car's right there." Cynthia indicated the location with a thrust of her chin. "We'll find them when we get there. If necessary, you can empty your purse on the . . ."

Debbie's ear-piercing scream drowned out the rest of Cynthia's words.

Cynthia jumped, dropped her load, grabbed Debbie's arm, and eliminated the space separating them. "What? What?" she gasped, louder than intended. In all the years she'd known Debbie, she'd never heard her scream, much less a tooth-rattling scream like that one. The guys they'd tried so hard to evade wouldn't elicit a scream like that, would they?

Debbie didn't answer. She stood frozen, horrified. She stared open-mouthed past the SUV parked on the passenger side of her car.

Cynthia stepped around Debbie, compelled to see what created that reaction from her unflappable friend.

A slender woman sat on the ground with her long legs tangled in front of her, propped up against the passenger door of Debbie's car. Her silver hair hung forward. Even so, it was too short to hide her hollowed cheeks and pointed nose. *That poor woman is as far past her prime as I am,* Debbie thought. *That could be me . . . dead!*

The woman's eyes were closed. Her mouth was pinched in a tight line. A large circle of blood covered the center of her loose-fitting, bright pink shirt.

Eyes wide and hands over her mouth, Cynthia backed away from Debbie and Debbie's car, adding a cushion to the distance between her and the woman on the ground.

Moving in the opposite direction, Debbie hurried toward the fallen woman, and hunched over her. "Are you okay? Can you hear me?" She reached out, touching the woman's cheek. It felt warm. That didn't necessarily mean anything. The air temperature was still in the nineties.

"Everything okay?" a deep voice called. Based on the way the voice carried, the person asking was located somewhere far across the parking lot.

Before Debbie or Cynthia could answer, a man ran up and pushed between Debbie and the collapsed woman. He bent over the woman and touched her neck. Then, without a word, he stood and took off running.

The collapsed woman provided no discernible reaction to Debbie's words or touch, or the actions of the strange intruder.

"What was that about?" Cynthia asked.

"Haven't the foggiest."

A moment later, two teenage girls ran to Cynthia's side. "Heard you scream," one of them said. Following Cynthia's gaze, they both saw Debbie and the reason for the commotion. Like Cynthia, they kept their distance.

A crowd formed at an amazing rate. Cynthia wondered where they all came from. Minutes ago, it seemed there were few people in the parking lot. "What should we do, Debbie?" she asked.

A woman standing near her said, "I'm calling 911."

Placing a hand flat on the back door of her Ford Fusion, Debbie steadied herself. She worried that the people closing in on her would knock her into the injured woman. Once braced, she cautiously reached out the other hand to feel for a pulse on the woman's neck.

Cynthia heard the woman who called 911 describe the scene. She told the operator that the woman's chin rested on her chest, and she mentioned the blood on the woman's shirt. "The 911 operator wants to know if she's alive," the woman said.

"I felt a pulse near her jugular. It seems pretty weak. Could be because it's hard to get to the right area. I don't want to take a chance on moving her head. Tell the operator she needs help, *now*!"

"Help's on the way," the woman said. "Take a deep breath, ma'am. You look like you're going to pass out."

"I need air, and so does this poor woman," Debbie told the people who stood uncomfortably close to her and the crumpled woman. The crowd had no appreciation for her personal space—or anyone else's. "Can someone please get these people to back up?" she asked.

The people closest to her attempted to comply. It seemed like a losing battle. As hard as they worked to push the crowd back, people in the back pushed to get a better look.

"The operator said we need to direct the fire department rigs to our location," the woman speaking with 911 said. "She said she'll keep me on the phone."

Afraid of passing out, Debbie sank to the tarred surface. She didn't allow the absence of a clean surface to dissuade her.

Their link to 911 continued talking.

Debbie heard little of what she said.

Confident that unconscious people hear what's happening around them, she attempted to reassure the collapsed woman. At the same time, she concentrated on staying calm, on taking deep breaths, on remaining conscious.

With hands clasped, Cynthia observed nervously from the sidelines. She chewed on her lower lip, while apprehensively scanning the building crowd.

Suddenly, the rise and fall of distant sirens silenced the spectators.

Stepping up in an effort to take charge, Debbie called out, "Can someone go to the entrance and direct them over here?"

Emerging from her distraction, Cynthia shouted, "Let me!" It came instantaneously, and far louder than intended. Face reddening, she pushed her way through the crowd, and wove her way to the entrance.

The parking lot covered more than an acre, and Debbie's car stood far down an aisle that ran parallel with Como Avenue. Cynthia had the wherewithal to count the rows as she ran to meet the emergency responders.

The blaring sirens halted mid-wail as the Advanced Life Support paramedic unit arrived at the parking lot entrance.

Cynthia waved frantically, trying to get the driver's attention.

Apparently he spotted her, and understood her actions—or the look on her face. He stopped, and lowered the window.

Before he could say anything, Cynthia pointed, "Fifth row past the motorcycles, right side. Lots of people. Can't miss the crowd."

Standing in the shadow of the ALS unit, she shuddered when she saw the two men she and Debbie spent the last few hours struggling to dump. The corners of her mouth turned up briefly, when the two men kept walking. Anxiety returned when she realized it might be a ploy. She found a modicum of security by staying within arm's length of the ALS unit.

The unit served as a powerful magnet, pulling in numerous followers along the way. Occasionally, the driver resorted to siren bleeps to move those impeding his progress.

"Rubbernecks," Cynthia muttered, while checking continuously for the two crazies. Failing to see them, she experienced both relief and surprise. It seemed they were the only two people not sucked in by the opportunity to view someone else's ill fortune. *Why not? Was this a trap?*

The driver of the ALS unit jockeyed into position in front of Deb's car.

Meanwhile, unwilling to permit the crowd to delay her response, the paramedic jumped out and ran to Debbie and the victim.

A minute later, the fire engine shadowing the paramedic unit pulled in behind it.

As the throng continued to grow and press in, it created a second challenge for the responders.

The four firefighters arriving in the fire engine worked to contain the crowd, and string crime scene tape. The tape helped establish a perimeter, protecting what appeared to be a crime scene. But the tape didn't dissuade some people from testing the limits of that boundary.

The EMT from the paramedic unit moved in close, talked to the victim and patted her face, attempting to elicit a response.

Simultaneously, his paramedic partner checked vital signs and put an oxygen mask over the woman's nose and mouth. Then, in order to check the source of the blood, she cut open the victim's shirt. Pulling the material aside, she glimpsed the ragged end of a stick. It protruded from the victim's abdomen. "Does that look like what I think it is?" she asked the EMT.

"Do you mean the sticks used by lots of food booths?"

"Yeah, wow. That's crazy," she whispered.

Blood covered the woman's abdomen, and leaked slowly from the wound.

In an effort to coagulate the blood and stem the bleeding, the paramedic applied TraumaDex powder. Then she used pads and tape to stabilize the position of the stick. While doing this, she told the EMT, "She's bleeding internally. Her abdomen's rigid. An artery may have been breeched. Thankfully, whoever did this didn't pull out the stick. It seems to be doing a decent job of plugging the hole. Otherwise, she could have bled out before we arrived. Too bad she's wearing hip riders. If her belt was higher, it might have blocked the stick."

"Yeah, but what was to stop her attacker from a second attempt?" the EMT asked.

"How about a broken stick, if the stick connected with her belt buckle?"

Fearing her location hampered their efforts, Debbie backed away slowly, head down. She mistakenly assumed the crime scene tape would tell her when she reached the crowd of observers. It didn't happen. She bumped into a man pressed up against the tape.

He grunted and frowned. He didn't relinquish an inch of space.

"I'll let you out here," the man next to him said, lifting the tape about a foot, and making room for her.

Looking around, Debbie figured there had to be at least eighty people crowded in a lopsided circle around the tape barrier. Her car and the SUV the collapsed woman faced were both inside that circle, and Debbie noticed people hanging all over her car. The dirty surface didn't deter them. That surprised her. There was a steady hum of conversation, almost everyone talking in hushed tones.

While Debbie stood, assessing the scene, a four-wheel all-terrain vehicle arrived. The St. Paul Fire Department used these rigs to provide emergency medical services at the fair.

Cynthia recognized the two men on it. She and Debbie had spoken with them this afternoon. She'd asked about firefighters using ATVs, and their role at the fair.

The men said they carried a lot of bottled water today. They were prepared to assist anyone overcome by the predicted heat. They'd explained that the firefighters on the ATVs learned of problems by constantly scanning both the State Fair 911 channel, and the fire channel.

That must be how they heard about it, Cynthia thought.

The driver parked alongside the fire engine, and the two men hurried to the other responders. While the firefighters from the ATV helped with crowd control, some members of the fire engine crew got a bodyboard out of the paramedic unit. Parked cars impeded their efforts, but they positioned it as close as possible to the victim.

More sirens preceded the arrival of three St. Paul squad cars. The officers hurried to the scene. One officer snapped photos of everything in the area. Another spoke with the crowd. The sergeant conferred with the EMT and the paramedic.

Debbie couldn't hear anything they said, but she saw the sergeant nod repeatedly and glance at her.

Then in a swift, smooth motion, the victim was placed on the bodyboard and loaded into the paramedic unit. The crew got in, and the sergeant instructed a uniformed officer to ride along in case the victim regained consciousness en route to the hospital.

As the paramedic unit made its way through the crowd, the driver used a series of siren bleeps to open a path.

Using outstretched arms, the firefighters from the ATV assisted. They ushered bystanders out of the way, applying force when needed. It was imperative. As little as a second or two could separate life from death.

TWO

While the sergeant contacted the senior commander of Robbery and Homicide, the other officer instructed the crowd. "Everyone, stay put," he said. "We want to speak with each of you."

After concluding her call, the sergeant asked anyone who witnessed the attack to raise a hand.

Not one hand went up.

"Okay, anyone who saw anything suspicious, anything that could aid our investigation in any way at all, please raise your hand."

Debbie, Cynthia, and three men raised a hand.

"No one else?" The sergeant scanned the crowd, and waited for anyone slow to react. After several seconds with no additional response, she continued, "Okay. The five of you, move to my left. The rest of you, please back up a few steps and wait. We'll get to you shortly."

The sergeant conferred with Debbie and Cynthia.

The other officer talked to the three men.

Debbie wondered about those men. The first time she saw them was after they raised their hands.

The sergeant asked to see Debbie's and Cynthia's IDs, obtained their phone numbers, and made notes. Then she asked for a complete description of what happened.

They had little to offer. Neither saw anyone in the vicinity as they approached Debbie's car.

"I'm afraid I wasn't paying much attention," Debbie admitted. "It never occurred to me that it would be important. I would have noticed someone hanging around my car, except I parked next to an SUV. I couldn't see my car, until we were almost all of the way to it. It would have been easy for someone to crouch down and sneak away as we approached. It could have happened before we reached the parking lot. I guess it might even have happened while we were checking out the sunset. Only, wouldn't she scream? I didn't hear a scream. Shouldn't someone have heard her?"

"I agree with everything Debbie told you," Cynthia said. "When I saw the woman, her eyes were closed. Because of all the blood and the way she slumped against Debbie's car, I thought she was dead. I thought maybe someone shot her."

"Did you hear gunshots?" the sergeant asked.

"I'm not really sure how they sound, but I don't think so. I suppose the idling busses could have drowned out the sound." Cynthia pointed to the row of busses lined up along the eastern edge of the parking lot.

"Did you hear raised voices or anyone arguing?"

The friends shook their heads.

"Did you see anyone running from the general vicinity of your car, either when you were close or from a distance?"

"No," Debbie said.

"Me neither," Cynthia said.

"But something weird happened, after we found her." Debbie mentioned the man who pushed her aside to check out the collapsed woman. "He ran away without saying a word or doing anything to help," she added.

"In which direction did he run?"

"I don't know." Debbie shrugged. "I was still crouched next to the woman. I couldn't see around the cars."

"He started out in the direction of Como, but I didn't pay any attention after that," Cynthia said. "Do you think he did it? If he did, would he be crazy enough to come back after we arrived?"

"Stranger things have happened," the sergeant said. "Describe him."

"He was about six feet tall, wore faded jeans and a bright-yellow T-shirt," Cynthia said. "He had brown hair and wore wraparound sunglasses."

"Were we looking at the same guy, Cynthia? I don't think he was that tall—maybe five-nine. Wasn't his shirt a bright orange, and his hair dishwater blond? I don't remember the sunglasses, but I was more interested in the injured woman than him. Is she going to make it?"

"Don't know. They're doing everything possible."

"Can we go now?" Debbie asked. It was pitch dark. She planned on being home by now. She had to work tomorrow.

"Which car is yours?"

"That one," Debbie said, pointing at the Ford Fusion inside the crime scene tape.

"You can go, but not in that car. It has to remain here until the scene is cleared.

"When will that be?" Debbie moaned.

"Can't say for sure. Possibly not until sometime tomorrow."

"How are we going to get home? I really need to get home. This is very upsetting. I need to sit down or lie down now, not tomorrow."

"Got a friend you can call?" the sergeant asked.

"Not really."

"There's no one?"

"Well, yes, but . . ."

"Take my word for it. It's your fastest way out of here. If you need to sit down, you can sit in the back of my squad." The sergeant pointed to it. "Make sure you leave the door open. Otherwise, you'll be stuck there until I return."

Debbie and Cynthia walked to the car she indicated, and sank gratefully onto the backseat.

"I'll call Gerald," Debbie said.

"Before you do, Debbie, I have to tell you something. The two men who wouldn't leave us alone passed me while I was giving directions to the ambulance driver. Debbie, they acted like I wasn't there. I've been looking all around, trying to see if they're still lurking. I don't think so. Even so, I'm glad Gerald is taking us home. They won't follow us if we're riding with a man, will they?"

"I'm not sure. I'll ask Gerald to walk each of us to our door and wait until we get inside. I wish I hadn't been so friendly when they started talking to us. Who knew they'd turn out to be such creeps?"

Debbie called her brother's cell. The call went to voicemail. She groaned and was leaving a message, when her phone beeped. The screen displayed her brother's name. Gratefully, she pressed the talk button.

"What's up, sis?"

"It's a long story, and I don't have enough time or energy to tell you right now. Can you pick up Cynthia and me at the State Fair? We're south of the fairgrounds, in the east Como parking lot."

"Ouch, bad timing."

"Please, Gerald. It's really important."

"Okay, I'll make a few calls. Should be there in about twenty minutes, depending on the traffic. I'll let you know when I'm close. Then we'll arrange a meeting place."

"Thanks. You're a life saver."

"Hang in there, sis."

Debbie hung up, tilted her head back, and blew out a long, slow breath.

In a New York minute, her head flew forward so fast it almost collided with the front seat. *Who knew what other heads had rested there*, she'd realized.

What a lousy way to wrap up a day at the fair, she thought.

Think you've got problems? Her mother was back. *Do you ever think of anyone but yourself? How would you like to be the poor woman you discovered?*

THREE

"What's your call, Grandma? Higher? Lower? Further to the right or left?" Pete Culnane referred to the location of the painting he held. For the last six days, he'd spent most of his off-duty, waking hours helping his grandmother get settled in her new apartment. Prior to the move, she lived in the house she and Pete's grandfather bought before he was born.

"Oh, hang on, Grandma. I've got a call."

Pete knew the nature of the call, the moment he glimpsed the display on his cell phone. He felt relieved it didn't come before he'd finished unpacking the boxes.

"What's up, Commander?"

Pete's boss, Senior Commander Lincoln, told Pete about the assault in the east Como parking lot. "As soon as I call Martin, I'll contact the Bureau of Criminal Apprehension to handle the crime scene," Lincoln added. "We're stretched pretty thin. I discussed it with the chief. He agrees it's a good idea."

After disconnecting, Pete turned to his grandmother and smiled apologetically. "Sorry, Grandma. I'm afraid that painting has to wait.

I've got to go. Got a case."

"Of course, Pete. I understand. Thanks for all your help. What would I do without you? You unpacked those boxes in record time. I'm so glad I won't have to look at them anymore. We can hang the pictures anytime. You'll be careful, won't you?"

"Sure will. I have pictures to hang." Pete smiled.

He gave his grandmother a gentle hug and kissed her before sprinting to his car. He was anxious to reach the crime scene, and he knew the State Fair traffic on Snelling would be mostly stop and an occasional go.

Any time but during the State Fair, the five-and-a-half-mile trip from his grandmother's Highland Park apartment to the Como parking lot took maybe fifteen minutes. After considering the alternatives, Pete decided to gamble on Hamline Avenue north to Pierce Butler, and Pierce Butler west to Snelling. He'd still deal with almost a mile on Snelling, but the time on Hamline and Butler should significantly shorten the trip.

Pete wished he had his unmarked car. The lights and sirens would have helped. He wondered how Martin was attacking the trip.

During the twenty-six-minute drive, Pete tapped nervously on the steering wheel and thought about a woman getting stabbed in the Como parking lot. It had to be a crime of passion, didn't it? Why else would someone choose a place and time like that?

* * *

Detective Sergeant Martin Tierney had his six-week-old daughter in his left arm and a bottle in his right hand when Commander Lincoln called.

For the first few weeks after they brought his daughter home from the hospital, Martin rarely helped with feedings. Back then, he stepped up mostly on weekends. No more. Now, he took care of the middle-of-the-night bottles and pacing almost as often as his wife. Necessity dictated the change. Initially, he thought the sleep interruptions explained Michelle's perpetual state of exhaustion. Not anymore.

"Hey, buddy, want to take over?" Martin asked his son Marty.

Marty sat across the room, slaving away on a LEGO concoction of his own creation.

"Heck yes, Dad!"

A few days ago, Martin noticed his son hanging unusually close whenever he was home. He wondered if it was a reaction to the distance Michelle seemed to be putting between herself and all of them. He'd planned to talk to Marty tonight when he tucked him in bed. Now that couldn't happen. He regretted not doing it earlier.

Marty plopped down on the couch alongside his dad, and Martin carefully transferred his daughter. Then Martin kissed Olivia's forehead, tousled his son's hair, and said, "See you later, sport. Don't forget to burp her."

Marty rolled his eyes. "I know, Dad. It's not like it's my first time."

This evening, getting to the fairgrounds wasn't the only thing on Martin's mind. His brain bounced back and forth between the trip and his wife. Michelle wasn't herself these days, and not knowing what was wrong weighed heavily on him. All efforts to get her to make a doctor appointment fell on deaf ears.

He didn't understand her reluctance. What was she keeping from him? At first he thought it was postpartum depression. Not any more. He feared it was even more serious than that. Now he had a new case that would keep him away from home. If anyone could speed the process, it was Pete Culnane. For the sake of his family, Martin hoped Pete would work his magic once again.

Approaching the east Como parking lot, Martin spotted the fire engine. Questions about the incident took over, displacing thoughts of Michelle. *What happened? Were there witnesses? Had to be, right? Why here? During the fair? Crazy! Weapon used? Was the victim alive when found? Did he or she share any information? Did he or she know the attacker?*

He glimpsed Pete standing near two squads and conferring with a couple of uniformed officers. That distracted Martin a second time. It occurred to him that the music from tonight's grandstand show might make it difficult to converse in hushed tones.

After parking alongside the fire engine, he joined Pete in time to hear the sergeant describe the victim's location, position, and injury.

Rubbing his upper lip with an index finger, Pete said, "Can't be premeditated. Agree?"

"Why?" Martin asked.

"Would a stick that by all indications came from one of the State Fair food booths be your weapon of choice?"

"Not likely. I'm surprised it was sharp enough."

"Good point, Martin."

"Pun intended?" Martin smiled.

"Ahh, no. But, if the person wielding it sharpened it, I retract the comment about it not being premeditated."

"I have the victim's purse," the sergeant said. "When I arrived, she still had the strap grasped tightly in her left hand. Robbery can't be the motive. Her billfold's inside, and there's eighty-seven dollars in cash, along with a half-dozen credit cards. Her name is Virginia Green. She lives in Highland Park. Her cell phone is in the purse. These keys were on the ground next to her right leg." The sergeant extended a gloved hand, holding a key ring. They're for that black Honda Pilot." She pointed at the SUV. "She collapsed facing it. Almost made it to her car before it happened. Might have made all the difference." She shook her head.

Pete and Martin made notes, while the sergeant brought them up to speed.

Then she motioned to the two women who still occupied the backseat of her squad. She explained who they were and mentioned the information they'd shared.

The second officer told Pete and Martin about the three men he interviewed. "As they entered the parking lot, all three saw a man stand up on the far side of that Pilot," he said, pointing, "and run in their direction. All three thought he looked panicky as he ran past them. One of them turned and saw the man run to the Como entrance to the fairgrounds. Unfortunately, their descriptions of that man ran the gamut. His shirt was described as yellow, gold, and orange. Two said it had a collar; one said it didn't. Hair color was two browns and a black. One said he wore a baseball cap. On the plus side, all three thought he was average height and build."

"He's probably the man I told you about," the sergeant said. "The guy who pushed aside one of the women who found the victim. He felt the victim's neck, supposedly for a pulse."

"We also interviewed all the people sucked in by the commotion," the sergeant continued. "Asked each of them if they saw anything that appeared relevant, and if anyone in the crowd seemed suspicious. The answer to both questions was a unanimous no. I watched each face as I asked the questions, looking for any indication the person was lying. Nothing."

"Ditto," the other officer said. "Of course a sociopath wouldn't give any indications."

Despite all the cameras the St. Paul PD acquired in preparation for the 2008 Republican National Convention, not one monitored the east Como parking lot. That wasn't surprising. Aside from the twelve-day run of the State Fair, the fairgrounds and this parking lot were used only for special events. All things considered, that totaled maybe forty days each year. Had this lot been monitored, the footage might have been invaluable.

While speaking with the uniformed officers, Pete saw the white motor home prominently displaying the Bureau of Criminal Apprehension (BCA) Crime Scene Team markings. The people onboard would handle the crime scene investigation.

Pete and Martin greeted the BCA agents and scientists, and hooked up with Jimmy Porter, the person assigned as their liaison.

"Caught the assignment, huh?" Porter said. "Guess that means the two of you drew the short stick."

"Obviously you didn't." Pete smiled. "How are Jackie and the kids, Jimmy?"

"Doin' well. The kids are ready to get back to school. For the last few weeks, Jackie's been counting the seconds 'til they do. Labor Day is Monday. Four-and-a-half days to go. "

Porter looked at Pete's faded jeans and polo shirt and asked, "Is this casual Thursday night? Can't say I've ever seen you dressed that way. You make him look like a real piker, Martin."

"I'd loan you my tie, Pete, but it clashes with your socks." Martin grinned. This had to be the first time he was dressed better than Pete.

While the other members of the Crime Scene Team set up auxiliary lighting and prepared to begin their investigation, Porter accompanied Pete and Martin to the sergeant's squad. He and Martin were almost running as they tried to keep up with Pete's long, brisk stride.

Moving close to the car, Pete squatted, elbows on knees, so he could see both women. "I understand you've been here all day," he said. "This is quite a way to wrap it up, huh?"

"You have no idea," Debbie sighed. "I'm exhausted."

Pete nodded, "I understand you found the victim propped up against your car."

"Yes. It was awful!" Debbie said.

"Did you start looking for or toward your car as soon as you reached the parking lot?" Pete asked.

"Not really. I knew where I'd parked. Didn't have to scan frantically to find it. Lucky thing. That SUV," Debbie turned in the seat and pointed at it, "blocked my view of my car until just before I got to it. That's when I saw the woman."

"How about you?" Pete looked at Cynthia.

"I was struggling with all the stuff I had to carry. I didn't pay much attention to the parking lot. Do you think it happened while we were nearby?"

"Don't know, at least not yet," Pete said. "Try reconstructing your trip through the parking lot. Can you think of anything? Anyone look nervous or suspicious? Anything at all?"

"No. I've tried. Really I have." Debbie frowned.

"Me neither," Cynthia said.

"The woman you found, did you see her while at the fair?" Pete asked.

"I don't remember seeing her," Debbie said.

Cynthia shook her head. "We passed a lot of people today, and nothing about her stands out. She isn't exceedingly tall or tiny. Her clothes resembled the stuff everyone is wearing. I mean, she wasn't wearing a snowmobile suit, and she didn't wear a hat with an umbrella attached. Don't get me wrong. What I mean is, I could have passed her a dozen times, and never noticed her."

"You found her a few minutes before the 911 call?" Pete asked.

"Yes," Debbie said.

"Can you give me an exact time?" Pete asked.

"It was about eight o'clock. I can't tell you the exact time. Do you know, Cynthia?"

Cynthia frowned and shook her head.

"How about sounds that might be linked to the attack?" Pete asked. "Did you hear a scream? A gasp? The sounds of a scuffle or of someone plopping down?"

"I heard a lot of screams," Debbie said, "but they all came from the Midway. From the people on the rides, I mean."

"And those busses make enough noise to cover up a lot of sounds." Cynthia pointed at the line of idling busses.

"My phone is ringing. It's probably my brother. He's picking us up. Is it okay if I answer?" Debbie looked pleadingly at Pete.

He nodded.

Before Debbie and Cynthia left, Pete and Martin gave each a business card, and instructed them to call if they thought of anything, regardless of the hour, and of how seemingly trivial.

Walking back to the roped-off crime scene, the two investigators told Porter what they learned from the St. Paul officers.

"It'll sure help if your folks find the rest of the stick used to stab her," Pete told Porter. "Or maybe the attacker left prints on one of the cars within the perimeter. Then the problem is linking the prints to the crime."

"I'd hate to have either of those things happen," Porter said. "It would take all of the fun out of it for the two of you."

"Anyone know who has the grandstand show tonight?" Martin asked. The words of the songs were indecipherable, but he heard the tune and felt the beat.

"Rascal Flatts," Pete said. "I saw you tapping your foot. Didn't know you're a country music fan."

"Rascal Flatts? Really? When my kid brother got married, my mom picked their song, "My Wish" for the mother-son dance. I'm not usually a country music fan, but the beat's contagious, don't you think?"

"Rarely after eight p.m. on weekdays," Pete said.

"How's it going?" he asked the crime scene personnel inspecting the area where the victim was found.

Looking up at Pete, a BCA agent said, "This is the victim's Pilot. Checked it out. Nothing obviously out of the ordinary, but we'll tow it in and check it more thoroughly. It looks like they swept the lot last night. Regardless, the amount of foot and car traffic complicates the finding of relevant footprints or tire tracks. We'll need to start with the shoes and tires, and work backwards to whatever we gather here. There's no blood spatter. We're looking for any trace evidence that might later be linked to the case. First take, aside from the remnants of the fair foods we're bagging, mighty slim pickings."

Pointing to Debbie's car, he said, "See the area where it appears the dirt was partially eliminated, like someone wiped it away? It appears the victim slid down that door, before coming to rest on the tarred surface."

Standing and stretching, the agent added, "Your sergeant said the stick used to stab her was broken. Some of our people are walking the lot and vicinity, looking for the rest of the stick. They're also gathering the contents of all garbage cans. I'm scouring the area for splinters. So far, I have three. They could be from that stick. They may even have traces of the attacker's DNA. Forensics will determine that."

FOUR

The paramedic unit sped from the State Fair parking lot to Regions Hospital—the closest Level I trauma center. Flashing lights and sirens alerted everyone along the way to its presence and the criticality of its mission.

Courtesy of an adrenaline rush, the EMT driver's heart raced. This happened every time he fought to keep the Grim Reaper at bay.

The paramedic inserted IVs and continuously checked the victim's vital signs. She conveyed readings and followed instructions issued by the emergency medicine doctor at Regions Hospital.

"I wonder if the stick was broken intentionally, permitting the attacker to escape with critical evidence?" the paramedic thought out loud. "Or was the break inevitable, due to the flimsiness of the stick? How could one of those sticks break the skin, and become imbedded in her? Do you suppose the person who did this sharpened it? Guess determining those things is the job of the Bureau of Criminal Apprehension and the medical examiner, huh?"

"Good questions," the police officer said. "Ever think you might be in the wrong line of work? Maybe you should get a job with the PD."

"Thanks, but I like what I'm doing. I like helping people."

"Ouch, that hurts."

"Sorry. I didn't mean it that way." The paramedic smiled apologetically.

"Do you think she might regain consciousness, before we get to Regions?" the officer asked. "It would sure help if she could answer a few questions. She may know who did this."

"When I have a minute, I'll see if I can get a response. Don't hold your breath. Chances are slim, at best."

The officer didn't permit that to dissuade him. "Ma'am, can you hear me?" he asked every few minutes. His efforts were no more successful than the EMT's had been back in the parking lot.

As soon as they reached the emergency room, the two responders rushed the victim inside.

The police officer followed close on their heels.

Thanks to communications between the paramedic unit and the hospital, Regions issued a trauma alert. For that reason, a trauma team stood at the ready when the paramedic unit arrived.

The team included a trauma surgeon, a senior staff physician, two emergency medicine residents, three emergency medicine RNs, radiology staff, a respiratory therapist, a lab tech, ER technicians, and a chaplain. Team members wore gowns, eye gear, and lead aprons. The last item protected them from the inevitable x-rays. At times like this, clearing the room before an x-ray wasn't always possible.

They displayed anticipation in a variety of trademark fashions. One relieved the tension by chatting nonstop. Another clenched and unclenched his fists. A third stepped nonstop from one foot to the other, performing some sort of rhythmless dance. Reactions rarely changed after months and years in their respective roles.

The EMT and paramedic rushed the victim through the ER to a trauma room.

The sixteen-by-twenty-foot room stood equipped for every eventuality. Supplies lined the walls, and an ultrasound, cardiac monitor, defibrillator, oxygen, suction outlets, and pyxis for distributing medicines were strategically located around the room. On hand were four units of O negative blood, two units of frozen plasma, and two units of platelets.

The senior staff physician inserted a central line in a major vein in the woman's neck. At her instruction, the RNs used this line to initiate a massive transfusion protocol. They also administered vasopressors, via the line. Through these efforts, they fought to stabilize the woman's blood pressure.

The surgeon watched as an x-ray tech did a CT scan, and the radiologist read it.

Having observed the scan, the surgeon knew the retro-peritoneal area was filled with blood. "Can't wait," he growled. "We've done all we can here. Gotta get her to the OR, *NOW*! Let's go! I need to open her up. We've got to stop the bleeding!"

"Not exactly the picture of calm, is he?" one resident whispered to the other, as they rushed the patient to the elevators.

"Who is?" his peer asked. "You ain't seen nothing yet. His bite is worlds worse than his bark. Besides, he's right. It's her only chance. Didn't you see the CT?"

While OR staff cleansed the victim in preparation for surgery, the trauma team put on surgical gowns and scrubbed for surgery. They knew from the CT scan that her abdominal cavity was filled with blood. They had to find and plug the leak before she bled out.

Once in the OR, the trauma surgeon removed the pads taped in place by the paramedic back in the parking lot. Leaving the stick in place, he moved with speed and precision, making a midline incision in the woman's abdomen. The incision relaxed the tension in her abdomen.

Blood and fluids gushed out. "Pads. Need pads, saline, blood, platelets, and plasma!" the surgeon ordered. "Can't see the source of the bleed. Too much blood. Need suction! More pads!"

Simultaneously, the anesthesiologist monitored the vital signs and struggled to stabilize the woman. He wished the surgeon would hurry up and find the source of all that blood. If he didn't, it was a lost cause.

There was a constant din, as the surgeon and everyone else in the

OR continued their efforts.

Suddenly, the victim's blood pressure began dropping, and her heart rate first decreased, then began increasing.

"More saline, plasma, blood, platelets," the surgeon ordered. A minute later, he shouted, "She's going into cardiac arrest!" He did a spectacular job of multitasking. While shouting orders, he continued concentrating on his search for the source of the bleed.

"Paddles, she's in cardiac arrest," the surgeon ordered.

The ongoing clamor in the operating room diminished as the anesthesiologist grabbed the paddles. Everyone took a step back from the table as he positioned the paddles over the woman's heart.

Her chest rose from the surgical table and dropped back with a dull thud, as the current traveled from the paddles to her heart.

It didn't work.

The anesthesiologist shocked her heart a second time—again without benefit.

"Epinephrine!" the surgeon yelled.

While the surgeon continued his frantic search for the bleed, a resident began chest compressions. Then the resident and the anesthesiologist took turns, using CPR and the paddles, struggling to revive the victim.

Those efforts persisted nonstop for twenty minutes. They failed.

The surgeon pronounced Virginia Green dead at 2059 hours.

The mood in the OR tanked. Everyone felt the shift from exhilarated to sullen, dejected. Each person was fully vested in saving the patient. Each felt like they'd failed—like they'd lost the big game.

Death didn't stop or slow the surgeon's efforts to find the bleed. He was tense. He'd lost the battle. He had to know what went wrong. He had to know why he'd failed.

The fact he wouldn't be the only one asking those questions didn't help. The death would be reported to the American College of Surgeons, and a detailed review of the OR processes would ensue. For the surgeon, that qualified as torture.

The scrub tech left the OR to find the uniformed officer who accompanied the victim to the hospital.

She found him in the family waiting area and shared the news.

FIVE

Pete Culnane was still at the crime scene and still speaking with Jimmy Porter from the BCA when he got the word from headquarters. Virginia Green died. It was now a murder investigation.

He shared the news with Martin Tierney and Jimmy Porter. "Let's contact her family," he told Martin.

They began with the contacts on Virginia Green's cell phone. In most cases, she used first names only. There were no Greens listed. Thankfully, this woman used the once popular ICE system. An acronym for "In Case of Emergency," ICE was sometimes used to designate emergency contacts for anyone finding a person with a cell phone and a medical or other problem.

Pete called ICE1, wondering who would answer.

A male voice said, "What's up?"

"My name is Peter Culnane. I'm an investigator with the St. Paul Police Department. With whom am I speaking?"

"Will Green. I don't understand. How did you get my number? What do you want?"

"I want to meet with you, Mr. Green. Where are you?"

"I'm at home. Why do you want to meet? Can't we discuss whatever you need over the phone?"

"We'll talk once I get there. How about an address?"

"Are you sure this isn't a telephone solicitation? Come on. 'Fess up. You're a door-to-door salesman, aren't you?"

Pete smiled. That was a first. "No, sir. Like I said, I'm with the St. Paul Police Department."

Will sighed and rattled off his address.

Martin was happy to move their investigation from the parking lot to a new location. He smelled hot cooking oil. That oil might be frying up fresh Tom Thumb donuts. He couldn't smell the donuts, but knew they were just out of reach. He wanted some in the worst way.

To avoid State Fair traffic delays, Pete and Martin took a circuitous but speedier route to Will Green's house.

Green's home was a two-story, half-timbered house, circa 1980s. It nestled in a middle class neighborhood in Roseville, a suburb north of St. Paul and the State Fair. Unlike some newer housing developments, the trees here were grown, and there was too much space between homes to reach out a window and touch a neighbor's house.

A man who appeared poised to leave middle age answered Pete's knock. His face was red and drenched with sweat. White hair thick enough to pass for a wig hung over the tops of his ears. Blue eyes fixated questioningly on Pete, then Martin, through thick, black-rimmed glasses.

Pete introduced himself and Martin as they flashed their badges and IDs. "Are you Will?" he asked.

Green's nod made him look like a bobblehead doll. "Is this about my daughter? Is Rachel okay? I called her right after I spoke with you. She didn't answer. She always answers. What happened to Rachel?"

"Unless Rachel is a nickname, we aren't here about her," Pete said.

"Then why?"

Pete swatted a mosquito.

"Sorry, come in." Will stepped back and held the door for the two investigators. He led them to the living room, wiping his face on a sleeve as he went.

After he and Martin settled in a couple of chairs, Pete said, "We're here about Virginia Green. You're related, correct?"

"Yes, she's my sister. Why?"

"I regret to inform you that . . ."

Green shot up out of his chair. "Oh God, no! Not Ginny. What happened? Will she be okay?"

"No, sorry, she died in surgery," Pete said.

"I spoke with her yesterday morning. She planned to spend the day at the fair. Was there an accident on one of the rides? I haven't had the radio or TV on all day."

"It didn't happen on a ride," Pete said. "Did she go with friends?"

"Wait. What happened to Ginny?"

Pete said, "She was attacked." He asked again if Virginia went to the fair with friends.

"What do you mean, she was attacked?" Will asked in alarm.

"She was murdered near the fairgrounds. I need your help to figure out exactly what happened."

Will blurted out, "But I didn't even know she was dead! How can I help?"

Pete explained, "Something you know may be important. Again— did she go to the fair with friends?"

"Yes." Will's expression conveyed a cautious willingness.

"Can you give me their names and contact information?" Pete asked.

"She didn't tell me who she was going with." Will sank back into the chair, closed his eyes, bit his lower lip, and shook his head slowly back and forth.

"What's your educated guess?" Pete asked.

"Her friends, Laura and Wendy."

"Last names?" Pete asked, pulling out his notepad.

"Laura Rushford and Wendy Wykoff. I don't know for sure if it was either of them, but they're the most likely."

Pete began a series of questions, gathering information about the victim and her family. "Was Virginia married?"

"Briefly. She's been divorced for decades."

"Any children?"

"No." Again Will shook his head.

"Do you have any brothers or other sisters?"

"Yes. I have a younger brother, Tim, and another sister, Caroline."

"Is Caroline single or married?"

Will asked with a tone of suspicion, "What difference does that make?"

"It could make a difference with her last name."

"Oh, yeah," Will shrugged. "I guess that's important. It's Campbell."

"How about Tim? Married or single?"

"No wife. He's married to his job."

"Where does he work?"

"IBM—in Rochester."

"Where do Tim and Caroline live?"

"Tim lives in Rochester. Caroline's in Apple Valley."

"When did you last see them?"

"This week. Mom died. Her funeral was Monday."

"My condolences."

"Mine also," Martin said.

"Thanks. It's been mighty tough."

Pete thought Will still showed signs of the strain. "When did Caroline and Tim return home?" he asked.

"Caroline commuted back and forth for everything. Tim left today. There's a lot to handle with Mom's estate, you know."

"I understand." Pete nodded. "What time did Tim leave?"

"Midafternoon. I think it was around two or three. I wasn't here at the time."

"Where were you?" Pete asked.

"At the fair. I went with some buddies. Turned out to be a mistake. I had a lousy time. Should've stayed home."

"Did you see Virginia at the fair?" Pete asked.

"No, but seriously, with all those people, what were the chances?"

Returning to the family, Pete asked, "Does Caroline have children?"

"Two daughters. One is married."

"Do Caroline's daughters live in Apple Valley?"

"No. Both are in south Minneapolis."

"What are the daughters' names?"

"Heather and Brittany."

"Which one is married?"

"Heather."

"Her married name is?"

"Bingham."

"What's her husband's first name?"

"Alex."

"You mentioned a daughter. Do you have any other children?"

"No, just Rachel."

"Are you married?"

"Yes." Will offered no additional information.

"Are you, your brother, and sisters close?" Pete asked.

"Tim and I love each other, but have little in common. Even less, now that Mom's gone." Will brushed away a tear. "I guess the same is true of Caroline and me. Ginny's been good to me. I was unemployed for a year and a half. Ran through our savings and was building credit card debt fast enough to make my head spin. Couldn't find a way out of it, until Ginny gave me an interest-free loan. Didn't have to make payments until I got a job. She used her network to help me land that job. Both of those things were huge!"

"Have you paid off the loan?" Pete asked.

"Yeah, a few months ago."

"Did Virginia have any enemies? Was she feuding with anyone? Did anyone have a grudge against her?" Pete asked.

Long pause. "You had to know Ginny. She didn't like anyone or anything getting in the way of achieving her goals. Unfortunately, in the process, I think she alienated a fair number of people."

"Including you?" Pete asked.

"We're normal. We have our fights, but I understand her and love her. I never raised a hand against her—not even when we were kids."

"How about Tim and Caroline? Did they get along with Ginny?" Pete asked.

"Yes. But Ginny and I were closer than she was to Tim or Caroline."

Stating it another way, Pete asked, "Was anyone angry with Ginny?"

"I don't know about angry. That may be a little strong. Some people in my family were unhappy with the way Ginny handled Mom's affairs. Even so, none of them would hurt her, if that's what you're asking."

"What do you mean when you say the way she handled your mother's affairs?" Pete asked.

"Some people thought she should have left Mom in her house, instead of moving her into an assisted living apartment."

Now it was Martin's turn. "Who thought that?" he asked.

"My daughter and Mom's brother, but I can guarantee neither would hurt Ginny."

Pete wondered how he could guarantee it. Few people can *guarantee* their own actions and reactions, much less someone else's.

"I need their names," Martin said.

"Believe me, neither one of them could or would hurt Ginny!"

"Regardless, I need their names."

"My daughter's name is Rachel. Rachel Lansing. My uncle is Tommy Wells." Once again, Will lifted an arm and dried his face on a shirt sleeve. "Sorry it's so warm in here. We subscribe to energy saver to reduce our electric bill. It helps save money. Unfortunately, on days like today, the AC can't keep up, even if it runs continuously."

"How about you? Did you agree with Rachel and Tommy?" Martin asked, already knowing the answer.

Will shrugged.

"Anyone else you can think of who might have been angry with your sister?" Martin asked.

"Aside from her ex-husband, I don't have any names or specifics."

"How about generalities?" Martin asked.

"Nothing I can think of. Like I told you, she irritated some people, but I can't think of any instances. Her friends or coworkers might be able to help."

"Where did your sister work?" Martin asked.

"For the state."

"What department?" Martin asked.

"Revenue."

Martin felt like he was pulling teeth. "Doing what?"

"I'm not sure. It has something to do with corporate tax filing, I think. When she talked about it, she usually ranted and raved. I usually tuned her out."

"Her ex's name is?" Martin asked.

"Howard Sunburg. Ginny dumped him and a short time later dumped his name."

"How about your father?" Pete asked.

"Deceased," Will sighed.

"How many siblings did your mother have?" Pete asked.

"Just Uncle Tommy."

"Your home isn't far from the fairgrounds is it," Pete said.

"Not far, but not nearly close enough to make a hefty chunk of change by parking the cars of fair goers in my yard."

"Do you go to the fair on a regular basis?" Martin asked.

"I usually go at least once a year. It has to be the best place in the state for people watching."

"With all that people watching, you got at least a glimpse of Virginia today, didn't you?" Martin said.

"No, didn't see her at all, but we aren't interested in the same types of things."

"What interests you?" Martin asked.

"I spend my time on Machinery Hill, even though the current version can't hold a candle to the way it used to be what it was like when I was a kid. I also like checking out the latest and greatest in the Merchandise Mart, watching the demonstrations in the Grandstand and the Education Building and, like I said, people watching."

"What did Virginia like to do at the fair?" Martin asked.

"She likes the Midway. I'm not about to throw money away on the Midway."

"When did you last speak with Virginia?" Martin asked.

"Like I said, yesterday. She had some stuff that has to do with my mother's estate."

"Who is the administrator of your mother's estate?" Pete asked.

"Ginny." A light seemed to go on in Will's head, when he realized, apparently for the first time, what that meant.

"Who stood to benefit the most, financially?" Pete asked.

"I assume my brother, sisters, and me."

"Did you drive or take a bus to the fair today?" Pete asked.

"Drove. I always drive."

"Where did you park?" Pete asked.

"On the street, east of the fairgrounds."

"Be more specific," Pete said.

"Near Midway Parkway and Hamline."

"How long did it take you to walk from your car to the fairgrounds?" Pete asked.

"Half an hour?"

"Did you walk or crawl?" Pete asked, raising an eyebrow.

"Maybe it only took fifteen minutes. I'm not sure." Will frowned.

"What time did you get home?" Pete asked.

"It's hard to say. I started walking to the car at around six thirty or so, but it was a pretty good hike. Then with the traffic and all . . . you know how it is." Will dried his face on his sleeve, then glanced at his watch. "Sorry, I'm worried about Rachel. She should have called by now."

"What's your best guess for the time you got home?" Pete asked.

"Seven or seven thirty."

"Where were you between then and nine?" Pete asked.

"You don't think I did it, do you?" Will sounded alarmed again.

"Did what?" Pete asked, wondering for a moment if a slip of the tongue might solve the case in record time.

"Hurt Ginny. I didn't do it!"

"Where were you from the time you got home until nine?" Pete repeated.

"Right here. I stayed home, once I got here."

Pete said, "I'll need the addresses and phone numbers for all the people we just talked about."

Both he and Martin took down the information.

Pete said, "That's all for now."

"Wait," pleaded Will, "you have to tell me what happened to my sister!"

"A fair goer found her, and she was taken to Regions Hospital. Unfortunately, like I said, she died in the operating room. I'm sorry for your loss."

Will's shoulders fell. He looked crushed.

Pete heard a car door slam.

Seconds later, a woman burst through the front door.

SIX

The short shorts worn by the woman who burst in on them accentuated amazingly long legs. She ran to Will and handed him a small, wailing child. "Take her, Dad. I have to get some bandages. She fell on the driveway. Be careful. Her knees are bleeding."

Will scooped up the screaming child. "That's my daughter, Rachel," he explained, talking loud enough to be heard over the child.

Pete felt like an intruder in this family moment, but stayed anyway. He wanted to speak with Rachel.

By the time Rachel returned with bandages, a moist cloth, and disinfectant, the little girl was calm and smiling. Her love for Will couldn't be more obvious.

"You have a real knack," Pete said.

Will grinned and nodded. "You're my buddy, aren't you, sweetie?"

The child's screams resumed with added strength as she fought her mother's efforts to cleanse her knees.

Will introduced the two investigators—over the screams.

Pete was impressed that he remembered both of their names.

"Why are they here?" Rachel asked.

"They came to deliver some very disturbing news. Your aunt Ginny was murdered."

Rachel gasped and grabbed Will's arm. "I'm so sorry, Dad. I can't believe it. I just saw her on Monday. What happened?"

"Someone attacked her."

Rachel's eyebrows shot up, and her jaw dropped. "You've got to be kidding."

"We have a few questions for you, Rachel," Pete said.

"Will it take more than a minute?"

Pete nodded.

"Okay, but first let me give Emma to Mom. She won't mind watching her, while we talk."

Will's wife was home? That surprised Pete. He hadn't heard her. Besides, how many people would hear a discussion coming from their living room and not check it out?

"Let me take her, honey," Will said. Looking at Martin, he asked, "You're finished with me, aren't you?"

Martin looked at Pete, and once again Pete nodded.

"Let me come with you and select a movie," Rachel said.

A moment later, Pete heard the sound of a television coming from the back of the house.

When Rachel returned, her mother followed.

Will's wife had ultra-short, salt-and-pepper hair. Her flip-flops snapped loudly with each step, as she crossed the room.

Pete and Martin were still standing, and continued doing so until the women sat down.

Mother and daughter settled in close proximity on a loveseat.

Pete and Martin returned to the two chairs they'd previously occupied.

"Were you and your aunt, Virginia, close?" Martin asked.

"Sure. She's my aunt. She doesn't have any kids, so she doted over me. I ate it up."

"Did that relationship change?" Martin asked.

"Of course. I got married, got busy, and we spent less time together."

"Tell us about your grandmother, your dad's mother," Pete said.

Rachel's head dropped. "She died."

Her daughter dashed into the living room, and made a beeline for Rachel's mother. "Grandma, can I have a cookie?"

Rachel didn't give her mother an opportunity to respond. "Not now, Emma. Grandma and I are busy. These men are busy, too, and they don't want to be interrupted. Go back and watch your movie. Stay in the den until Grandma and I are finished. I'll get you something to eat, after these men leave."

The little girl made a face. Then, looking at Pete and Martin, she asked, "Who are you?"

"We're police officers," Pete said.

"No you're not. You aren't wearing police clothes."

"Emma, go back and watch your movie right now. If you don't, you won't get a cookie later, either."

Emma pouted, spun on a heel, and sashayed down the hallway toward the back of the house.

Rachel smiled at Pete and Martin and said, "Sorry for the interruption."

"No need to apologize," Pete said. "I understand your grandmother was a vital and active woman."

"That was true, until the last year."

"What happened to change that?" Pete asked.

"Aunt Ginny decided Grandma needed more help than she could provide. She moved Grandma out of the house where she and Grandpa lived for almost fifty years. She put her in an assisted living apartment."

Thinking of his own grandmother, Pete asked, "What was your reaction?"

"At first I assumed Ginny knew what she was doing."

"Then?" Pete asked.

"Before long, I knew it was the worst thing she could have done to Grandma." A tear welled in the corner of Rachel's eye, and she brushed it away.

"Why was it the worst thing?" Pete asked.

"After Aunt Ginny moved her into an apartment, Grandma gave up. She no longer had a garden to take care of, and she no longer took daily walks. She lost interest in everything. She just sat in that stupid apartment, watching TV, and staring out the window. Ginny said Grandma would enjoy the daily activities at the new place. Well, Grandma never did." Rachel looked angry.

Her mother's expression indicated agreement.

"Did that create the first breech in your closeness to Ginny?" Pete asked.

"No."

"What did?" Pete asked.

"Like I said, I got busy, and we went our separate ways."

"How did your dad react to what happened with his mother?" Martin asked.

"Why don't you ask him?"

"Because I'm interested in your take on it."

"He remained in Ginny's corner. I tried to talk to him. So did Uncle Tommy. We wanted to force Ginny to move Grandma back into her house. She could have. It's still empty. Dad acted like we didn't understand."

Her mother nodded.

"Did you speak to your husband about it?" Pete asked Rachel's mother.

"I broached the subject a few times. Made some remarks about Emma's deterioration. Will refused to talk about it. Every time I opened my mouth, he walked away."

"Tell us about Will's relationship with Ginny," Martin said.

"She's his big sister," Will's wife said. "She helped us when Will lost his job. She gave us money and helped him find another job. He owes her. His loyalty is unshakable." She frowned.

"Who is handling Emma's estate?" Martin asked.

"Ginny," Will's wife said. "She has more money sense than Will. I guess it may now fall on Will's and my shoulders." She sighed deeply. She looked concerned.

"Your uncle, Tommy, was the only person who took your side in this disagreement with Virginia?" Pete asked.

"Well, Tommy, Mom, and me," Rachel said, glancing at her mother.

Her mother's head bobbed.

"Was Tommy as unhappy as you about the whole arrangement?" Pete asked.

"I guess," Rachel said. "He did his best to change things. He tried to get Dad to intervene. Dad was probably the only person who could have changed Ginny's mind." Sigh.

"Did your discussions or your uncle's discussions with your dad get heated?" Pete asked.

"Mine did. I only know that Tommy's didn't anytime I was around. Even so, I'm sure they talked about it when I wasn't there. It was the single, overriding topic of conversation between Dad and me for the last few months. The more Grandma went downhill, the more adamant I became. I'm sure that's true of Tommy as well. He spent a lot of time with Grandma. He saw what was happening. But, if you're thinking Tommy or I did this, you're wrong! Neither of us would attack Ginny. And surely not after Grandma was gone." More tears welled up, and she brushed them away. "What would be the point? It's too late to do any good anymore. It's over and done. I'm not a violent person. Neither is Uncle Tommy. He's a teddy bear. He wouldn't hurt a fly."

"Any idea who would hurt Ginny?" Pete asked.

"My money is on her ex-husband," Rachel said.

Her mother nodded.

"Do you know where Howard Sunburg works?" Pete asked.

Both women shook their heads.

Pete thought they looked like perfectly timed puppets.

SEVEN

Pete didn't relish the idea of knocking on doors after ten at night. "What do you say we call it a day, Martin?"

"That's the best idea I've heard since I offered you my tie."

On their way back to the Como parking lot where they'd left Pete's car, Pete asked Martin about his kids.

"Marty is the penultimate big brother. He loves to hold Olivia and give her a bottle. Olivia must be growing. She looks the same, but she's definitely heavier than when we brought her home."

"That's good news on both counts. How about Michelle? Is she doing better?"

"No. If anything, she's worse. I'm really worried about her. She has no energy, no ambition. Sometimes I worry she might not be feeding Olivia. She does when I'm home, but . . . Guess she must, otherwise Olivia wouldn't be putting on weight, would she?"

"Not unless Marty is stepping in."

"Good point. I'd planned to talk to him tonight. Should have before now. I've been dragging my feet. I'm so worried about blowing it, about saying it the wrong way. What if everything is fine and my questions scare him? What if he tells Michelle what I ask and upsets her?"

"Don't you think what's happening with Michelle might be scaring him?"

"Guess I've been trying to find comfort in the fact he hasn't said anything."

"But Martin, maybe he thinks saying something would betray his mom."

"You're sure a bearer of glad tidings, aren't you? Guess I better talk to him. Unfortunately, it's too late to do that tonight. I used to see him every morning before I left. Not anymore. We have to wrap up this case. Until then, I may not be home while he's awake."

"What time does he get up these days?"

"Eight, nine, sometimes later."

"You could come in late tomorrow."

"A little late, yes. Late morning, I don't know. I wish Michelle would see a doctor. Don't know why she's refusing. It's so unlike her. Everything about her is so unlike her."

"If there's anything I can do, Martin, let me know."

"I appreciate it, and I will. But other than handcuffing Michelle and taking her to the doctor, I don't know what it would be."

* * *

Driving home, Pete thought about Martin, and his predicament.

Martin and Michelle spent years trying to have a second child. After Michelle got pregnant, Martin's anticipation reminded him of a kid waiting for Santa. He didn't blame Michelle. How could he? But he hated the toll her problems now took on Martin. Even so, he felt jealous of his partner. He so wanted kids of his own.

Incapable of finding a solution for Martin, Pete's thoughts swung to his grandmother. Would the move from her house to an apartment cause her to deteriorate the way Will's mother did? His grandmother's new place was a far cry from assisted living. Still, it was a

radical change from having her own house. Was it a positive or negative change?

Everything happened so fast. Too fast.

His folks were on a European cruise when the time came to move
her into the apartment. They'd made the reservation almost a year
ago and couldn't change the dates.

His sister and her family were on an end-of-summer trip to the
Black Hills. She offered to stay behind. He couldn't let her.

That left him to orchestrate the packing and unpacking and to
help his grandmother get settled in her new home. He was happy to
help in any way possible. It made him feel good, and he enjoyed their
time together. He was relieved a case hadn't interfered.

When he first heard about her plans to sell the house, he asked if
it was what she wanted. She assured him it was. He didn't pursue it.
Now he wondered what triggered the decision. It seemed to come out
of the blue. She seemed to get along fine in her home. Was the decision to move some sort of cry for help? Did she feel pushed? Was she
putting a positive spin on it for his benefit? He hoped not, but he
wasn't certain. He should have asked more questions.

He had to talk to her again. He had to insure this was what she
wanted. He had to intervene, if necessary.

She couldn't return to her house. It sold within a week after it was
listed. If necessary, there had to be another solution. One, of course,
was making an offer the new owners of his grandmother's house
couldn't refuse. Rubbing his upper lip and shaking his head, Pete
knew he'd fail miserably if he tried to pull that off. The godfather he
wasn't.

EIGHT

The following morning, Martin arrived at headquarters at the usual time.

Pete wondered what, if anything, that meant.

"I'm due at the Medical Examiner's Office at nine o'clock, Martin. Beforehand, I have to go to the Bureau of Criminal Apprehension to get the stick used to stab Green. Since the ME will take photos of the stick, I'll forward some to you. While I'm gone, how about going to the fair and collecting sticks? It'll help to know which booth sells which stick or sticks. If we can determine which booth sold the stick, we'll talk to everyone who worked there yesterday. It may be pie in the sky, but maybe someone noticed something suspicious."

"True. Maybe when the attacker bought the food on that stick, they said, 'Hey, thanks. I think this stick is perfect for stabbing this friend of mine.' Want me to bring anything back for you, Pete? Walleye on a stick?"

"Since you're asking, how about bringing me a pony? I always wanted a pony."

"Getting it into the unmarked might be a problem."

"True. You better leave right away. I'll walk you to the parking lot."

* * *

Pete arrived at the ME's office at eight fifty. He proceeded to the autopsy room, where he joined the forensic pathologist, forensic technician, and a scientist from the St. Paul Crime Lab.

The room had a drop ceiling, terra cotta floors, and tile walls. Five stainless steel sinks stood along the four walls.

Pete watched the forensic technician remove Green's body from the cooler, roll the stainless steel cart across the room, and connect it to a sink. That connection permitted body fluids to drain from the cart into the sink.

The pathologist took the standard set of twelve photos, with the victim both face up and face down, and from every angle. The photos documented the condition of the body, and included pictures of Green's face, hands, and arms. Then he removed the hospital gown and took a series of close-ups of the wound.

With the gown off, Pete saw the stitches used to close the incision made in the operating room.

Next, the technician weighed and measured the body and took x-rays, including a whole body x-ray.

After taking the stick out of the box Pete collected at the BCA, the pathologist removed the cloth protecting it. He set the stick on a table, and lay measuring sticks and a label reading ME2012-2202 alongside it. The label designated the ME case number, and tied the photos to this case. He took several photos, documenting the shape and dimensions of the stick.

The pathologist conducted an external exam of every inch of the victim's body, looking for other wounds and trace evidence. He knew trace evidence was unlikely, because Green's body was scrubbed in preparation for surgery.

The external examination took an hour. In the process, the pathologist found no defensive wounds. He learned Green didn't have her attacker's skin, or anyone's, under her fingernails. She did have blood on her right hand. It could be hers or her attacker's. He collected a sample.

The technician drew enough vials of blood for all the necessary tests, including toxicology, DNA, and tests for diseases.

A running commentary filled the autopsy room. The pathologist explained his activities and findings. In the process, he noted that, regrettably, the path of the stick was compromised by the incision made in the operating room.

The investigation was a team effort, between the PD and the ME's office. Pete did his part, telling about the progress thus far with the investigation. He mentioned the information gathered the previous evening from the victim's brother and his family. He said he had the names of the people who may have attended the fair with the victim, and that they were next on the list of priorities. Since at this phase, everything was relevant, he also mentioned the victim's marital status.

Once the preliminaries were completed, less pleasant sounds took over. First came the high-pitched whine of the autopsy saw. It filled the room as the technician, under the supervision of the pathologist, cut the sternum and ribs, making a Y from the shoulders to the pubic bone.

The odors in the room deteriorated markedly when the stench of the open body cavity and the bowel overpowered the smell of tissue and blood.

During this portion of the exam, the pathologist named the stomach contents. They included bits of green olive, cheese, beef, pickle, and a doughy substance.

"Most items on a stick are coated with a batter," Pete said. "She may have purchased the stick used to kill her."

"Have you spoken with the food vendors at the fair?" the pathologist asked.

"Martin Tierney's doing the preliminaries right now."

"Good idea. If she purchased the stick, her attacker might have been with her at the time. She may have looked nervous, anxious, frightened," the pathologist said.

"And if the attacker purchased the stick, and she wasn't nearby at the time, that person might have looked nervous, anxious, angry," Pete said. "Something might have made an impression on the vendor. Once Martin has the sticks, we'll submit them to the BCA to narrow the field of vendors. Seems unlikely, based on the size and shape, but this stick may not even have come from the fair. The BCA will determine the type of wood. That might help, but it could take weeks. The stick suppliers might also sell them to other, non-fair locations. Thing is, our stick efforts might be futile. On the other hand, they may not."

"Another problem is that so many things are served on a stick," the pathologist said. "The good news is that this stick may be longer than most."

"Too bad there aren't traces of the food on our portion of the stick," Pete said.

"I agree, but like I said, the size and shape of the point may significantly narrow the field."

The pathologist determined the cause of death was a sharp force injury, and the weapon was a stick. Reconstructing the path as closely as possible indicated the sharp end of the stick pierced Green's abdomen approximately 2.7 centimeters below the navel. It penetrated 9.2 centimeters, in an upward angle of fifty to fifty-five degrees. The stick penetrated the inferior vena cava.

The pathologist concluded that the broken edge of the stick and the puncture and tearing of Green's inferior vena cava indicated one of two things. After the stick pierced her abdomen, either Green turned left, away from her attacker, or the person holding the stick pushed the stick to the left. If it was the latter, the attacker held the stick in his or her right hand.

The pathologist said the person who stabbed her was strong, but could be a man or a woman. Based on the angle of entry, that person was not less than four feet tall.

Pete would return the stick to the BCA for safekeeping and to maintain the chain of evidence.

He liked the folks at the ME's, but this was always an unpleasant way to spend time.

Apparently Martin felt that way also. He didn't argue about who would do what this morning.

NINE

As he'd promised, Pete emailed photos of the stick removed from Virginia Green to Martin.

Martin had them by the time he reached the fairgrounds. He saw the message, but didn't open the files until he reached the Administration building.

En route, he caught a whiff of some of the delicacies served at the fair, and thought about the smells bombarding Pete at that moment. Realization of his relative good fortune elicited a smile.

After asking numerous questions of a lot of people in the admin building, Martin got some of the information he needed. He learned there wasn't a list of vendors providing the sticks used by the food booths. Each booth made its own arrangements. Admin couldn't identify the sticks used by any of the booths, so the photos Pete sent wouldn't result in a quick answer.

On the plus side, a page on the State Fair website listed all food booths, and the foods sold at each. Martin explained a printed copy would be helpful.

After several minutes, he obtained a printed list of all food booths, showing their locations. Then, thankfully, the person helping him reminded him about the booths selling food across Snelling Avenue from the fairgrounds.

"Oh yeah." He shrugged and walked away. So far, he had no proof the stick came from a State Fair or a Snelling Avenue food booth. He could, hopefully, at least narrow it down by getting a sample of every stick used and sending it to the BCA for analysis.

He needed help to accomplish that. A logical resource was the police officers who came from all over the state to work at the fair. For that reason, he met with the State Fair police chief. After Martin explained his mission, the chief made copies of the vendor list, and rounded up nine officers.

Each wore the uniform of his or her respective department.

Martin told them he needed a sample from every food that comes on a stick served at every food booth.

"Sounds like a dragnet," one officer chuckled. That drew a few snickers.

They divvied up the list of vendors, and the chief handed Martin and each uniformed officer a clear plastic bag for the sticks they collected.

As the officers headed out, a female with sergeant's bars and a Hibbing patch asked, "Do you want these sticks with or without food on them?"

"Hold up, everyone!" Martin called out. He spent several seconds trying to determine what Pete would do, then said, "Good question. Get them with the food. Feel free to eat the food. If you do, leave some traces. And don't forget to label each stick. If it's the type we're looking for, we need to know the source. Also, do *not* share what I told you about this case with *anyone*."

After walking to the Snelling entrance, Martin passed through the gates, crossed the street, and began canvassing the food vendors with stands in the front yards. Once he identified himself, by and large, the vendors willingly complied with his request. Each handed over their foods on sticks and waved off his money. One asked why he wanted it. Martin said only that it was part of an investigation.

Making the rounds, he regretted that Tom Thumb donuts didn't come on a stick.

The pronto pup took up a lot of space in the bag, so Martin treated himself to a sample. Deciding his credibility as a stick collector might suffer if the next vendor saw him eating the wares, he slowed to look at the booths. There were paintings, tie-dyed shirts, baseball caps, literature, and pennants—for starters.

He knew it took years to get a booth on the fairgrounds. The rent out here must be significantly lower, but so was the traffic. There were too many entrances. He wondered if the people setting up these booths did so out of necessity or by choice. Could go either way, he decided.

Eight of the nine officers were back at the police department by the time Martin returned. Looking at their bags, he figured he had enough work to keep the BCA occupied for hours or days, even after they separated out the sticks not matching the photos Pete sent. He smiled when he noticed most of the officers scored a free lunch.

Glancing at his watch, he realized it was almost noon. Pete might be back at headquarters by now. He stepped out in the parking lot, hoping to spot the last officer. Scanning the crowd in front of the Grandstand, he heard a voice behind him.

"Looking for me? Hope I didn't hold you up. There was a problem at the coin toss. Had to break up a fight. Sorry."

"Not a problem. After all, that's why you're here. Thanks for your help. Encounter any uncooperative vendors?"

"No. The uniform opens a lot of doors—at least here. That's not always true back home."

Martin hustled to his car. He was anxious to deliver the results of his morning's efforts and find out what Pete learned during the autopsy.

TEN

When Martin walked into Pete's office with the bags of sticks, Pete whistled. "That's a lot of sticks."

"Yeah. There are several lengths, and the shape of the point varies. Both should help the BCA narrow the field."

They drove the sticks to the BCA headquarters.

A man with shoulder-length blond hair, wearing a burnt-orange Weezer T-shirt and cowboy boots exited the building as Pete and Martin approached the entrance.

"Pete Culnane!" the man said, extending a hand. "It's been a long time!"

"It has, Virg. How's the fishing?"

"Great, but the fish aren't always biting." The man smiled.

As they walked into the building, Martin asked, "Who was that cowboy?"

"Sorry, Martin, I thought you knew him. I'd have introduced you. That's Virgil Flowers. He's a BCA investigator. He has quite a reputation."

Handing the sticks to a forensic scientist, Pete asked if they'd gotten to the case.

"Before you took off with the stick, we found traces of DNA on the ragged edge. Don't yet know if it's from the person who stabbed her, or the victim herself. Found trace evidence on her shirt. Based on the location, could have been left there by the attacker while stabbing her. Could also be from her. Won't know until we compare it to her DNA. Won't have an answer for at least a few days. You'll be the first to know. That's all so far."

Before leaving, they checked in with Jimmy Porter, their BCA liaison on this case. They learned the BCA obtained a search warrant. The search of Virginia Green's house stood high, but not at the top, of the list of priorities.

Back at headquarters, Pete and Martin went through Virginia Green's cell phone contacts. The women Will thought she attended the fair with, Laura Rushford and Wendy Wykoff, weren't listed. Curious. Could they be ICE2 and ICE3, Pete wondered.

He gave it a try, calling ICE2. Jackpot! It was Wendy.

Martin spent several seconds contemplating his plan of attack, then called ICE3. Another hit. He connected with Laura Rushford.

The investigators obtained locations for the women, then left headquarters for face-to-face meetings.

Wendy Wykoff met them in the reception area of the Ecolab complex in downtown St. Paul. Pete pegged her as late fifties and wondered how anyone walked without teetering on high heels like hers. Her gray-streaked, shoulder-length hair hung behind her ears, highlighting large, dangling earrings.

Pete explained why they wanted to talk to her.

Wendy's jaw dropped. "That's not possible!"

"We have positive identification," Pete said, "Will identified his sister's body last night."

Wendy confirmed that she and Laura attended the fair with Virginia yesterday. There were two other friends in this group. She provided their names and contact information.

"Virginia didn't ride with the rest of you?" Pete asked.

"No, she drove separately. She planned to go a bit later than the rest of us."

"What time did you meet?" Pete asked.

"We were supposed to meet in front of the Dairy Building at ten. Ginny was a few minutes late."

"Did you leave the fair together?" Pete asked.

"Yes. The other four of us took a bus from a park-and-ride lot. Ginny walked us to the bus. She left as soon as we boarded."

"You caught the bus by the west Como parking lot?" Pete asked, familiar with the layout.

"Yes. Ginny offered to give us a ride back to our cars, but we had round-trip tickets. Our bus was there when we got to the lot. There was no sense taking her that far out of her way."

"Did Ginny have any arguments, any confrontations while you were with her yesterday?" Pete asked.

"She told one of the vendors his prices were outrageous, but that was Ginny. He ignored her. He probably hears stuff like that all the time."

"Which vendor?" Pete asked.

"A guy selling cloths that are supposed to pull spills out of carpet and dry sweaters like magic. That sort of thing. I don't know the name of the product, but he was in the Merchandise Mart."

"Any other arguments?" Pete asked.

"I wouldn't call that an argument." Wendy shook her head emphatically. "It was more like a remark that was ignored. You had to know Ginny. She stated her mind. It's part of the package. It's also true you couldn't ask for a more loyal friend. You have to take the bad with the good. Life is like that. I can't believe she's gone! What could she possibly have done to deserve this?"

"The question isn't whether she deserved it, but whether something she said or did triggered it. Were there any other incidents either before or at the fair that might point us in the right direction?" Pete asked.

"Nothing I can think of. While at the fair, we mostly talked among ourselves and enjoyed the food and the rides. That was why we went. It was good for Ginny to get away. She's been taking her mother's deterioration and death pretty hard."

Wendy's eyes grew moist. "Planning the funeral was a daunting task. Her mother didn't do any advance planning and never made her wishes known. It was awful. Ginny was a basket case." Wendy frowned. "I feel so sorry for poor Will. He was relying on Ginny to handle their mother's estate. Now he'll probably have to handle both Ginny's estate, and their mother's. I'm not sure he has the where-withal to accomplish that. Maybe his wife and daughter will help."

"What about Will's brother and other sister?" Pete asked.

"Oh yeah. I forgot about them. Ginny was closest to Will. She rarely talked about her sister and the other brother."

"Were there hard feelings between Ginny and that brother and sister?" Pete asked.

"I don't know. If there were, she didn't talk about it."

"Would she have talked about it?" Pete asked.

"Depends on the nature of the problem, or problems. If it was because of something she did, probably not."

"Putting the fair aside, did Ginny ever mention any problems, confrontations, enemies?" Pete asked.

"She had some problems at work. She's task, not people oriented. I guess that sometimes irritated her co-workers."

"How about some specifics?" Pete asked.

"Don't really have any. I'm afraid the names didn't register. They didn't mean anything to me."

"How is her relationship with the other members of her family? I mean other than her brothers and sister," Pete asked.

"At her mom's wake, things were a bit icy between Ginny, her uncle Tommy, and her niece Rachel. I think she usually gets along fine with both of them. Neither stepped up to help her make the arrangements. Don't know what they had to be peeved about."

"Did you see a man in a yellow, gold, or orange shirt following Virginia yesterday, either before or after she dropped you off at the bus?" Pete asked.

"Didn't notice that before, and I wasn't really paying any attention after. We were busy getting on the bus and finding seats. Never saw her after I found a seat."

Pete and Martin each handed Wendy a business card, and Pete said, "If anything else comes to mind, anything at all, please contact one of us. Sometimes the seemingly insignificant things can be critical to solving a case."

"Do you think it was planned?" Wendy asked.

"That's part of what we're trying to determine," Pete said.

Progressing to ICE3, Laura Rushford, Martin drove to West St. Paul. Laura managed the Target store located there.

Petite, with searching hazel eyes, she wore a frown while introducing herself. Before they had an opportunity to explain why they were there, she said, "Wendy called. I can't believe what happened to Ginny. We were with her all day. We should have taken the ride she offered. If we had, this would never have happened."

There was likely some truth to that, Pete thought. Since the weapon of choice wouldn't work on more than one victim . . . On the other hand, if the attacker had access to other weapons . . .

Like Wendy, Laura didn't notice anyone following Ginny either before or after she dropped them off at the bus. She did know that Zachary Esko, one of Ginny's subordinates, qualified as a perpetual thorn in Ginny's side.

"Ginny said he was forever filing union grievances, and accusing her of forcing him to do her job. I think they had it out on a weekly basis. It got so she wouldn't meet with him, unless there was a third party present. She said she had to protect herself against his trumped up accusations."

"Do you know if things have gotten worse or if she's been winning most of their recent battles?" Pete asked.

"No, sorry."

"How about her family? How was her relationship with them?" Martin asked.

"Okay I guess."

"Was she close to any of them?" Martin asked.

"She was closest to Will and his daughter Rachel. She had a special tie to Rachel, especially when Rachel was young. I think they drifted apart, once Rachel had a family of her own."

"I understand there may have been some hard feelings over the way Virginia handled her mother's affairs," Martin said.

"Got me, I didn't see it." Laura shrugged.

"Did anyone else have a bone to pick with Virginia?" Martin asked.

"Ginny could be pretty acerbic. She was a cut-to-the-chase kind of person. That left some people cold."

"Why did you put up with it?" Martin asked.

"Because she had a good heart. She would knock herself out to help, and she was there as soon as she sensed a need."

"Anyone at all who might have had it in for her?" Pete asked.

Laura's shoulders rose, held there a few seconds, then dropped. "Not that I know of. Sorry I can't be more helpful."

Pete and Martin ran through the drill with the business cards, and left the store. The aisles teamed with bargain hunters, taking advantage of the before-school sales.

ELEVEN

"Next?" Martin asked on their way back to the unmarked car.

"Let's talk to the two other women who went to the fair with her. Then we'll check out her co-workers."

"Did you notice how Ms. Rushford identified Esko as Virginia Green's subordinate?" Martin asked. "Do you think that has something to do with a store manager's constant awareness of the pecking order, or just coincidental?"

"Don't know, but I think Target has team leaders, rather than managers. Why didn't you ask her?" Pete chuckled.

"Sure thing, and why didn't I tell her I was surprised to see a female store manager? You bet!"

Pamela McGregor and Amy Tracy were the other two friends. While Martin drove, Pete contacted them. Neither answered their home phone. Both answered their cells. Both would meet whenever convenient for Pete and Martin. Pete got their locations. Pamela worked at the Central Library in downtown St. Paul. Amy worked at the Revenue Department, across I-94 from downtown.

At Revenue their questioning would go beyond Amy, so they decided to start with Pamela.

Reaching the main lobby, Pete and Martin passed through the monitors that blew the whistle on anyone trying to escape without checking out a book. They continued another dozen steps to the checkout counter. It was self-serve, so Pete waited impatiently for someone to acknowledge him. Eventually that happened, and he asked for Pamela McGregor.

A moment later, a woman emerged from a door along the far wall. "I'm Pamela," she said, extending a hand. Her long-sleeved shirt was buttoned at the wrists. Even so, her hand felt ice cold. Pete wondered if the way she dressed was a fashion statement or a way of coping with the cold air that greeted him as he'd opened the library door.

Pamela led them behind the counter and to her office. "Have a seat," she said, pointing to the chairs across the desk from her.

She already knew the reason for this meeting and didn't waste time on small talk. "Where did it happen and how? Was she shot? Stabbed? Beaten to death?"

"It's an active investigation," Pete said. "All I can tell you is that she was found in a parking lot near the one where you boarded the bus."

"What time?" Pamela asked.

"What time did you leave her?" Martin asked, wondering who was questioning whom.

"I'm not sure. Between seven thirty and seven forty-five, I think."

Pamela knew about Virginia's problems with Zachary Esko and the hard feelings over her mother's death. "But I can't imagine any of those things providing sufficient reason to murder someone, can you?" she added.

"Is there ever sufficient reason?" Pete asked.

"No. Of course not, but obviously some people disagree."

"Did you get both Ginny's perspective and her family's on the situation with her mother?" Pete asked.

"Well, no. I only heard Ginny's version."

Pete asked if she saw anyone following them at the fair, or if

Ginny antagonized anyone yesterday.

Pamela mentioned the man in the Merchandise Mart. "In the scheme of things, it was mighty insignificant, don't you agree?"

There she goes again, Martin thought.

"Can you think of anyone who might have a reason to attack or murder her, regardless of whether it was valid or seemed sufficient?" Pete asked.

Pamela rested her chin on the heel of her left hand and stared into space.

Pete watched her flip through the pages of her memory bank.

After a minute she said, "Two people." Holding up an index finger, she continued, "First, her ex. I think she took him to the cleaners."

"But she divorced him decades ago, didn't she?" Pete asked.

"True, except a year or so ago she heard about a piece of land he owns in Costa Rica. Turns out he bought it while they were married, using some money he squirreled away. She was awarded half the value of that property."

"How did she find out about it so long after the divorce?" Pete asked.

"Turns out she has a friend who is friends with her ex's current girlfriend. Howard and his girlfriend went to Costa Rica. He's building a house on the land. Apparently he bragged about hiding the land from Ginny. The girlfriend made the mistake of telling Ginny's friend, not knowing about the connection. Word got back to Ginny. She hired someone to research the purchase records, and so she wrote." Pamela smiled, apparently getting a lot of satisfaction out of knowing Howard was caught and punished.

"Her ex was furious when he got slapped with the papers. After all that time, I'm sure he thought he'd gotten away with it."

"Who else?" Pete asked.

"Her landlord. She's been reporting him to the city for some kind of code violations. She's gotten city inspectors out there. He's jumping through a lot of hoops these days. She said he was so angry he was spitting nails."

"Do you know his name?" Martin asked.

"First name only. It's Brendon."

"Anything else you can think of?" Martin asked.

"'Fraid not."

TWELVE

"The list grows," Pete said as he and Martin slid into the un-marked for the short trip to the Minnesota Department of Revenue. "Soon I'll need a legal pad, rather than this three-by-five notepad."

"You're not complaining, are you?"

"Not a chance. It's the leads we fail to uncover that bother me."

"That and the times you're lead around by the nose?" Martin said.

"Yeah. Have you noticed what the ring is doing to my nostrils? I'm afraid if Katie notices, she'll trade me in for another model."

"Aren't you the modest one? Now you think you qualify as a model? Let me know when you have your first runway event. I'll get a bunch of the guys together. We'll come to see your legs and bare chest."

"I think women will be more interested than the guys."

"True. I'm jealous. No one wants to see my bare chest. Not to change the subject, but since they both work at Revenue, do you think Amy Tracy knows Zachary Esko?"

"Don't know, but we'll soon have an answer."

A four-story granite building, topped with a red-tile roof, housed the Department of Revenue. Built in 2001 it resembled some of the oldest buildings in the capitol complex. It's a new kid on the block in a neighborhood that includes Regions Hospital.

The street in front of Revenue was torn up due to construction of the light rail's central corridor. It wouldn't open for almost two years, but ultimately that route would connect downtown Minneapolis to downtown St. Paul.

Amy Tracy met the two investigators at the security desk on the first floor. Dressed for casual Friday, she wore capris and a T-shirt. They followed her to the elevator and got off at the third floor.

It was obvious Amy got the lowdown from her friends. She had no questions about why they were there or what happened to Virginia.

When all three were seated, Pete began, "Tell us about Virginia's job responsibilities."

"She worked in corporate income taxes."

"Are your responsibilities linked to hers?" Pete asked.

"We're peers. We have the same classification in different divisions. I'm in individual taxes."

"What kind of relationship did Virginia have with the other Revenue employees?" Pete asked.

"Like most of us, she liked some. Others, not so much."

"Was there animosity between Virginia and some of the other staff?" Pete asked.

"Animosity, yes. Hatred, no."

"Animosity with whom?" Pete asked.

"Zach Esko is the first who comes to mind. He and Ginny didn't get along at all. That's no secret."

"Who else?" Martin asked.

"She often complained about her supervisor, but that's par for the course."

"What did she say about her supervisor?" Pete asked.

"She said he had no organizational history, but thought he had all the answers. She said he huddled with the brown noses and made life miserable for everyone who refused to kiss up. I told her to kiss up and make her life easier. She refused."

"Was her relationship with Esko also par for the course?" Martin asked.

"No, not by any stretch."

"What was going on between them?" Martin asked.

"Like all of us, Esko's job duties include, and I quote, 'Other duties as assigned by the division director.' Zach claimed he was being dumped on. He said Ginny forced him to do things that far exceeded what someone in his classification should be required to do."

"Any merit to his claim?" Martin asked.

"I don't know. I'm not familiar with what he was being asked to do."

"I understand Virginia was also having problems with her niece and her uncle. Are you aware of that?" Pete asked.

"Somewhat. They stayed clear of her at the wake and the funeral. A few times I noticed her uncle staring at her, but only when she wasn't looking."

"What caused the problems?" Pete asked.

"Ginny said everyone was ready to second guess the things she did for her mother, but no one was willing to step up and lend a hand."

"Can you provide any details?" Pete asked.

"Kind of yes, kind of no. Ginny moved her mother, from the home where she was raised, into an assisted living apartment. She said her mother had trouble doing all the things of everyday life. She thought it would be easier if she didn't have to try to take care of a three-bedroom house all by herself. Ginny and Will helped her when they could, but they couldn't always be there. Ginny said her mom was going downhill pretty fast, so it was the only reasonable action."

"What happened with her mother's home?" Pete asked.

"I heard it's sitting empty. Guess it has been since she moved. It was the perfectly wrong time to put a house on the market, pricewise. I don't think Ginny had a single offer. The asking price may be over-inflated. I don't really know."

"You took time off to go to the fair on a Thursday. Why didn't you go on the weekend?" Pete asked.

"It's known as crowd avoidance. We wanted to spend some time in the Midway, and we didn't want to spend most of that time waiting in lines."

"It worked as planned?" Pete asked.

"Yes, we had a terrific time!" Her smile sagged. "Guess it may have gotten Ginny killed, huh?"

"Did anything happen at the fair that might explain what happened to her?" Pete asked.

Amy shook her head. "Nothing I can think of."

"Did you notice anyone following you?" Martin asked.

"Everyone is following everyone at the fair. With all those people, it's like a moving mass of bodies."

"Does anything stand out?" Martin asked.

Amy sighed. "Nothing comes to mind."

"Did you notice a man in a yellow, gold, or orange T-shirt in your vicinity too often for it to be a chance occurrence?" Martin asked.

"With all those people wearing all those colors, do you have any idea how impossible it is to answer that question? Had someone dressed in orange or yellow knocked me down or said something nasty, it might have registered. That didn't happen."

"Did anyone in any color act suspiciously?" Pete asked.

"Define suspiciously."

"Followed you, stared at you and your friends, made you uncomfortable," Pete said.

"No. At least not that I noticed."

"We'd like to speak with all of Virginia's subordinates. With whom should we arrange that?" Pete asked.

Reaching for her phone, Amy said, "Let me call her supervisor."

After a brief conversation, Amy hung up and said, "Come with me, I'll take you to Russell Winger. He's . . . he was Ginny's supervisor."

Winger was shocked to learn of Virginia's death. He fell all over himself, attempting to accommodate Pete and Martin. He gave them his office. He arranged for them to speak with Virginia's subordinates one by one, in a steady stream.

All of her subordinates acted amazed by the news. All were aware of the problems between their supervisor and Zachary Esko. A few sided with Virginia, but most sided with Zachary.

"She actually picks on him," one said. "Sometimes I think he intimidates her, and it's her way of bringing him down a few notches. I told him to shut up, and she'd get over it. He was either unwilling or unable to do that. Have you ever known someone who is capable of pressing all the right buttons?"

And how, Pete thought.

After about ninety minutes of several different spins on that interpretation, Zachary Esko walked in.

THIRTEEN

With a smile as painted on as a clown's, Esko introduced himself to Pete and Martin. He was Pete's height, six-two, and had a similarly slender build. His black hair covered his head with tight ringlets. He had cold brown eyes and a cleft chin.

"Tell me about working for Virginia Green," Pete said.

"Hated it!" Zachary laughed.

"Guess that means you're relieved she's gone," Pete said.

Zachary's smile disappeared. "Relieved? Perhaps. Glad? No."

"There must have been times you could have strangled her," Pete said.

"Is that what happened?"

"Answer my question," Pete said.

"I sometimes attacked her verbally, but would never attack her physically. I'm not that kind of person."

"What kind of person are you, Zachary?" Pete asked.

"I believe in an honest day's work for an honest day's pay. I don't believe in taking advantage of the state, and I do my best not to let it screw me over."

"Virginia was trying to do that?" Martin asked.

"Absolutely! I had to do my job and large chunks of hers. She was dead wood. She was walking into the sunset, and taking her sweet time about it. That happens when people get to be her age, you know."

"Did you do anything about it?" Martin asked.

"I tried. I went to the union. They tried, but couldn't do anything. There's this mandatory, catch-all phrase in our job descriptions. It allows supervisors to screw employees. Virginia used it that way."

"So what did you do?" Martin asked.

"I told her I didn't have enough time in a forty-hour week to do my job and hers. I told her she had to prioritize my projects."

"And?" Martin asked.

"And she did. Her duties usually took precedence."

"And?" Martin asked.

"And I accomplished what I could in a forty-hour week. I didn't work one minute more or one minute less than forty hours each week."

"Were you at work yesterday?" Pete asked.

"Yes."

"What hours do you work?" Pete asked.

"Eight 'til four thirty. Speaking of which, I get off in," he looked at his watch, "exactly two minutes. Sorry, gotta go, or I'll break my rules." Esko stood and turned to go.

"Sit down, Zachary. We're not finished," Pete said. His tone left no room for discussion. "What did you do yesterday after work?" he asked.

"I went home."

"You're wearing a wedding band. Was your wife there last evening?" Pete asked.

"No, she works the three 'til eleven shift at Regions. She's an ER nurse."

"Can anyone vouch for your whereabouts?" Pete asked.

"I live in a condo. My neighbor may have heard my television. Otherwise, no."

"Got a phone number for that neighbor?" Martin asked.

Esko pulled a cell from his trouser pocket, touched the screen a few times, and recited the number. "It's his cell. You can probably reach him right now. Speaking of right now, it's four thirty-one."

"And we aren't finished," Pete said.

Esko pouted.

"What's your home address?" Pete asked.

Esko mumbled an address in Falcon Heights. It was a stone's throw from the fairgrounds, and a brisk ten-minute walk to the east Como parking lot.

After Esko left, Pete called the neighbor he'd mentioned. He explained who he was, and that he was in the middle of an investigation. "I have a question for you. Do you know if Zachary Esko was home last night between seven and nine?"

"Sorry, I have no way of knowing."

"Can you hear him moving around or hear his television?"

"I can only hear his television when I'm in the hallway. Unless he's making a lot of racket, I don't hear him moving around."

"Is there anyone who might?"

"I live next door to him. It's possible the couple that lives below him hears him. I'm on the top floor, and I'm not sure how much the people below me hear. All I know is that so far they haven't complained."

"Do you have a phone number for the people who live below him?"

"All I have is their names. They're Connie and Curtis Foley."

"Any idea of the likelihood of finding them at home at this hour?"

"Both are retired, so there's probably a good chance."

Using his phone, Pete searched the web for a Curtis Foley in Falcon Heights. He found one and dialed the number. Several rings later, an elderly sounding voice said, "Hello." It sounded more like a question than a declaration.

"Is this Curtis Foley?"

"Yes. Is this a telephone solicitation? I don't accept . . ."

"No, sir. This is not a telephone solicitation." Pete explained who he was, and what he wanted. "Did you hear any noise coming from the condo above yours last evening?"

"Naw. The only time I hear anything out of him is when he's hanging pictures."

"Did you see Zachary arrive or depart yesterday?"

"No, but I don't spend much time staring out the window. Other than traffic, there's rarely much to look at around here. Besides, he would probably have taken the back stairs to the garage. There's no way I can see that stairway. Unless I'm standing outside my backdoor, that is."

Pete thanked Curtis for his time and hung up.

"Well?" Martin asked.

"He can't vouch for Esko."

FOURTEEN

"Would like to have asked him if he ever had a personal phone call or text, during the forty hours he so carefully tracks," Martin told Pete, referring to Esko.

"Martin, of course not. Remember, he doesn't work a minute less than forty hours per week."

"Right, and I hate sweets." Martin smiled.

Pete and Martin had one last person to question before leaving Revenue. That was Virginia Green's supervisor—the guy who arranged all of the other meetings then disappeared. Pete wondered if Winger subscribed to Esko's philosophy and fled the premises at four thirty. They were in Winger's office, but Pete didn't see a briefcase. Did he move it to another location, before giving them his space? Surely someone at his level carried a briefcase, right?

One way to find out.

"Stay here, Martin. I'm going to look for Winger."

The bullpen area mimicked a ghost town.

Pete checked the offices in the vicinity of Winger's. A lone person occupied each of two of them. Neither knew where he could find

Winger. As he walked toward the offices on the other side of the bull-pen area, the first one stuck her head out her office door and called after him, "Try the conference room." She pointed toward a room in the direction he already headed.

Winger sat at the far side of a conference table, typing away on a laptop. A briefcase lay open on the table, answering Pete's question. "Finished?" Winger asked, as Pete approached the door.

"Not quite. We also want to speak with you."

"Of course, no problem. Give me a minute. Can't lose my train of thought."

Ten minutes later, Pete was unwilling to continue waiting. As he took a step toward the door, Winger appeared.

Amy Tracy told them Russell Winger liked people who kissed up, and got even with anyone who didn't fall in step.

In about ten seconds, Pete pegged Winger as the ultimate dictator and know-it-all. That fit nicely with Amy's assessment.

"Didn't want to influence your plan of attack," Winger said. "Now that you're finished with those people, I'll give you the lowdown on Virginia and each of them. You'll need that to contextualize what they said. It will give you an idea of what they didn't say. I can also fill in some of those blanks for you. Where should I start?"

"By telling us about your relationship with Virginia," Pete said.

"It was strictly professional, of course."

"I'm asking about your working relationship," Pete said.

"Oh. It was fine, as long as she remembered who is in charge. At times, she either didn't understand or didn't respect the fact that that's me. She often had her own agenda. That forced me to monitor her more closely than I would have liked."

"What was her agenda?" Pete asked.

Winger frowned and stared into space, tapping his upper lip with an index finger. Then he said. "She was egocentric. She always looked at this place through her own lenses. She evaluated my policies and procedures, based solely on how they affected her. She was bent on doing it her way, regardless of the policies and procedures I established. She wasn't a team player."

"I'll bet that made your job more difficult, made you angry," Martin said.

"Not really. I make the decisions. Those decisions rule." Winger emphasized the last word, and closed the comment with a smile.

"Even so, having to deal with the opposition must have been exasperating at times," Martin said.

"I refused to let it be." Winger crossed his arms, and the furrows in his forehead deepened.

"Where were you last evening, between seven and nine?" Pete asked.

"Home. I work long days. I'm tired by that time."

"Anyone there with you?" Pete asked.

"No. I live alone. Divorced."

"Did anyone see you arrive at home?" Pete asked.

"Got me." He shrugged.

Enough, Pete thought. "Thanks for your time. We won't keep you any longer."

"Okay. Don't hesitate getting back to me if you need my help again."

After he and Martin exited the building, Pete said, "How would you like to deal with that on a regular basis?"

"Funny, he reminds me a lot of you."

"Ouch, thanks. Whom shall we honor with our next visit, Martin?"

"The ex has my vote."

FIFTEEN

Pete called Virginia's brother Will, hoping he knew how to locate her ex-husband.

"Howie works for Ecolab in downtown St. Paul," Will said. "I think he still lives in the house he and Ginny built in Vadnais Heights. I heard he got the house, and she got everything else."

"Did Wendy Wykoff introduce your sister to Sunburg?" Pete asked.

"I doubt it. If she had, the demise of her marriage might have ended Ginny's friendship with Wendy. It was that acidic. I think she met Wendy at some Ecolab function she attended with Howard."

Not surprising, Will didn't have Sunburg's phone number.

"While I've got you, do you know the last name for Virginia's landlord?"

"Yes, Humboldt. Brendon Humboldt. I'm sure his phone number is in the contacts list on her phone."

Pete shared the information with Martin.

"Huh," Martin said. "Too bad we didn't know about Sunburg, when we were at Ecolab. By now, especially since it's a Friday, he's probably gone."

"True, but this way we have an opportunity to see the house he and Virginia built. In the process, we might learn something important about her."

"Right. Solving this case could depend on knowing whether she prefers brick or vinyl siding."

"I'm glad to hear you're learning the finer points of this business, Martin."

"You bet. When do you think the BCA will get around to checking out all those sticks, Pete? I hope collecting them wasn't a waste of time. The fair ends on Monday. Besides, in another day or two, will anyone remember if there was something special about one of their customers?"

"Unfortunately, we don't set priorities for the BCA. If the person who bought Virginia Green's stick stood out, there's a pretty good chance someone will remember them. If the person didn't stand out, it's unlikely anyone would remember him or her five minutes after their purchase."

"Yeah, you're right. You know, I could have immediately eliminated a lot of the sticks collected. Based on the photos you sent, many of them were too short to qualify. Also, a lot of them were too thin, or the points were wrong. Wish I'd taken the time to figure out which ones were possibilities."

"Don't worry about it. We have enough to keep us busy for a while, and our current efforts may be more fruitful than trying to determine the source of the stick."

"True. I wonder how they're doing with the search of her home. Her computer could contain some interesting messages . . . or maybe the person sent her a letter."

"Right, and the letter probably contains a return address."

"Of course it would. You wouldn't want something like that floating around." Martin smiled.

Pete used his cell phone to search for a phone number for Howard Sunburg. He came up empty-handed. "Either he doesn't have a home phone, or the number is unlisted."

Before initiating a potentially fruitless trip to Vadnais Heights,

Pete called the central number for Ecolab. It was three minutes after six, so he wasn't surprised when greeted by a recorded message.

As soon as he hung up, Pete's cell vibrated. He couldn't help but wonder if there was news about the sticks or Virginia's apartment.

The caller ID said it was Pete's boss, Commander Lincoln.

No word on the search of the victim's home, but Lincoln called to put things in perspective for Pete and Martin. He told Pete that, on average, a half-million corndogs are consumed each year at the fair. The figures for hot dish on a stick were iffier, but were estimated at thirty thousand per year. In other words, looking only at those two items, an average of more than forty-four thousand sticks were circulated each day of the fair.

Pete shared the news with Martin.

"Guess that means there'd be no benefit in trying to get a description of all the people who bought something on a stick yesterday," Martin said. "It must include almost everyone who walked through the gates. What was yesterday's attendance?"

"Just a minute. Should be able to tell you." Using the browser on his phone, Pete had the answer in little more than a minute. "It was 101,379. Sounds like the predicted heat discouraged a lot of people. The record for the second Thursday of the fair was set in 1995. It was 155,183."

"Since you're in the mood for trivia," Martin said, "I should use our trip to Vadnais Heights to teach you a few things. First, did you know that Teddy Roosevelt said, 'Talk softly and carry a big stick,' for the first time at the Minnesota State Fair Grandstand? It was in 1901, when he was still McKinley's vice president."

"Seriously?"

"Yup."

"Okay. Do you know what the State Fairgrounds was used for, before it became the fairgrounds?" Pete asked.

"Farmland?"

"Nope, it was the Ramsey County Poor Farm, and the first time the fair was located at the current site was in 1885."

"What happened to the poor farm when the land became the fairgrounds?"

"I think Ramsey County moved it to White Bear Avenue, near Frost. The barn is still there. It's listed on the National Register of Historic Places."

"What's it used for now?"

"I don't know," Pete said.

"I could assign that project to Marty."

"Good idea. I'm sure he'd like to contribute to our investigation."

"That depends on whether he considers the assignment of my making or his." Martin laughed.

Martin was in better spirits today.

Pete figured the discussion Martin wanted to have with his son didn't happen last night or this morning. He decided not to broach the subject. Martin was happier today, and he didn't want to spoil it. Instead, he said, "Tell me what's happening with your matrix, Martin." He referred to a device Martin created a year ago to track suspects and assist in solving cases. Martin was sold on it, and still hoped for his endorsement.

"I'm adding suspects at a record pace, and not eliminating anyone from consideration. It seems almost everyone she knew had a problem with Ms. Green. In most cases, those relationships don't seem volatile enough to end in murder, but that's often true in the cases we investigate. Most of the people we're interested in don't have anyone to corroborate their alibis, and I don't trust most of those who do. I keep hoping that, if we talk to enough people, something will jump out at us."

"I agree on all counts. I feel like I'm chasing my tail."

"Does Katie know you have a tail, Pete? She may prefer to marry someone who has evolved a step or two beyond that."

Twenty minutes after they began this trip, Martin pulled up in front of Sunburg's home. The street view of the ranch-style home was dominated by a three-car garage. That was a common malady of modern construction, Pete thought.

There were no cars in the driveway, but with three garage stalls, why would there be?

Martin parked on the street, and the two investigators walked to the front door.

Pete rang the doorbell, while Martin positioned himself several steps behind him. Both men stood stiffly, waiting for a response.

During about six months out of every year, it would be dark by now, and turned-on lights might indicate if anyone was home. Days were getting shorter, but the uncooperative sun wouldn't set for more than an hour.

Pete waited a minute, then tested the screen door. It was unlocked, so he opened it and rapped on the front door with a heavy hand.

After a delay long enough to test the patience of both men, the door opened, and the overpowering smell of fried onions almost bowled Pete over.

The man who stood in the doorway was six feet tall and bulky. His head was shaved, and he wore a brown and gray goatee.

"You don't look like missionaries. What do you want?" the man asked.

"Are you Howard Sunburg?" Pete asked.

"Yes, why?"

Pete explained who they were and told the man about Virginia Green's death. He didn't explain the circumstances.

"No kidding?" Sunburg smiled. "What a loss to society." The guy actually laughed.

"I can see you're all broken up over it," Pete said. "Where were you between six and nine o'clock last night?"

"Right here."

"Can anyone vouch for that?" Pete asked.

"Depends on how snoopy my neighbors are. One of them may have seen me drive in."

"I understand you weren't on good terms with your ex-wife," Martin said.

"If this is going to take awhile, why don't you come in? I don't see any sense in air conditioning the neighborhood."

The two investigators followed him through the foyer and into the living room. Virginia either took all the furniture, or he threw it out and started over after the divorce. With minimal, dark-colored leather furniture, hardwood floors, no area rugs, and vertical blinds as the only window coverings, it definitely looked like a bachelor pad.

Sunberg ushered Pete and Martin to a couple of chairs. He said he'd be back in a minute, and waddled toward the kitchen.

Pete heard hushed tones coming from that direction, but couldn't decipher what was said.

A minute later, Sunberg returned. "My girlfriend's fixing dinner," he explained. "It's almost ready. Hope this won't take long. What do you want to know?"

"I understand you and Virginia Green had a feud long after the divorce was finalized," Pete said.

"Yeah." Sunberg looked like he'd been busted.

Neither investigator responded. Eventually, red faced, Sunburg added, "It was all a misunderstanding. I thought the land was part of the divorce settlement."

"But with her help you got it straightened out?" Pete asked.

"With her help, I was taken to the cleaners a second time." Sunburg scowled.

"And all of that renewed the hard feelings between you and Ms. Green?" Pete asked.

"Put yourself in my place. Tell me you would have warm feelings for the bitch!"

"You've been divorced since when?" Martin asked.

"Since 1977."

"How long were you married?" Martin asked.

"Three years. I married her in 1974."

"What destroyed your marriage?" Martin asked.

"I grew tired of her negativism, her nagging, and her efforts to control my every thought and action. She was a control freak. Living with her was like living in prison."

"It took three years to discover that?" Martin asked.

"No, it took until the end of our honeymoon—literally. At first, I needed her. Guess I even found some comfort in knowing someone cared enough to pay that much attention to me. My parents pretty much let me raise myself. Ginny's tactics started getting old after a year or so, but at the time I couldn't afford to escape. Listen, if I was going to kill her, it would have been at that point, not now."

"Any idea who might have had it in for her?" Pete asked.

"I can't give you any names, other than maybe her brother Will. She dominated him the way she attempted to dominate me. Maybe he got tired of it, too. Other than him, I'd guess anyone who was exposed to her on a regular basis. She was vindictive, malicious, domineering, ostentatious, egocentric, obstreperous, narcissistic, and superficial. And those are some of her better qualities. It's beyond me how she managed to have any friends at all."

SIXTEEN

"Don't know about you, Martin, but I'm going to have to air myself out on the clothesline as soon as I get home."

"Really? I think the smell of fried onions is an improvement." Martin laughed.

"Does that mean you don't like my new after shave? They had a big sale at Fleet Farm. I bought a whole pallet of the stuff. Would have gotten more, but it was all they had."

"What does Katie Benton think of it?"

"I'd hoped to find out tomorrow night. We'd planned to go to the fair. Now, I'll have to wait awhile for her endorsement."

"Or for her to run the other way."

"Come on, Martin, seriously?"

"No. But it's good to know you're interested in my opinion."

"Martin, every morning I wonder what you'll think of my outfit."

"Right, and Barack calls almost daily to run ideas past me."

"Oh? How fast does he run?"

"Fast enough to escape this discussion." Martin smiled.

"Where does your matrix think we should next channel our efforts, Martin?"

"My matrix is a finely tuned machine, but it doesn't yet speak. Recently, however, it started mimicking Olivia's cooing. If you're interested in my recommendation, I say the landlord. Can't you see it? A demanding tenant drives a poor, accommodating slumlord over the edge?"

"Brendon Humboldt it is." Pete found a Brendon on the list of contacts taken from Virginia Green's cell phone. When he reached Virginia's landlord, Pete learned he didn't occupy the other half of the Highland Park duplex where Virginia had lived. He had a single family home that was also in Highland Park.

Sliding the phone back into his pocket, he said, "After we talk to Humboldt, let's call it a day. I'm sure you'd like to get home."

Pete wanted to give his partner an opportunity to address the problems on the home front. "By the way," he continued, "what's the baby's schedule these days? Does she sleep through the night?"

"You're kidding, right? Michelle said she's colicky. All I know is, unless Michelle or I hold her and don't stop walking between midnight and two in the morning, she screams her lungs out. The whole time, her face is pinched in a tight little knot. Don't get me wrong. I love that kid. You should see her smile when I hold her and talk to her. I know she recognizes my voice. Speaking of kids, Pete, what's happening with you and Katie Benton? Are you ever going to propose to her?"

"I've thought about it—a lot. I'm not sure she'll say yes. Just as important, I don't know if she can deal with my lifestyle day in and day out. How does Michelle deal with the uncertainty of your hours and the constant canceling of plans?"

"She knows it's a part of the package. Of course there are times when it causes friction. And, hard as it is to believe, after a long day, I'm not always easy to be around. Our marriage requires a lot of give and take. Admittedly, she does a lot more of the giving than I do. I guess the bottom line is: she thinks I'm worth it. If Katie has a head on her shoulders, she knows you're worth it, too."

"But a lot of cops' spouses start out thinking it's worth it, then change their minds. I don't know what I'd do if we got married, and she left me."

"You'd do what all divorced cops do. You'd get up in the morning, get dressed, and go to work. You'd get so absorbed in the job that for at least awhile, you'd forget about it. The next day, you'd do the whole thing all over again. You've already canceled a lot of things you planned with her at the last minute. It isn't like Katie doesn't have a feel for what it would be like being married to you."

"True, but she isn't coping with it day after day after day."

"But, Pete, neither are you. Our hours aren't always crazy."

"True."

"Have the two of you gotten far enough to talk about having kids?"

"She knows I want kids. I know she wants to have some, too. I'm just not certain she wants to have mine."

"Well, there's one sure way to find out."

"I know. One other thing bothers me, Martin. I don't think it would be fair to stay in my home. Katie may feel she's moving into another woman's territory. Andrea decorated that home. Much of the time, I still feel her presence."

"But Pete, she died more than two years ago."

"Doesn't matter. I still feel that way."

"In that case, I think you should move."

"I agree, and that's sort of holding me back. I love that house. I love the location, and the neighbors. It's been home for a dozen years."

"Tell me, Pete, would you rather have an empty house to which you've grown attached or a new home to share with someone you obviously love?"

"I know you're right. I'm just having a lot of trouble getting off dead center. Guess I'd better ask her first, huh? I'd hate to sell the place and end up alone in a strange place."

"I have an idea. You could ask her to go house hunting with you. Tell her you want to find a new home for the two of you."

"That's not a bad idea, Martin. I'll think about it . . . as soon as I'm able to stop thinking about this case."

"Sounds like a delay tactic to me." Martin chuckled.

* * *

Humboldt lived on James Avenue, a block from the fenced-in campus of St. Catherine's University. Like the others in this St. Paul neighborhood, his house appeared to be circa the 1930s or '40s. The ecru-colored two-story structure stood out in a neighborhood where white exteriors were the first, second, and third most popular choices. During the summer months, the homes here benefited from substantial shade cast by a variety of elderly trees. Humboldt's home was compact and, in keeping with the homes up and down the street, well maintained.

Martin pulled over to the curb, and the two investigators ascended the four steps to the front door. This time, Pete stepped back, and Martin rang the doorbell.

A sixtyish man who looked like an elf with an overactive pituitary gland answered almost before Martin's hand left the doorbell. He wore a black polo shirt that appeared a size or two too small for his belly. His gray hair hung down over the collar. "Police, I assume," he said.

"Yes, sir." Martin nodded, and flashed his badge and ID.

"Come in." Humboldt stepped aside for the two investigators.

The front door opened into the living room. The decorating displayed a woman's preferences.

"I understand Virginia Green rented an apartment from you," Pete began.

"Yes, why?"

"She was murdered last night," Pete said.

"No kidding?" Humboldt grinned. "She rented half of one of my duplexes, much to my chagrin. She's the worst renter I ever had, hands down."

"How so?" Martin asked.

"Nothing was ever good enough or ever quite right."

"For instance?" Martin asked.

"She said her key stuck in the front lock. I took graphite over and worked it into the lock. Next thing you know, she said I owed her for the cost of dry cleaning her coat. She claimed her key got graphite on it. She said the bathroom faucet leaked. I showed her how turning the on-off knob to the warm position prevented it. Didn't matter. Every other week I got a call from her, saying the dripping sound drove her crazy. For her, that would have been a very short trip. She called the city. Claimed the plumbing wasn't up to code. I have no idea where she got that idea. She was wrong, of course, but I had to take time to meet with the inspector. That's a minute sampling. Shall I go on?"

"So there was no love lost between the two of you," Martin said.

"That, sir, is an understatement."

"Where were you last evening between six and nine?" Martin asked.

"I was right here."

"Can anyone vouch for that?" Martin asked.

"Yeah, my wife. Her book club is meeting tonight. Want me to call her?"

Martin nodded.

Humboldt grabbed the cordless phone that sat on an end table. As soon as he finished punching in the numbers, Martin held out a hand. Understanding the meaning of that gesture, Humboldt gave him the phone, without first speaking to his wife.

After getting Humboldt's wife on the phone, Martin explained he was with the St. Paul Police department. "I have a few quick questions," he said. "Do you know where your husband was last evening, between six and nine?"

"He was home with me. Why?"

"I'm in the middle of an investigation. Do you know what time he arrived home yesterday?"

"We were together all day. We spent the afternoon at the fair. Got home around five o'clock. We planned to stay longer, but it was too hot."

Martin hung up and asked Humboldt if anyone else could vouch for his whereabouts yesterday.

"Either you or I can check with my neighbors, I guess."

"I understand you ran into Virginia Green yesterday, while at the fair," Martin said.

"No. I didn't even know she was there. Is that where it happened?"

"Can't say," Martin said, and he and Pete left.

"You know, of course," Martin said under his breath, as they walked to the unmarked car, "his wife may be covering for him."

"Yeah. Wouldn't be the first time, Martin."

SEVENTEEN

Back in the privacy of the unmarked car, Martin said, "Virginia Green didn't have much of a fan club, did she?"

"She had her share of detractors. But if we believe everything we're hearing, the dislike was never intense enough to lead to murder. At the same time, those close to her seemed to understand her and accept her shortcomings. I guess all friendships rely on those two things, don't they?"

"True, because few people are as lovable as you and I."

"Lovable *and* humble. Unless something happens to change our minds, Martin, let's start with Tommy Wells tomorrow."

After driving Pete to headquarters, Martin headed home to his family.

On his way home, Pete thought about walking into an empty house. Then he thought about Katie Benton. Was she the solution? Usually, thinking about her made him smile. Not this time. He grappled with how to proceed. Should he ask her to marry him? Was it the right thing for him—for both of them? He thought so. Or did he just want to believe it? He knew he loved her. The last six months had gone really well. They liked many of the same things, and laughed about the same things. She put up with his sense of humor. He liked her family, and they liked him. Just as important, his family liked her. It was a conundrum. The wrong decision could be devastating all around.

He decided to call his buddy, Chris Gannon. Sometimes it helped to talk these things out. Chris was a good sounding board and rarely steered him wrong.

Despite the pressing desire to get off dead center and make a decision, procrastination took charge. Instead of calling Chris, he fixed dinner. While eating, he rifled through the mail. After putting the bills in their designated holding place, he recycled the rest. Then he picked up the novel he started reading a week ago and found little time for. Before he'd read a full page, the phone rang.

"Pete, I've been thinking about you. Decided to call and see how you're doing."

"Been thinking about you, too, Katie. Today was crazy. I'm working on a new case."

"The woman who was attacked at the fair?"

"Yes, but it happened in a parking lot across the street from the fairgrounds."

"I heard about it. Right away, I wondered, why there? I'm afraid you're affecting my thought processes. Scary, isn't it?" After several seconds of silence, she said, "Pete, are you there?"

"Yeah, sorry." Speaking to Katie drove his conundrum back to the forefront. Should he ask her to go house hunting? No! Not before he talked to Chris.

"Guess you're working a lot of hours these days, huh?" When several seconds passed without a response, she said, "Pete, are you falling asleep?"

"No, sorry. I'm a bit distracted."

"Is it the investigation? I've never seen . . . or heard . . . you this preoccupied."

"That and a few other things. It's not looking good for tomorrow night, Katie. I'm afraid I'll have to beg off. I'm really sorry. I do this far too often. Unfortunately, I can't imagine being able to hang it up early enough to get together. I hope you understand."

"Of course I understand, Pete. It's your job. I'm happy to take the bad with the good. You're worth it."

"Thanks. Katie, I've been thinking about doing some house hunting. Would you like to come along?"

"But Pete, you love your house."

"Yeah, even so, the time feels right. I won't have an opportunity before we wrap up this case. Once we do, would you like to help?"

"Sounds like fun. Are you looking for a woman's perspective?"

"One particular woman's, yes. I think black vinyl siding is attractive. How about you?"

"Well, it's a neutral color, and it would stand out—except at night." She laughed.

He smiled. He loved the sound of her laugh. It was infectious. "I'll find a realtor first chance I get."

After hanging up, Pete thought about Katie's remark. Did she really mean it? Was she willing to cope with his schedule? Would she mean it after they were married for ten years? Ten? What about five . . . or two?

What came over him? He was going to talk to Chris Gannon first.

He ran a hand back and forth through his hair and decided that worrying about it was a waste of time. It was too late to undo. Katie knew what he was asking, didn't she? Of course. She must know.

Shaking his head, Pete returned to his book. That lasted about thirty seconds. After reading the same paragraph six times, he inserted the bookmark, and snapped the book shut.

He walked to his bedroom. He got ready for bed and slid between the sheets. By the time his head hit the pillow, he was sound asleep.

EIGHTEEN

On Saturday morning, Pete got up at six, completed his four-mile run, read the newspaper, and was at his desk at headquarters when Martin dragged himself in at eight. Pete noticed the dark circles under Martin's eyes and said, "Looks like last night was your night to pace with Olivia."

"Yeah. I already drank four cups of coffee. Didn't help."

"Maybe you should start training Marty to step up to the plate."

"With school starting next week? Not going to happen."

"Maybe Michelle could homeschool him. Then he wouldn't have any excuses."

"You're full of good ideas this morning, aren't you?" Martin laughed. "Guess that means one of us had a good night's sleep. I need some more strong coffee."

"Grab a mug, and we'll plan our day."

Martin returned a few minutes later with a large mug of coffee and two sweet rolls. "I brought you a treat." He held out a roll.

Pete waved it off. "Thanks, I already ate."

Martin didn't argue. He knew when he grabbed two that Pete was unlikely to eat one. It was a rare occasion when Pete Culnane splurged. Fortunately, he was willing to sacrifice his figure to help with Pete's weight control. He shrugged and devoured both.

"We have a change of plans, Martin. Thanks to your efforts, the BCA determined the vendors using our stick. They narrowed it down, based on the length and diameter of the stick, and the point. I have a list of seven vendors."

"What food or foods?"

"Foot-long or twelve-inch corn dogs. Different vendors call them different things."

"Wish you'd told me we were going to the fair, before I ate both rolls. What if I don't have room for Tom Thumb donuts?" Martin smiled.

"You've never let me down before, Martin."

Prior to leaving, they marked the vendor locations on a map. Because they spread from one end of the fairgrounds to the other, they made a copy of the map and divided the work.

On their way to the headquarters parking lot, Martin half-ran to keep up with Pete. In retrospect, he regretted eating two sweet rolls.

As they entered the fairgrounds, through the main Como entrance, Pete said, "Martin, this is your second trip through the turnstiles, and my first. We're totally screwing up the attendance records. Wonder what I should do to fix that."

"I'd start with the governor."

"Good idea, Martin. Since you thought of it, I'll let you handle it—and take credit."

"Or the blame. I'll get right on it—as soon as I'm the commander, and you're the sergeant." Martin chuckled.

After splitting the workload, it still took more than an hour to cover the seven booths that sold the right corn dogs. They spoke with almost everyone who worked last Thursday.

While they did, the lines of patrons in front of those booths grew, and the managers and owners grew irritated. In the process, both investigators elicited and ignored a wealth and variety of inhospitable body language.

They asked the workers the questions Pete discussed during the autopsy. They also covered the ones he and Martin talked about on their way to the fairgrounds.

Pete knew it was a longshot, but he hoped someone stood out. If the person who stabbed Green bought the stick for that purpose or already had murder on their mind, it was reasonable.

If no one stood out, it could mean a lot of things. For example, was that person a sociopath? At the time of purchase, they had no idea how the stick would be used? The stick was discarded, and the attacker found it? Green had the stick when she was attacked? The booth was too busy for the staff to pay attention to customers? There were a million other explanations.

Martin arrived as Pete finished the questioning at the last booth.

When they reached the unmarked car, Pete pulled the small spiral notepad from his suit coat and looked up Tommy Wells's address and phone number.

A woman answered.

Pete explained who he was and asked to speak with Tommy.

Before long, a gruff voice said, "What can I do for you?"

Pete explained.

"How long will it take?"

"An hour or so."

"Better come right over. I have to be out the door no later than ten."

On the way, Pete called the four women who attended the fair with Virginia Green. Once again, he started with Wendy Wykoff.

After explaining he had a few more questions, he asked, "Did any of you buy a foot-long corn dog on Thursday?"

"No."

"Did any of you buy anything on a stick?"

"Sure, lots of things."

"Including?"

"Deep fried olives, a pickle, and cheese, for starters. Why?"

"Was Ginny still eating anything or carrying one of those sticks when she walked you to the bus?"

"No."

"You're certain?"

"Positive"

Next, Pete called Laura Rushford and asked the same questions. The only answer that differed from Wendy's was the foods on a stick they bought that day.

"Two down, two to go," he told Martin.

"And?"

"Tell you as soon as I finish."

When Pamela McGregor answered, he asked, "Was Ginny eating something that came on a stick or carrying one of those sticks when she dropped you off at the bus?"

"No. We hadn't bought anything like that for hours."

Amy Tracy made it unanimous.

NINETEEN

Tommy Wells lived in a ranch-style house on Walnut Street in a working class neighborhood in Lauderdale—a suburb sandwiched between Minneapolis and St. Paul. Alongside the driveway, a gigantic tree hid much of the house from view. Homes up and down the street repeated that tactic.

A woman, sounding like the one who answered the phone when Pete called, came to the door. "Come in," she said. "Tommy will be with you in a moment. He's getting ready for work. Have a seat." She motioned toward the living room. "Can I get you anything?"

"No, but thanks for offering," Pete said.

The house smelled like freshly baked chocolate chip cookies. Martin would have liked to take a few of them off her hands. Even so, he let Pete's response suffice.

The two investigators sat and waited for Virginia Green's uncle. It was a short wait.

Tommy Wells filled the doorway as he entered the living room. A hulk of a man, he stood close to Pete's height and had massive shoulders and large hands. He wore knee-length plaid shorts and a polo shirt.

Eyewitnesses rarely paint a consistent or reliable picture of the people they describe. Even so, Pete figured it was a stretch to think this man could be the person who checked Virginia Green's status prior to the arrival of the paramedics. Finding that man could be important to the case.

Media outlets interviewed Commander Lincoln from the crime scene on Thursday night. He mentioned the man who stopped to check on the victim and asked that man to call the PD. To date, they hadn't heard from him, nor from anyone else offering information about him.

"Tommy Wells," the man said, holding out a hand first to Martin, then Pete. He had a grip like a vice. "Have a seat. Please, make yourselves comfortable."

Tommy plopped down on the couch. "Would you like something to drink? Mary Ann is making cookies. Would you like some? She makes a mean chocolate chip. Hers beat Sweet Martha's hands down. Too bad it's impossible to get a booth at the fair. With her baking them and me selling them, we could add a nice cushion to our retirement." Tommy smiled.

"Thanks, I couldn't," Pete said.

"How about if I have Mary Ann fill a bag for each of you?"

"Kind of you to offer, but no. Thanks anyway," Pete said.

Martin knew all about Sweet Martha's cookies. He'd love to have an opportunity to compare Mary Ann's cookies to Sweet Martha's. For a fleeting moment, he thought about swapping Pete for a partner who ate like a real person. Remembering Pete's unsurpassed track record for solving cases, he ignored his stomach and succumbed to peer pressure.

"Mary Ann said you were getting ready for work," Pete said. "Where do you work?"

"At the fair."

"What do you do?" Pete asked.

"I work in a booth, selling Midway tickets. On days like last Thursday, I'm grateful the booth is air conditioned. Couldn't do it otherwise."

"You worked at the fair last Thursday?" Pete asked.

"Yes, I work all twelve days. Have for the last ten years. It gives me and Mary Ann a little mad money. I understand Will told you about my sister's death. Due to her funeral, I went in late on Monday. That was the first time ever that I failed to work my full shift."

"Do you always work the same shift?" Pete asked.

"Yes, from four in the afternoon until the Midway closes at midnight."

"But you said you have to be out the door in an hour," Pete said.

"Yes, it's Saturday. I always take my grandson Tommy to his baseball games on Saturdays. He's responsible for the treats today, so I have to take him shopping first. Tommy's my namesake. He makes me proud." Wells beamed.

"Did you see Virginia at the fair last Thursday?" Pete asked.

"No. Sorry to say, I didn't."

"I understand she spent much of her time in the Midway. I'm surprised you missed her," Pete said.

"Do you know how many people are there on an average day? The ticket booth where I work is one of seven, and it has multiple windows. Even if she came to my booth, there's only a one in five chance I'd wait on her. I see only the people who pass in front of my window, and I see them only when there's a lull. Most of the time I'm too busy selling tickets and making change to notice anyone."

"I understand you weren't happy about the way Virginia managed your sister's life, especially over the last year," Martin said.

"I was more than unhappy. Ginny killed her mother. My sister lost her will to live after Ginny shuffled her off to that apartment. I couldn't believe how fast she went downhill. I confronted Ginny. I told her we had to get Emma back in her house. The house was empty. It would have been better for the house and for Emma."

Tommy shook his head. His face grew redder with each proclamation. "Ginny said her mother was no longer capable of taking care of herself. That was bull! I dropped in on Emma at least once a week. I always did that—both before and after Ginny moved her into assisted living. Emma was eighty-four, but both physically and mentally she was a decade or two younger. I tried to tell Ginny that. She said I wasn't qualified to judge."

Tommy pulled a hanky from a back pocket and mopped his face.

"Sorry. I get a little overheated when I talk about it. Emma aged at least a year for every month she was in that dungeon. Ginny either couldn't see it or didn't care. I honestly don't know which. Bottom line: Ginny's actions killed my sister. When I told her that was happening, she told me that Emma's doctor agreed with the move. If that's true, he's an idiot!"

Tommy mopped his forehead, again.

"It's obvious you and your sister were very close," Pete said.

"She was twelve years older than me. She was like a second mother. She taught me how to ride a bike. If I skinned my knee, she was as likely as my mother to patch it up. She taught me how to dance. When I was too shy to talk to girls, she taught me how to break the ice. Emma was there for me my whole life."

"Sounds like there wasn't much love lost between you and your niece," Pete said.

"Not for the last year. Before that, she was like a daughter. She spent half of her childhood riding around on my shoulders. I loved that kid. I don't know what changed her. She's not the person I once knew."

Tommy frowned and rubbed his forehead. "Giving her the benefit of the doubt, maybe feeling responsible for Emma was too much for Ginny. Maybe it changed her. She insisted what she did was the best thing for my sister. She might actually have believed it. Guess we'll never know now, huh?" Tommy looked glum.

"How many booths did you say sell Midway tickets?" Martin asked.

"Seven."

"Do you always work in the same one?" Martin asked.

"Yes."

"Which one?" Martin asked.

"Booth number six. It's near the center of the Midway."

"Does someone supervise the people selling tickets in those booths?" Martin asked.

"Of course. There are several supervisors and two superintendants."

"What's the difference?" Martin asked.

"All of the ticket booths are split between the two superintendents. A supervisor oversees only one or two booths."

"What's your supervisor's name?" Martin asked.

"Gary Henderson."

"Does he supervise one booth or two?" Martin asked.

"Two."

"Do you have any breaks when you work at the fair?" Pete asked.

"Yes, one. It's from nine until nine thirty."

"It's always the same time? It doesn't vary from day to day?" Pete asked.

"Some people go at different times. I always go from nine until nine thirty, give or take a few minutes."

"How did you spend your break time on Thursday, the day before yesterday?" Pete asked.

"The same way I always do. I used the facilities and grabbed something to eat."

"Did you leave the fairgrounds while on break that day?" Pete asked.

"No. It takes too long to get to and from any of the gates. Besides, I had no reason to leave."

"Any idea who might have wanted to hurt Ginny?" Pete asked.

"Where do I start? Like I said, she's not the person I once knew. There's her ex-husband. There's this guy she was dating, borrowed a substantial sum from, and stopped repaying." Tommy counted them off on his fingers as he went. "I understand she undermined a guy she was competing with for a promotion. I also hear some of her staff hated her. I had problems with her, but hurting her wouldn't have solved anything." He didn't use a finger to count himself.

"She bragged about making life miserable for her landlord," Tommy continued. "What kind of person revels in making life miserable for everyone around them? Sorry, that's a rhetorical question. Off the top, those are all of the people I can come up with. Did you ask Will?"

"Yes," Pete said. "Do you know the name of the man she was dating and borrowed the money from?"

"No. Will probably does." Tommy looked at his watch. He was getting restless.

"Did she mention the name of the man with whom she was competing for a promotion?" Pete asked, figuring he already knew the answer.

"Probably, but I didn't pay any attention. I'd be hard-pressed to come up with it."

"Did she ever express a concern for her safety? Did she think she was in danger?" Pete asked.

"I never heard her say anything like that. Was it premeditated?"

"We're in the process of determining that," Pete said.

"Are we almost finished? I don't want to be late. Tommy's expecting me."

"Just a couple more questions," Pete said. "Where do you park when you work at the fair?"

"In the employee lot. They bus us to and from the fairgrounds from a spot near Heritage Square."

"Where's the employee lot?" Pete asked.

"Northwest of the fairgrounds, near Larpenteur Avenue and Highway 280."

"Did Ginny have a will or a trust?" Pete asked.

"I have no idea. She was usually well organized, so it seems likely."

"Do you know if she has a safety deposit box?" Martin asked.

"I have no idea."

"Where did she do her banking?" Martin asked.

"I don't know that, either."

"That's all for now, but don't go anywhere," Pete said. "We may want to speak with you again. In the meantime, take our business cards." He and Martin each handed one to Tommy. "If you remember either of those names, please call one of us—anytime."

TWENTY

Martin waited until they reached the street to say, "That guy definitely has the strength to ram a stick a half foot into someone's gut. He has thirty-plus years on me, but I wouldn't want to take him on. How about you, Pete?"

"Hell, Martin, I wouldn't take you on." Pete laughed. "I want to speak with Tommy's supervisor and co-workers. I'd also like to get my hands on Virginia Green's will or trust, assuming she has one or the other. If getting her money was the motive, the location for the attack seems perverse. For that reason, it isn't a priority. Even so, I think we should keep it as a consideration."

"Since she doesn't have a husband or children, her brothers and sister seem to be the most likely beneficiaries. From what we've heard, sounds like Will could be at the top of the list. Her niece Rachel is another reasonable recipient. If Virginia currently has a boyfriend, he might have made the cut."

"On the other hand," Pete said, "I suppose Virginia could be giving everything to charity."

"Okay, which charity or charities are most likely to knock her off to get at the money, and why didn't they wait until she had her hands on her mother's assets?"

"While you work on that, Martin, I'll call Amy Tracy. She didn't mention Virginia being in a fight to the finish for a promotion. I wonder why. Cell phones are wonderful, aren't they? They make our job so much easier—when they aren't making us too accessible. If you don't want to tackle the charities, how about asking Will for the name of the boyfriend who loaned her money? If her uncle knows about it, Will should."

"Then?"

"Since it's Saturday, today might be the best time to check out her ex's and her landlord's neighbors. Let's see if anyone witnessed their returns at the times they claimed on Thursday."

* * *

Amy Tracy's cell phone didn't make her accessible. Pete left a message, asking her to call ASAP.

Martin was more successful reaching Will Green. "Did your sister borrow money from someone she dated in the recent past or is currently dating?"

"Just a minute."

Martin heard a muffled conversation in the background. Eventually, Will said, "Sorry. Are you still there?"

"Yup."

"We think his name is George. George Dover or Dexter or Dawson. It's something like that. I'm almost positive his first name is George, and his last name begins with a 'd.' You have the contacts from Ginny's cell phone don't you? She may not have gotten around to deleting him from her contacts . . . or she could have left him there to identify him if he tried to reach her."

"She was no longer seeing him?"

"No."

"Did she pay off the loan?"

"I'm not sure, but I don't think so."

"In other words, it's reasonable to assume that she didn't," Martin said.

"Not reasonable, but probable."

"Was she dating anyone when she died?"

"I don't think so. She didn't bring anyone to Mom's funeral."

Martin thanked him for his help and disconnected. Then he scanned his list of contacts from Virginia's phone. There was one George. No last name. "Got it," he told Pete. "Do you want to call him or should I?"

"My track record isn't all that hot, but I'll do it. What's the number?"

Pete dialed as Martin recited it. He got George Dawson's address and arranged to meet him in about forty-five minutes. He estimated it would take that long to get from Lauderdale to Mendota Heights.

En route, Pete made a courtesy call to the Mendota Heights Police Department. He gave them a heads up, in case they wanted to have a representative at the meeting with Dawson. No surprise. They begged off.

Martin beat his estimate by three minutes. Dawson lived in a brick bungalow with a single-car garage. There was a lot of foliage out front, but it couldn't compete with the forest in the backyard. A couple of massive trees dwarfed Dawson's house.

A woman answered the door. When Pete asked for George, she said, "Love, there's someone here to see you."

A mousy little man emerged through a doorway that led to the kitchen. His long pointed nose and wispy mustache contributed to that image. He was bespectacled and had thinning gray hair. "Are you Peter Culnane?" he asked.

Pete nodded. "Like I said, we have some questions."

"Yeah. Let's talk in the kitchen. Betty, you won't be interested in any of this. I'll see you around four o'clock. That'll give you enough time to fix dinner, right?"

Betty harrumphed and snatched her purse off a chair. After giving Pete and Martin the once-over, she sniffed and stomped out the front door.

The three men sat around the kitchen table. George folded his hands on the table and looked expectantly at the two investigators.

"We're here about the attack on Virginia Green," Martin said.

"Yeah, I heard about it on the news. It happened in the State Fair parking lot? It had to be a wacko. Who would attack someone there?"

"We thought you might have an idea who would want to hurt her," Martin said. "I understand you used to date her."

"I have no idea who would do it. I can't begin to imagine it."

"Does that mean that, to the best of your knowledge, she didn't have any enemies?" Martin asked.

"I didn't say that," Dawson snorted. "She had plenty of enemies. I was added to the ranks several months ago. I just don't know of anyone who would solve it by killing her. It seems a bit extreme."

"That depends," Pete said. "If someone owes you money and refuses to pay it back, a person can get pretty riled, can't he, Mr. Dawson?"

"Hey, I was furious when she decided that there was no need to repay me, but I wouldn't kill her over it. That wouldn't get my money back. I filed a claim in conciliation court. And I got the money ten days ago. Guess no one told you about that part, huh?"

"Were you seeing Ms. Green when her mother was placed in an assisted living facility?" Pete asked.

"Yes."

"Tell us what effect that had on the other family members," Pete said.

"As far as I could tell, everything went smoothly. Ginny had to do all the work. She had to go through her mother's things and decide what furniture to take to the new place. It was hard on Ginny—a very emotional time. I helped her move the furniture. Her mother was in her new home for a month or two when all hell broke loose. Ginny's brother and uncle and niece all got on her back. No one lifted a finger to help with the move. Everyone jumped in and condemned Ginny after the fact."

"Which brother?" Pete asked.

"Will."

"What effect did the move have on Ginny's mother?" Pete asked.

"I don't understand the question."

"Did her mother thrive in the new environment?" Pete asked.

"She was old. Do people in their eighties thrive anywhere?"

Trying again, Pete asked, "Did you notice a deterioration in Emma Green's physical or emotional condition, after the move?"

"Once we got her moved into the apartment, I rarely saw her. I don't think I'm qualified to have an opinion."

"Describe Ginny Green," Pete said.

"Ambitious, hard driving, dedicated."

"Yet she had a lot of enemies?" Pete asked.

"I don't know if enemy is the right term. A lot of people didn't like her. Hell, a lot of people don't like me, either. I took her to conciliation court to resolve a dispute, but she wasn't my enemy."

"Can you name any enemies she had?" Pete asked.

"No. I think that term is too strong."

"Okay, can you think of anyone who might want to hurt her?" Pete asked.

"Her detractors varied from day to day. People get angry and might want to lash out. They usually calm down and get over it without taking any action."

"Can you think of anyone who might have at some point in time wanted to lash out against Ms. Green, regardless of whether or not they actually did?" Pete asked.

"The only person I can think of is her mother."

"Where were you last Thursday evening between six and nine?" Pete asked.

"I was here."

"Was anyone here with you?" Pete asked.

"No, I was alone."

"Did you see a neighbor or someone who could vouch for your whereabouts?"

"Not that I'm aware of."

"Do you have a home phone?" Pete asked.

"No, why?"

"Never mind," Pete said.

Pete handed Dawson their business cards and said, "Call one of us if you come up with *anyone* who could have, on a whim, hurt Virginia Green."

When they were out of earshot of Dawson's home, Martin said, "Do you think Dawson dismissed his girlfriend, so she wouldn't hear about Virginia?"

"Yup."

"I love the way he arranged to have her return in time to fix his dinner. If that's the status quo, I wonder what Virginia saw in him."

"Maybe she dated him to gain access to his bank accounts. If so, he must have more money than his home suggests."

"Pete, that's a despicable thing to say about a murder victim. I'm shocked!" teased Martin.

Pete smiled. "I didn't say it happened. I'm looking at all the possibilities. That's my job. Let's see if any of Dawson's neighbors know if he was home between six and nine on Thursday."

TWENTY-ONE

Pete and Martin split up and knocked on every door on Dawson's block and the block facing his. It took just under thirty minutes. When they finished, they had no confirmation that Dawson was home during the relevant hours. They did have a list of the homes where no one answered and one more tidbit.

A woman who lived across the street said Virginia and George fought all the time. "He took a swing at her at least once. Gave her a black eye. She called the police."

"She told you that?" Pete asked.

"Yes. I saw the police cars, and a few days later I saw her black eye. I asked her about it, and she told me the whole story."

"What did she tell you?"

"She said he was drinking and went off on her, after she burned their dinner. How crazy is that?"

"How well do you know George?" Pete asked.

"Not well. I say 'hi' when I see him in the yard. That's about it."

"Did that incident happen around the time they stopped seeing each other?"

"I don't really know. It might have. You have to ask George."

Pete made notes. He'd check the police report, and he might talk to George about it—later.

Martin got another spin on that story from the first neighbor to the left of George's home. After the cops showed up at George's, this guy asked George about it. George told him Ginny started the whole thing. He said she threw a glass of wine in his face.

"Guess that means Dawson remains on your matrix, at least for now," Pete said.

"Yeah, along with Virginia's ex, Howard Sunburg; her landlord, Brendon Humboldt; the subordinate who disdained her, Zachary Esko; her brother Will; his daughter Rachel; and her uncle, Tommy Wells. And that's just for starters. What next?"

Pete pulled out his cell and said, "Let's see if I can reach Amy Tracy." The subsequent look on his face and the way he shoved the phone back in his pocket announced a second failed attempt.

"Maybe we should go to the fair," Martin said. "We could sample the food, talk to some people, and sample the food."

"And while there, we could sample the food." Pete laughed.

"Exactly!" Martin smiled.

"Not quite yet. I want to get there in time to make sure Tommy works in the ticket booth he mentioned, and I want to see where and when he goes on breaks. Tommy went to his grandson's baseball game. Is Marty playing this afternoon?"

"Yeah, at three."

"We're not far from Highland Park. Let's talk to Humboldt's neighbors. Depending on how long that takes, we may have enough time to go to Vadnais Heights to check with Sunburg's neighbors. Then you can drop me off at headquarters and go to Marty's game. I can handle the surveillance of Tommy's booth."

"You're saying that so you can pig out at the fair without witnesses, aren't you?"

"Yeah, but don't tell the guys. I have a reputation to maintain."

"How about if we do it this way, Pete? I'll drop you off at headquarters, and I'll meet you at the fair between five thirty and six. That way, I can help track Tommy."

"I like it."

* * *

Fewer people were home in Highland Park. No one knew that Humboldt and his wife went to the fair, much less what time they got home or if they were home between six and nine.

"I saw lights over there around eight thirty, but have no idea if they were there from six o'clock until then," one neighbor said. "If you wanted to know about those hours in November, I could be more helpful. Well, that's only if they don't use those gadgets that turn lights on and off at set times. I don't think they do. I've never noticed their lights always going on and off at the same times."

She was right about the lights being a tip-off in November. Today the sun set at seven fifty. Daylight savings ended the first Sunday in November. Once that happened, the sun would set before five.

Pete knew that Humboldt had time to stab Virginia Green, and get home by eight thirty.

* * *

On the way to Vadnais Heights, Pete mentioned, "Saturday isn't the optimum day to do this, especially when it's Labor Day weekend. Just the same, I hate to wait until Tuesday. The further we get from the day in question, the less likely people will remember what happened and what they observed."

Martin didn't utter a word during this trip, and Pete wondered if he was thinking about his wife, Michelle. He was torn between asking and letting Martin broach the subject, when he was ready. Patience won.

Pete noticed Sunburg's girlfriend's car when they reached Sunburg's street.

Martin parked on the corner.

Pete looked at his watch. "We should be fine time-wise. Worst case, or would it be best case, this shouldn't take more than an hour."

"Marty will be thrilled to see me," Martin said. "His batting average is over three hundred, if you only count the times I'm there."

"He's a terrific kid, Martin."

"Yeah," Martin sighed.

Walking to the first house, Pete tried to decipher that sigh. *Are things worse with Marty or Michelle? Or was it just a sigh?*

The sound of laughter and the smells of meat grilling reminded Pete of his hollow stomach. Martin usually ensured they didn't miss many meals. Apparently Pete's partner was deep into this case—or too distracted to think about eating.

Once again, the two investigators came up empty-handed. One neighbor knew Howard was home at six, but not if he left sometime after that. Another thought he was home at nine, but didn't know what time he arrived.

Most neighbors thought Howard was friendly, but none were close to him or spent time with him.

"He doesn't have much to do with the guys around here," one man said. "In fact, he seems to be drawn exclusively to the female persuasion. I never see guys over there. Some of the women I see over there are actually pretty. With a face like his, I don't understand how he does it."

TWENTY-TWO

For a reason Pete could only speculate about, Martin was more talkative on the trip from Vadnais Heights to headquarters. Did the thought of going to Marty's game cheer him up?

"There's no sense in wasting this trip to headquarters," Martin said. "I have more trivia for you. First, who was Dan Patch?"

"All I know is that he was a horse."

"He was more than just a horse. He was a legendary pacer. In 1906 he set the record for pacing the mile at our State Fair. That record still stands. That's why the street the Grandstand is on is named for him. In fact, the current Grandstand was built in 1909 to accommodate the huge crowds he drew to harness racing. They refer to it as the house Dan Patch built."

"What year was the first Minnesota State Fair?" Martin continued.

"Well, Minnesota became a state in 1858, so 1858?"

"Close, but no cigar. It was 1859."

"Foul. What's a year?"

"Three hundred and sixty-five days." Martin laughed. "Unless, of course, it's a leap year. Who are the State Fair mascots?"

"That's easy. Fairchild and Fairborn."

"Which came first?"

"The egg?"

"Ha, ha."

"Okay, I don't really know. Fairchild?"

"Good guess. On average, how many cheese curds, not orders of cheese curds but individual cheese curds, are sold each year?"

"Do they get any easier?"

"No, but this is the last one, at least for now."

"Two million?"

"Good guess. It's 2.6 million."

Martin deposited Pete in the parking lot at headquarters and left for Marty's game.

Pete spent a little under an hour glued to his desk, attempting to make a dent in the paperwork. At a quarter to three, he hung up his suit coat and tie, grabbed a logo-free baseball cap, walked to the parking lot, and drove to the fairgrounds. During the fair, this drive qualified as a trip from hell—at best.

He turned into the east Como parking lot, fully aware that Debbie Brookston and Cynthia Lockhart discovered Virginia Green here. It took a few minutes to find a parking space. The Saturday of Labor Day weekend, the final weekend of the fair, again proved a bad time to attend the fair if you hated crowds—or wanted a parking space.

Crossing Como, Pete entered the fairgrounds through the Como gate, and contributed to the daily attendance.

Following Clough Street and approaching Judson, he saw an information booth on the right. Stopping there, he picked up a map. He knew, in general terms, how to get to the Midway. He wanted the most direct route.

After studying the map, he turned and looked west down Judson. Food booths packed both sides of the street, and brightly colored fluorescent signs shouted "Try me!" A mass of humanity filled the street from curb to curb, spilling over onto the sidewalks. Weaving and pushing his way through the crowd, Pete knew the fair presented a perfect opportunity for pickpockets. With both hands strategically positioned, he safeguarded his valuables, including his Smith & Wesson.

He passed the Lee and Rose Warner Coliseum, catching a whiff of the stench emanating from the Cattle Barn. It overpowered the smells disseminated by the food booths. He took a right onto Liggett Street, hoping to find something more appealing to his nostrils.

Since the new route took him past the Horse Barn and the Sheep and Poultry Barn, he succeeded only in trading one obnoxious odor for another. The Midway loomed to his left, just beyond the Horse Barn. The map referred to it as "The Mighty Midway." Music from the rides and the screams of patrons bombarded his ears. He saw the Grandstand. Thanks to Martin, he knew how the street there got its name.

A block upwind and past the livestock barns, Pete whiffed a variety of foods. Heavily buttered corn on the cob and deep-fried pronto pups again reminded him that he missed lunch. He thought about buying a pork chop on a stick but decided not to waste time in a line. Besides, he should wait for Martin.

If the map indicated the location of ticket booths, Pete failed to decipher the key. He ended up scouring The Mighty Midway, pen in hand, making an "X" on the map to designate each location as he passed. Thankfully, the layout, colors, and flags made the ticket booths easy to spot. He found all seven.

In the process, he heard the carnival barkers trying to attract customers to test their skills at a variety of carnival games. He saw a fair number of people, usually women, carrying stuffed animals. Maybe the odds of winning weren't as bad as he thought.

From a distance, and with the baseball cap pulled low on his forehead, Pete observed the beginning of the shift change at the ticket booth where Tommy Wells claimed to work. Sure enough. At five minutes to four, he saw Wells approach and enter the booth. His next mission: identify and intercept Tommy's supervisor as he went from one of his booths to the other.

During a seemingly interminable delay, Pete rubbed his neck, shifted from one foot to the other, and bit his lip. It looked like a lost cause.

He glanced at his watch—the one that once belonged to his grandfather. His dad gave it to him two years ago. Every morning, when he put it on, he thought about both his grandfather and his father. He remembered his grandparents' fiftieth anniversary. He recalled how vital they both were that day, and for the next few years. He thought of the devastation he experienced when he learned of his grandfather's death.

As a kid, he spent a lot of time with his grandparents. Without fail, his family visited them every Sunday back then. He remembered going on vacations with his grandparents, going fishing with his grandfather, and helping him with yard work. The watch would always be one of his most prized possessions.

Pete's thoughts transitioned seamlessly to the present when he saw a man walk to the door to Tommy's booth and use a key to get inside. He didn't want to approach the man while he was at the booth, so he continued watching.

He was still there, observing, when he glimpsed Martin out of the corner of his eye.

"I didn't know we were going incognito," Martin said, looking at Pete's baseball cap and dressed-down clothes.

"Seemed advisable. Don't worry. I think the bag of Tom Thumb donuts makes you look like just another fair goer." Pete smiled.

"How about bringing me up to date? What's happened since you arrived?"

Pete provided the details and indicated the locations of the other six ticket booths on his map. "His supervisor followed this path when he walked to this booth." Pete traced the path on the map. "Presumably his next stop will be back at his other booth. Why don't we split up? That way we can keep an eye on this booth and intercept him, regardless of the direction he goes when he leaves it. I don't know their procedures or protocols. If he's transferring money or tickets, I'd assume he has a police escort. Just in case, be careful not to spook him. This will be a waste of time if you get shot, and I have to rush you to the emergency room."

"Thanks for your concern. It's heartwarming. No wonder I like working with you." Martin chuckled. "If something does happen to me, will you stop long enough to get me another bag of Tom Thumb donuts? They could give me the motivation to hang on."

Pete shook his head and rolled his eyes.

Ten minutes later, the man they waited for did as Pete predicted. He strode down the path where Pete stood nonchalantly endeavoring to look like he was engaged in Will Green's favorite State Fair activity—people watching.

"Gary Henderson? My name is Pete Culnane. I'm a St. Paul police officer. I have a couple of questions."

"How do you know my name?"

"Got it from Tommy Wells."

"You're not in uniform." Henderson fidgeted nervously.

"I'm plain clothes, Mr. Henderson. Hate to draw attention by flashing my badge here. Can, if you insist."

"The State Fair has its own police department. The St. Paul Police Department doesn't have jurisdiction here."

"I'm aware of that, Mr. Henderson. I'm here about a crime that occurred in the east Como parking lot. That is our jurisdiction. I have a few questions about one of your employees."

Henderson seemed to relax a few degrees.

"I can't talk now," Henderson sputtered. "Look at these lines. I have my hands full. We'll have to talk later."

"When do you get off?" Pete asked as Martin joined them.

"The booths close at midnight, but it's another ninety minutes before I get home. Want me to call you then?"

"You could, or I could call you tomorrow morning or afternoon. What time do you get up?" Pete asked.

"Sometime between nine and ten."

"I'm willing to wait, if you commit to talking tomorrow. Will you call me, or should I call you?" Pete asked.

"I'll call you." Henderson held out a hand, expecting a business card. He got two.

Henderson hurried away, and Martin turned to Pete. "When's the last time you ate?"

"Breakfast."

"Every food you've ever imagined is served on a stick around here. How about if we grab something?"

"Sure, what's your pleasure?"

"It's pretty unlikely that 'my pleasure' will be something you'd eat. That's the beauty of the fair. We don't have to get something from the same vendor. Let's head down Dan Patch. I'm positive we'll both find something to tickle our palates."

"You go first, Martin. I'll keep an eye on Tommy's booth. I want to know every time he leaves, and where he goes when he does. When you get back, you can watch while I go on a scavenger hunt."

Martin bought a corndog and cheese curds.

When his turn came, Pete followed through on an earlier idea. He bought a pork chop on a stick. He didn't regret it. It was grilled and moist, and coated with just the right combination of spices.

The two investigators watched Tommy's window while they ate. If Tommy noticed them, he didn't show it. However, he had few opportunities to do anything but collect money and hand back change and the tickets.

While eating his pork chop, Pete asked about Marty's game.

"They lost. Trying to get the batter out at first, Marty threw the ball over the first baseman's head. By the time the first baseman retrieved the ball, the tie run scored from third, and the go-ahead run scored from second. Marty's face turned scarlet. He looked like he wanted to crawl in a hole. I talked to him after the game. Told him the pros do it on a regular basis, even the All-Stars. I tried to convince him he shouldn't let it bother him."

"Did he listen?"

"I don't think so."

"There's no need for both of us to stand here until midnight, Martin. If you leave now, you can be home by eight."

"I feel guilty about abandoning you. It doesn't seem right that you get all the overtime."

"Funny, Martin. Why don't you hang around home tomorrow, until you hear from me? I'll talk to Tommy's supervisor and keep trying to reach Amy Tracy. I'll also work on our plan of attack. You can work on that from home. When I'm ready to proceed, I'll call."

"Sure. 'Til tomorrow, then." Martin ambled away, in no apparent hurry to get home.

By watching the ticket booth until Tommy's shift ended, Pete learned several things. At least for tonight, Tommy occupied the same window from the time he reported in until he went home. He took one bathroom break, and a half-hour dinner break a few minutes after nine. He didn't leave the fairgrounds during his dinner break. Instead, he walked down Dan Patch, and bought two ears of sweet corn, one at a time, from a booth a short distance past the Grandstand.

Regardless, what he did today might have no relation to his actions two days ago. If Virginia Green drove his actions that evening, the attack that killed her eliminated any need for repetition.

TWENTY-THREE

Pete got the report on the Bureau of Criminal Apprehension's search of Virginia Green's home a little before nine on Sunday morning. The BCA didn't uncover a single clue to point Pete and Martin in the right direction. There were more than a thousand emails in her inbox, but nothing even remotely threatening. Martin would be disappointed to hear that also applied to the printed mail.

Tommy's supervisor, Gary Henderson, called Pete at ten. "What do you need to know?" he asked.

"Do you supervise all of the Midway ticket booths?"

"No, just two."

"What shift does Tommy Wells work?"

"Four 'til closing."

"And closing is at?"

"Generally, midnight. When things are slow, I let some staff leave a little earlier."

"What's the earliest you might dismiss them?"

"Eleven."

"Did Tommy work the fair last Thursday, that is, three days ago?"

"Yes. With rare exceptions, my staff must commit for all twelve days. Usually, the only exception is illness."

"Was Tommy ill last Thursday?" Pete asked.

"No, he was there."

"Do the people working in your ticket booths get breaks?"

"Yes, they get a thirty-minute break, and of course they get restroom breaks. If the fair traffic and the number of people buying tickets lags, I allow additional breaks. Forcing them to sit in the booth, staring at their hands, wouldn't accomplish anything. They coordinate the extra breaks amongst themselves."

"Did they get additional breaks last Thursday?"

"You have to ask them. I can't be watching their every move."

"Do the people have assigned times for their thirty-minute breaks?"

"No. They work it out amongst themselves, based on the traffic."

"Do some of your staff tend to stick to specific break times?"

"I don't know. I have to coordinate the efforts in two booths. My staff has to be intelligent enough to plan those things."

"Have you noticed any patterns among some of the members of your staff?" Pete asked.

"I don't have time to babysit these folks. I would know if any of them created problems. I'm not likely to know if they're doing their jobs and getting along fine."

"Are the same staff always assigned to the booth Tommy is in?"

"Yes."

"So it's likely they're familiar with each others' patterns," Pete said.

"I suppose."

"I need the names and contact information for the four people who worked the booth with Tommy last Thursday."

"I can't give you that information. It's available only at the personnel office. Besides, all I have is a list of names."

"A list of names and phone numbers, you mean, don't you?"

"Well, yes."

"Read the list of the four people who worked with Tommy last

Thursday, slowly. I'll make notes."

"I'm not allowed to share that information. There are privacy concerns."

"I'm a police officer, so you have some leeway. My other option is to show up today and pull the people out of the booth one by one, regardless of the number of people lined up to buy tickets."

"You can't do that! This is Labor Day weekend. It's one of our busiest times."

Left fist clenched tightly, Pete worked to maintain an even tone. "Tell me what you want to do. Do you want to read the list of names and phone numbers, or do you want me to show up at four o'clock today?"

Henderson rattled off the names and phone numbers.

Pete couldn't write that fast, but abbreviated the names and jotted down the numbers. He filled in the missing information as he read the list back to Henderson. "Thanks for the help," he said.

Henderson hung up without responding.

Pete called Martin and shared the information.

"Do you want me to call one or two of those people?" Martin asked.

"Thanks. Not necessary. I'll get back to you if there's anything noteworthy."

Pete started at the top of the list. Based on the sound of the woman's voice, he woke her up. After explaining who he was, he began asking his list of questions.

Yes, she knows Tommy Wells. Yes, they work the same shift in booth six. Yes, Tommy was there last Thursday. They all were. Yes, many of them have preferred break times. Yes, she thought Tommy did, too. She thought he usually took his break around nine o'clock. No, she didn't know if that was the time he took his break last Thursday. Yes, because of the heat and diminished crowds, they had some extra breaks last Thursday. No, she didn't know when Tommy took the extra breaks. No, she never got off before eleven o'clock. No, she didn't know if Tommy saw his niece at the fair last Thursday.

Pete thanked her and dialed the second number.

The man said he had no idea what Tommy Wells's schedule was last Thursday. He said that wasn't his job. He had enough trouble taking care of himself. He didn't even remember what he ate for supper last night. He had no way of knowing if Tommy saw his niece at the fair last Thursday.

Pete shook his head and dialed the third number.

That person didn't answer.

The fourth said, "Tommy's a doll." She knew he tried to take his breaks about the same time each day. She said he got lightheaded if he went too long without eating. Yes, nine o'clock is his chosen hour, and the exceptions are rare. His break was probably at nine o'clock on Thursday, but she couldn't guarantee it. Yes, she had some extra break time on Thursday. They all did. No, she couldn't remember when or how Tommy used the extra time. She was confident she'd know if Tommy saw his niece. If he did, it must have been while she was on break. She took her breaks at seven and ten. Both were thirty minutes, or a little longer.

"Why are you asking all these questions about Tommy?"

"It's part of an investigation."

"Did Tommy do something?"

"Has he been acting like he did something?"

"He hasn't been himself. It's probably because of his sister's death. They were very close, you know."

"That's what I understand. Can you tell me when you noticed a difference in him?"

"Some time last week, I think. Can't say for sure."

Running a hand through his hair, Pete called Martin. "Here's my report, a compilation of what I obtained from three of the four people who work the fair with Tommy. He usually goes on his break at nine o'clock. He probably took his break at nine o'clock on Thursday. He took another break that day, but no one knows when. He may or may not have seen Virginia at the fair last Thursday."

"Well, that was worthwhile," Martin laughed. "Don't you love an exercise in futility?"

"When it comes to exercise, I prefer running."

"Not me. I like keeping my right elbow in tiptop shape. I do that on a regular basis by loading up a fork and bending the elbow as it moves between the plate and my mouth."

"Sorry to cut you off, Martin. I've got to go. Amy Tracy's returning my call."

TWENTY-FOUR

Pete told Virginia's friend and co-worker, Amy Tracy, "I heard Virginia created an enemy while competing for her last promotion."

Tracy didn't respond.

"Did she?"

"People who get passed over are usually unhappy about it. It's a fact of life. Some of them blame the person who got the job."

"Did the person who was passed over blame Virginia?"

"I guess."

"You didn't mention this the last time I spoke with you."

"It's not exactly earth shattering."

"Did Ms. Green subsequently supervise the person who was passed over?"

"No. He demanded a transfer."

"Is that also the normal course of events?" Pete asked.

"Not really."

"What's his name?"

"Jason Proctor."

"Does he still work at Revenue?"

"Yes. Now he works for me."

"Then you know him fairly well."

"I guess."

"Does he still bear a grudge against Ms. Green?"

"Yes."

"But it didn't occur to you to mention him when my partner and I were there on Friday?"

"No. I thought you were interested in Zachary Esko, and Ginny's other staff."

"Do you have his phone number?"

"Yes, at work, and no, I can't get it before Tuesday."

"I want to talk to Proctor on Tuesday. Do you know if he'll be at work?"

"He didn't submit a leave slip, so he'll be there—unless he's sick, of course."

Oh, the joy of telephone interviews, Pete thought. He considered asking if she wanted them to find the person who killed her friend, but thought better of it. After tucking away his spiral notepad, he called Martin. "Let's talk to Ms. Green's neighbors."

"Meet you at headquarters?" Martin asked.

"Yeah. Can you be there in a half hour?"

If weather dictated his dress today, Pete would put on a swimsuit. After trading the comfort of a pair of worn jeans and a T-shirt for a suit, he grabbed his keys and hustled out the door. On the way to headquarters, he mulled over the progress made or, more accurately, not made with this case.

After meeting at headquarters, Pete and Martin traveled west on I-94. On the way, Pete noticed the haze over downtown Minneapolis. He figured the high humidity kept the particulate matter, or whatever they called the junk that made it look this way, close to the ground.

He also noticed the way his partner looked. Today he had to speak up. "Martin, you look more rested but more stressed out. What gives?"

"I'm a wreck, Pete. I told you a few days ago that Michelle is always tired, barely eats, and is depressed. When we got up this morning, she also felt dizzy, and she didn't know what day it is. On top of all that, she ached all over. I grabbed the keys and said we were going to the hospital. I told her we have to find out what's wrong. She started crying. She insisted it isn't that serious. She begged me to put down the keys. She promised to go to the doctor on Tuesday. I said that wasn't soon enough. I told her that we need answers, now. She kept crying and begged to wait until Tuesday."

"Marty saw her crying. He started crying, too. I told Michelle I'd stay home today and tomorrow. She objected, strenuously. A few hours later, she seemed better and said she felt much better. She told me I had to go if I heard from you. I said only if she promised to call if she began feeling worse. I feel sure she will. As you know, Pete, I've been meaning to talk to Marty. Couldn't delay it any longer. We talked for a long time. For weeks, he's known there's a problem. He said he often stays home in case she needs him. He started crying, again. He's scared, Pete. I told him to call me right away if he thought she was worse or needed me for any reason. I feel guilty about putting so much on his shoulders."

"Martin, he'll survive this. He might become a stronger and more caring person because of it. If you hear from Michelle, we'll stop—wherever we are. You'll head right home."

"But how will you get back to headquarters and your car?"

"That's not important."

"It is to me."

"I'll commandeer a vehicle? Well, maybe not. I'll catch a cab. I know you'd do the same for me, and right now it's not the key issue."

Pete waited a few minutes, then changed the subject. He told Martin about his conversation with Amy Tracy and added, "I'd like to check with some of the people who live in Emma Green's assisted living complex. Then let's speak with Tommy, again."

Virginia Green's neighborhood was a mixture of retail and residential. Were it not for the side-by-side front doors, the duplex might be mistaken for a single family dwelling. The exterior was a dark gray sideboard. A huge tree in the front yard tilted ominously toward the house.

Both sides of the street in front of and alongside the duplex were packed with cars. Pete knew the Vikings played Houston on Thursday, so that wasn't the reason for the gathering. He wondered which house was party central. All he had to do was open the car door to get the answer. The noise came from the duplex where Virginia Green had lived.

While pressing the doorbell, Pete wondered about the likelihood that anyone inside could hear it. Perhaps the unchanged volume of the noise answered that question.

"Want me to kick down the door?" Martin offered with a smile, and Pete thought the distraction the case provided might be helping.

"No, I'm afraid you might hurt yourself. Then I'd have to carry you back to the car. No offense, but I could break a fingernail."

Martin chuckled.

Pete welcomed the sound.

"I wouldn't want to compromise your immaculate appearance," Martin said. "Your delicate ego might not survive the affront."

Changing tactics, Pete banged a heavy fist on the door. The outcome was no more successful than his first effort. After allowing more than enough time for someone to get from the furthest reaches of the home to the front door, and that was about a minute, Pete pounded on the door again. This time, the hammering on the door was accompanied with, "Police, open the door!"

A dramatic reduction in the noise level indicated Pete had someone's attention.

A man opened the door a few inches and asked, "Did you knock?"

"Do you live here?" Pete asked.

"Yeah, did my neighbor complain about the noise?" He motioned with a thumb toward Virginia Green's front door. "I told her I was having a party today. It's my thirtieth birthday. She promised to find a place to hang, so the noise wouldn't bother her. Why would she call you, instead of complaining to me?"

"Your neighbor didn't call, and we're not here about the noise," Pete said. He identified himself, and he and Martin displayed their badges and IDs.

"Then why are you here?"

"We have a few questions. Come out here. I don't like talking through doors," Pete said.

"Just a minute. Let me get a shirt and shoes." He closed the door in their faces.

The music returned to its previous decibel level. A long minute later, the door opened, and he stepped outside. Shoes untied, he smelled of booze and cigarettes.

"Okay, what's up?"

"Your neighbor was attacked last Thursday," Martin said.

"Virginia?"

"Yes," Martin said.

"No way!"

"Living in such close proximity, do you know if she had any enemies?" Martin continued.

"Had? Does that mean what I think it means?"

"Probably," Martin said. "Did she?"

"Guess she must have, huh?"

"If you suggested she spend the day elsewhere, she must be able to hear what goes on in your apartment," Martin said. "Is that only when you have a party, or can you hear her as well?"

"I hear her a lot better than I'd like, but Ginny's usually pretty quiet."

"When do you hear her?" Martin asked.

"Mostly when she's arguing, fighting, whatever you want to call it."

"What would you call it?" Martin asked.

"Fighting, I guess."

"Is that a frequent occurrence?" Martin asked.

"Not really."

"Were there any arguments over there in, say, the last month or two?" Martin asked.

"The one that sticks out was three weeks ago tomorrow. I remember when it happened, because I was afraid it was going to go on all night. I had to get some sleep. I had an early meeting the next morning. The racket started at about ten o'clock. I wanted to call and tell her to move the fight to another location. I decided that would be too nasty, due to the nature of the conversation."

"What was the nature of the conversation?" Martin asked.

"Based on the shouting, I think her mother must have been dying."

"Do you know who was with her that night?" Martin asked.

"I didn't recognize the voices, but I recognized the cars. Her niece's yellow Beetle was parked out front. It's hard to miss. Her brother's and her uncle's cars were there, too."

"What does Virginia's brother drive?" Martin asked.

"An Impala."

"What color?" Martin asked.

"Red."

"When you said her uncle, you meant Tommy, correct?" Martin asked.

"I'm pretty sure that's his name."

"What does Tommy drive?" Martin asked.

"A blue Chrysler 200."

"How would you describe her relationships with the members of her family?" Pete asked.

"For the first few years I lived here, they seemed really close. Not so much the last while, but I can't give you a time frame."

"Was the deterioration of her relationships true across the boards?" Pete asked.

"If you're talking about her uncle, niece, brother, and sister-in-law, yes."

"She has two brothers. Which one?" Pete asked.

"The one with the red Impala. Will."

"How do you know what kind of cars they drive?" Pete asked.

"I met them a couple of times, when they came to visit."

"Other than the incident with her family, did you ever hear arguing coming from her side?" Pete asked.

"Just once. That was with our landlord."

"When was that argument?" Martin asked.

"It's really hard to say. It was probably a weekend. Can't narrow it any further than that."

"Was this a recent event or did it occur some time ago?" Martin asked.

"At least a month ago."

"Was Ms. Green dating anyone over the last several months?" Pete asked.

"Well, a guy came over on a regular basis, but I don't know if they were dating or just friends."

"Define a regular basis," Pete said.

"Every weekend."

"Describe him," Pete said.

"Around six feet tall. Carries a few extra pounds. Most people her age do. Black hair."

"Did you ever hear the two of them argue?" Pete asked.

"No."

"Do you know what kind of car he drives?" Pete asked.

"One time I saw him getting out of a Lincoln MKX. Another time it was a Cadillac Escalade."

"Did you happen to notice the license plate numbers?" Pete asked.

"No." He shook his head and smiled. "I wasn't that interested."

"Since this place is anything but soundproof, did you happen to catch this man's name?" Pete asked.

"No, can't help you there, either."

TWENTY-FIVE

"Guess Green's neighbor either wasn't here or was in a fog when the BCA searched her side of the duplex," Martin said.

"And he must not talk to his neighbors. I'd be surprised if the arrival of the BCA didn't raise a few eyebrows."

Since they were in the neighborhood, Pete and Martin decided to knock on a few doors in search of more information about Virginia Green.

They discovered Ms. Green had little to do with her neighbors. The few they found at home on this holiday weekend said they'd know her if they passed her, but knew nothing about her, including where she worked. Two of her nearest neighbors had met her brother and her uncle. One said, "Tommy is a real hunk." The look in her eye and tone of her voice indicated, at least to Pete, that she coveted this uncle.

The endeavor to learn more about Ms. Green was a rousing failure.

"Let's see if Emma Green's neighbors will be more helpful," Pete told Martin.

At the time of her death, Emma Green lived in a large, recently constructed, three-story assisted living complex in Roseville. The landscaping provided a variety of walking paths and sitting areas, and seemed welcoming. The powers-that-be obviously sought to create an atmosphere that, at least on the surface, provided an ideal place if you found yourself needing some level of care. Apparently that wasn't enough to cut it with at least one resident—Emma Green.

Pete and Martin passed through the accommodating outermost doors, which opened as they approached. A second set of sliding glass doors still separated them from the residents. On the wall between the two sets of doors, the security system included a list of resident names and the office, a code number for each, and a keypad for entering the numbers.

Pete entered the number for the office, hoping someone would respond.

"How may I help you?" the speaker next to the keypad asked.

"I'm Peter Culnane. I'm with the St. Paul Police Department. My partner, Martin Tierney, and I want to speak with Emma Green's friends."

"I'll be right there," the speaker said.

A woman came out of a door on the left side of the reception area. The sliding glass doors opened as she approached.

Pete and Martin showed her their IDs and badges.

"Come to my office. I'll write down some names and apartment numbers."

As the two investigators followed her, Pete noted the efforts to continue the welcoming motif. The lounge through which they passed included a fireplace, baby grand piano, upholstered chairs, and coffee tables adorned with flower arrangements.

By contrast, the office she entered held little more than a desk, computer, printer, and a few chairs, presumably for residents or potential residents and their families.

"Please, have a seat, while I write down the information. I also need a minute to familiarize you with our facilities and our residents."

I don't want to live here. I just want to talk to a few people, Martin thought.

"Emma lived in apartment 214. That's up one level and to the left. It's important you understand that some of our residents may not remember that she died. Please keep that in mind as you speak with them. Her best friends live in the apartments closest to hers. Those are the people she got to know, because she passed them on her way to and from her mailbox and when she came and went. She didn't attend any of our activities, nor did she eat in our dining room. It's a shame she missed out on so much of what we offer. Anyway, as a result, she didn't mingle with most of the other residents. You are, of course, free to talk to anyone you wish."

Pete and Martin thanked her, walked to the elevator, and Martin pressed the up button. "How did you like her sales pitch?" he asked.

"I think I can take care of myself for another year or two."

"But in three or four years, it would be better than living in the streets, I guess."

"Perhaps, but I'm not sure Doc would agree with you."

"You mean the homeless guy who helped you solve the case last year? The one where the victim was a homeless guy wearing a diamond ring?"

"Yup. Tell me, Martin, would your parents want to live here?"

"No. Too many old people. At least I suspect they're all old. Who else would live in assisted living?"

"Maybe someone who's disabled. But how about ten or fifteen years from now? Let's say when that time comes, you sell your parents' home and move them here. How would they react?"

"Mom would disown me. She loves where she and Dad are right now. She also treasures her independence. Dad would like to get rid of the yard work and shoveling, but not enough to move into a condo. You're right. This place isn't for them. Their mindsets would have to do a one eighty, before they'd accept it as their home. But obviously they aren't the norm. These places are going up all over. If they weren't being filled, the construction would cease."

The two investigators took a left off the elevator and checked the first apartment number: 224. A dozen paces ahead, the hallway took a left. They walked to that point and knocked on the first door—apartment 220.

A tiny, bent woman with white hair and glasses answered the door.

"Do you know Emma Green?" Pete asked.

"Oh my, yes. She was such a dear. Very quiet, but very sweet. She didn't like it here. Did you know that? All she wanted to do was move back home. I'm sorry. I shouldn't leave you standing out there. Come in and sit down. Take a load off, as my son would say."

She led the two men into a compact living room that overflowed with furniture. "Have a seat. Can I get you something to drink? I have coffee and tea and pop. What sounds good?"

"Nothing for me, but thanks for offering." Pete smiled.

"Nothing for me either, thanks," Martin added, then continued, "Emma didn't like it here?"

"No, the poor thing. I tried to get her involved. We have exercise classes and crafts. She didn't want to do any of those things. I think she was depressed about losing her home. That's a common ailment here. Some of us resign ourselves and decide to make the most of it. Eventually, she may have been able to do that, too. Unfortunately, she never had the chance."

"Do you know what happened to her?" Pete asked.

"I heard it was a blood clot, but I'm not positive. Sometimes sitting too much causes blood clots, you know. Emma told me she used to walk a lot. She said at least a couple of miles each day. Before moving her here, Emma's daughter told her she didn't want her to live alone anymore. She said there was too good a chance she'd fall and die before anyone found her. Emma told me that made her afraid. She started shuffling along, thinking that way she wasn't as likely to fall. She spent a lot of time doing nothing but reading. People our age need exercise. Use it or lose it, you know. I saw her grow weaker and more frail as the months passed. Sure, it comes with age, but it doesn't have to happen that fast. Especially if you stay in shape. I tried to tell Emma that. She agreed, but did nothing. It's such a shame."

"Did she talk about her family?" Pete asked.

"All of the time."

"Was she angry with them for putting her here?" Martin asked.

"Only with her daughter. She said it was all her daughter's doing. She said her brother fought tooth and nail to keep it from happening. I heard her son didn't want to second-guess his sister. That makes no sense to me."

"So her brother and her daughter fought about it?" Martin asked.

"All the time, according to Emma. I think that bothered her, too."

"Do you know who else around here was particularly close to Emma?" Pete asked.

"Yes, Betty in 210, and Louise in 215, but I don't know if either is home right now. They could be at bingo."

Louise was home. Betty was not.

Louise said Emma's daughter should be shot. "Emma's mind was perfect. Her daughter had no business trying to run her life. This is America. I've heard of people dying of a broken heart after they lose their husband or wife. Emma died of a broken heart after she lost her house. She barely ate anything. I think she lost about thirty pounds between the time she moved in here and when she died. And Emma didn't have the weight to lose. That wouldn't hurt me, of course," she said, patting her stomach. "Honestly, what makes some people think they have the right?"

"Was she active while she lived here?" Martin asked.

"Goodness, no. She sat in her apartment, watched TV, and read. The only time I saw her was when she went to get her mail or walked out front to go somewhere with a family member."

"Her family came often and took her places?" Martin asked.

"Her brother Tommy was always taking her on what he called excursions. As they walked out the front door, on a couple of occasions I heard him say, 'Let the adventure begin.' I think he did his best to make her laugh. She didn't do that much. I told her to go to her doctor and get something for depression. One afternoon, when I saw Tommy alone in the hallway, I even told him to take her and get her something."

"What did he say?" Pete asked.

"He said he'd done everything he could think of to get her to talk to her doctor. He said she refused. He said she said this was her life now, and she had to get used to it."

"Did she get used to it?" Pete asked.

"Not a chance. She didn't like it any more last week than she did the day she moved in. She just closed herself off and dried up. It's a crying shame. I did everything I could think of to get her to take an interest and get involved. Nothing I said or did made a difference. Poor Emma felt like the rug was pulled out from under her. She begged, cajoled, and cried. And Ginny was deaf and blind to all of it."

"Listen to me, you," she said, pointing a crooked index finger at Pete. "You, too." She swung the finger toward Martin. "People my age need to feel like they have some control over their lives. If they still have their right minds, you can't start calling all the shots. You have to include them in the decision making. Think how you'd feel if someone did that to you. Adding several decades doesn't change anything. No one likes to be railroaded."

The two men thanked her for her time and returned to the elevator.

"I think I've heard enough," Pete said. "How depressing is that? I know sometimes people have to put their parents in places like this for safekeeping. Virginia may have truly believed that this was the only option for her mother. If Emma's friends and family know what they're talking about, Virginia was sadly mistaken. Tommy may be right. Virginia may have been instrumental in shortening her mother's life."

Martin shook his head. "I'll bet you'll think about this case if you're ever forced to move your parents into assisted living or a nursing home."

"Yeah, no kidding." Pete grimaced. "I can't even bear to think about it. I may never face it, but that doesn't keep me from dreading the thought of broaching the subject with them. I know what their reactions would be, and it wouldn't be pretty. It might take a stick of dynamite to get them out of their home. I'm not sure there's anything I could say to change that."

He didn't mention it to Martin, but thought also of his grand-mother. He continued to worry that uprooting her and moving her from her home into an apartment may have started a downward spi-ral.

"Let's talk to Tommy's wife," Pete added.

"I thought we were going to talk to Tommy."

"We were, but he'll be on his way to the fair by the time we get to his house."

As they walked out the front door, Pete called the Ramsey County Medical Examiner's Office. He knew, thanks to the Bureau of Crimi-nal Apprehension, that there was no blood splatter on the ground in the vicinity where Virginia was found. He needed one more piece of information. He thought he knew the answer, but hoped his instincts were wrong.

TWENTY-SIX

Pete asked an investigator at the ME's office if there might have been blood splatter on Virginia's attacker. The investigator said, between the plugging action of the stick and the absorbent qualities of her shirt, that was highly unlikely. So, unfortunately, Pete's instincts were spot on.

When the two investigators reached Tommy's house, his wife Mary Ann, answered the door. She was tall and solidly built. Gray hair framed her face. She seemed surprised to see the two investigators. "Tommy's already gone," she said. "Today and tomorrow, and he'll be done for another year. I don't know how he does it. Twelve straight days for a seventy-five-year-old is pretty tough. He's really dragging today."

"We have a few questions for you," Pete said.

"Oh?" She looked surprised. "Do you want to come in?"

"Sure, it won't take long," Pete said.

They settled in the living room.

Mary Ann sat with fists clenched.

"Who are Tommy's best friends, Mary Ann?" Pete asked and pulled out his notepad.

Mary Ann relaxed markedly. "Most of them are either college classmates or neighbors. There's also a man he worked with. I'd also say our children are some of his best friends." Considering that, she smiled.

"I'd like the names and whatever contact information you have for each of them," Pete said.

"Our children's names are Tom, Bill, and Pat. Pat's a girl." She smiled again. "Her last name is Medford." Mary Ann rattled off the addresses and phone numbers for her children.

"The guys from college that are still close to Tommy are Mike Jenkins, Scott Peterson, and Alan Norwood. Mike is the only one who lives around here. He's out in Woodbury. Scott lives in Maryland, and Alan is in Seattle. Tommy has their addresses, but I don't know where. The neighbors he's closest to are Paul Zimmerman, Don Kent, and Rick Vernon. The Zimmermans live directly across the street," Mary Ann pointed. "The Kents live on this side of the street. If you're facing our house, they're two houses to the left." She pointed. "Again facing our house, Rick lives three houses to the right." For the third time, she pointed in the applicable direction. "Tommy and Eddie Adams, a man he worked with, still get together at least once a month. I don't have an address for Eddie, either. All I know is that he lives in Afton."

"How about phone numbers?" Pete asked.

"Tommy has all of them on his cell phone, and he has it with him. He wears it like an essential piece of clothing—like shoes or socks." She smiled and shrugged. "If you like, when he gets home, I can call you with all the addresses and phone numbers."

"If we need them, one of us will get back to you or Tommy," Pete said. "Tommy's retired?"

"Yes. He has been for quite some time."

"Where did he work?" Pete asked.

"He was a mechanic for Northwest Airlines. Thank goodness he retired before the merger with Delta."

"He has uniform shirts for working at the State Fair?" Pete asked.

"Yes, T-shirts."

"How many does he have?" Pete asked.

"Three, but one has long sleeves. He hasn't been able to wear that one this year. As a result, I have to wash the short sleeved ones every other day."

"You wash them in the morning?" Pete asked.

"Yes." Mary Ann looked puzzled.

"Did you wash them Friday or yesterday?" Pete asked.

"Yesterday, why?" Mary Ann looked uncomfortable.

"When you washed the shirts yesterday, was one of them more stained than usual?" Pete asked.

"Tommy wears another shirt under his State Fair T-shirt. He always takes the T-shirt off, before he gets something to eat. The T-shirts are usually sweaty, but I wouldn't call them dirty."

"No stains on either the uniform or other shirts you washed yesterday?" Pete asked. He had the answer from the ME's office, but Virginia could have collapsed into Tommy as she went down.

"No." Again, Mary Ann looked puzzled.

"Was Tommy upset, nervous, or jittery when he got home after work on Thursday?" Pete asked.

"I don't know. I was asleep. I heard him come into the bedroom, but I was still half asleep. We didn't talk. I drifted right off."

"How about when he got up the next morning?" Pete asked.

"He's been upset for months about his sister, and about Ginny's unwillingness to listen to him. He was, of course, distraught when Emma died. I think Tommy told you that. He and Emma were so close."

"Yes, I understand. Was it bothering him more than usual when he got up on Friday morning?" Pete asked.

"That's hard to say. It's a roller coaster, of course. Lots of things happen that renew or increase the pain. Then things even off again."

"When did Tommy hear about Ginny?" Pete asked.

"On Friday."

"What time on Friday?" Pete asked.

"Around ten or so. Will waited until he knew Tommy would be

awake."

"What was Tommy's reaction to the news?" Pete asked.

"He was shocked, of course."

"Tommy was shocked *and* on edge, wasn't he?" Pete probed further.

"Let me think." Suddenly, her eyes went wide. She jumped out of the chair so fast, it looked like she'd been launched. "Wait a minute! You don't think he hurt Ginny, do you? Tommy would never do that!" She shook her head excitedly from side to side, accentuating the pronouncement.

Pete considered her reaction and wondered if it was overdone.

TWENTY-SEVEN

Tommy's neighbors now topped Pete and Martin's agenda. They started with Paul Zimmerman, the friend who lived across the street from Tommy.

Paul answered the door, napkin in hand.

Pete said, "We'll give you a chance to finish eating. See you in about thirty minutes."

Returning to Tommy's side of the street, they went to Don Kent's home. Smells of bratwurst and sauerkraut seeped out the door when Kent opened it, but Pete saw no indications he was still eating.

Pete introduced himself, showed his badge and ID, and said he had a few questions.

"What about?"

"Give us a chance to ask the questions, and you'll know," Pete said.

"Okay, come on in and have a seat."

The three men sat in the living room. Someone was talking in the kitchen and stayed there.

"I understand you and Tommy Wells are good friends," Pete began.

"Yes." The answer sounded more like a question.

"When did you last speak with him?" Pete asked.

"Friday morning. I saw him mowing his lawn, and I went over. I needed to borrow a ladder."

"How early was that?" Pete asked.

"Just after eight. He always waits until eight to keep from disturbing our neighbors. Well, at least most of our neighbors. A few would be disturbed even if he waited until ten. The people next to me stay up all night and sleep half the day."

"I understand he was pretty upset when you saw him on Friday, huh?" Pete asked.

"Yes. He's still upset about his sister's death."

"Did he mention what happened on Thursday?" Pete asked.

"What happened on Thursday?"

"I think it's better if I let him tell you," Pete stood and added, "Thanks for your help."

"Wait, you can't just leave me hanging."

Pete could and did.

The two investigators went to the second home on Tommy's side of the street.

A woman answered the door, and Martin asked for Rick. She called "Rick" over her shoulder, then turned back to Martin and said, "Give him a few seconds. He's doing email."

She'd barely finished saying that before a man stepped into the room and asked, "You looking for me?"

"Rick Vernon?" Martin asked.

"That's me." The man smiled. "What can I do for you?"

Martin identified himself, and Rick's smile disappeared. "What do you want with me?"

"We have some questions," Martin said. "Only need a few minutes."

Rick stepped outside, closing the door behind him. "What do you want to know?" he asked.

"Did you speak with Tommy Wells on Friday or yesterday?" Martin asked.

"No. Not since Thursday."

"Before he went to work on Thursday?" Martin asked.

"That's right."

"I understand he's taking his sister's death pretty hard," Martin said.

"That's probably the understatement of the year."

"Does he blame anyone?" Martin asked.

"Yes, his niece—with good reason. I heard someone attacked her at the fair. I don't think Tommy will shed many tears at that funeral."

"If you haven't spoken with Tommy since before it happened, how do you know about his niece?" Martin asked.

"Mary Ann told my wife."

"Have you seen Tommy when he's riled?" Pete asked.

"Rarely."

"Does he get physical at those times?" Pete asked.

"Not anymore."

"What changed that?" Pete asked.

"His age. We're not getting any younger." Rick smiled.

"I hear Tommy was angry enough to attack his niece," Pete said.

"Verbally, yes. Physically, no. If you think he hurt his niece, you're wrong. Why would he? It was too late to fix things for his sister."

"We'd like to speak with your wife," Martin said.

Rick shrugged, went in the house, and returned with his wife.

Standing in the doorway, she looked petrified.

"What was Mary Ann Wells's reaction to Virginia Green's death?" Martin asked.

"Shock."

"Perhaps, but she knew Tommy was happy about it, didn't she?" Martin pushed.

"All I saw was shock."

"When did Tommy find out about it?" Martin asked.

"On Friday."

"Do you know when on Friday?" Martin asked.

"No. She didn't say, and I didn't ask."

Martin thanked her.

Turning and facing the Zimmerman home, Pete and Martin saw Paul sitting on the front steps.

They joined him, standing at the foot of the stairs.

Taking a guess, Pete said, "I understand you spoke with Tommy on Friday morning."

"Yes, and again after I saw you drive away yesterday. Tommy's having a rough time. Why don't you give him a break and hassle someone else?"

"Our mission isn't to hassle Tommy or anyone else," Pete said. "It's to determine who murdered his niece."

"Well, you're wasting your time, if you're looking at Tommy. I know Tommy, and I know that as angry as he was with Ginny, he would never have lifted a finger against her."

"People sometimes do the unexpected in a moment of rage," Pete said.

"That may be, but if Tommy did it, I'd know."

"How so?" Pete asked.

"He tells me *everything*."

Pete and Martin walked to the unmarked car.

"Okay, Martin. Do you want to fly to Maryland or Seattle?"

TWENTY-EIGHT

He and Martin started this investigation three days ago, and the lack of progress frustrated Pete. A distraction might be the best thing for him. He had two priorities. As soon as he got home, he changed from his suit into jeans and a T-shirt. Then he dialed the first number.

"Grandma, how are you?"

"Pete, it's so nice hearing your voice. I'm well. Getting settled and adjusting to my new surroundings. I met a few of my neighbors. Everyone is so nice. One neighbor wants to introduce you to her granddaughter."

"Did you tell her I'm married?"

"No. If you want me to say that, you'd better make the move. I can't lie for you, Pete. By the way, when are you going to stop stalling and ask Katie? I've seen the way you look at her and vice versa. It's obvious you're both head over heels. Besides, I'd like to be healthy enough to enjoy the wedding." She laughed.

"I'll see what I can do, Grandma. In the meantime, I have a few hours. Is there anything you need? Want me to finish hanging your pictures?"

"There's no rush, and my neighbors might complain if you start pounding nails at this hour. I think some of them are already in bed."

"Do you miss your house, Grandma?"

"Sure. After all those years, who wouldn't?"

"Sorry you moved?"

"Not really."

"Will you tell me if you start hating your new place?"

"It wouldn't be fair to unload on you, Pete."

"I want you to unload on me. Were you pushed into moving, Grandma?"

"I was nudged, but not pushed."

"Do you feel like you're losing control over your life?"

"No, why would I?"

"You might if you felt like someone else was making the decisions for you."

"Don't worry, Pete. I'll *never* permit that to happen."

"If it begins to feel that way, promise you'll tell me—right away?"

"Sure."

"Promise?"

"Okay, but Pete?"

"Yes?"

"Don't worry. I'm fine."

"That's good news. I'll see you soon."

After disconnecting, Pete contemplated for a few minutes. Then he dialed the second number.

"Pete! Dare I ask?"

"We've asked a lot of people a lot of questions. So far, much to my chagrin, no discernible progress."

"I'm sorry." Katie's tone conveyed that as well.

"Yeah. How about you, Katie? What are you up to?"

"Crocheting. My new nephew made his appearance! I'm making a blanket for him. Had my sister-in-law been courteous enough to find out his sex beforehand, I could have done this at a more relaxed pace." She laughed.

"Congratulations. When was he born?"

"Last night."

"Have you seen him, yet?"

"Saw him today. He's a doll. I held him—briefly. His mom's pretty possessive. I think that's because he's her first. Can't wait to hold him again."

"Yeah," Pete sighed, wishing she could hold their kid. *Someday?*

"All of his dark brown hair reminds me of you, Pete."

"Only my hair doesn't stand straight up."

"Yes, it does. Every time you pull off your ski cap—and whenever you're concentrating and run your hand back and forth through it."

Pete smiled. He thought about mentioning house hunting again, but decided to hold off for now. "I still don't know when we'll wrap up this case, Katie. Don't know when I'll be able to see you."

"Guess that means you don't want to come over now, huh?"

"Sorry. I'm wiped out."

"I understand, Pete, and I have my crocheting."

"It hurts to know I can be replaced by a stick and a ball of yarn."

"Not just any yarn. I'm working with the finest Sun Valley fibers."

"Good. I feel much better, knowing that." Pete laughed.

"I'm glad. Like I've said before, I hate to threaten your fragile ego."

If only you knew, he thought. *It's far too fragile to come right out and ask if you'll have my children.* "Tomorrow's Labor Day, the unofficial end of summer," he said. "What happened to our plans to go to the Boundary Waters?"

"Guess a few other things took precedence. Life is like that."

"Yeah, my life is. Sorry, Katie."

"Don't worry, Pete. We have plenty of time for those things."

TWENTY-NINE

Despite several attempts and one message, Pete didn't reach the last person who worked the fair with Tommy until Labor Day morning. That man was Gene Clements.

When Pete mentioned Tommy Wells, Gene said, "Ahh, yes, Tommy. I've worked the fair with him the last five years. He's so friendly, so accommodating."

"Do you remember when Tommy took his breaks last Thursday?"

"One was probably at the usual time."

"What time is that?"

"Around nine o'clock or so."

"I understand he also went on break around seven thirty."

"Did he?"

"When the fair traffic is down, do you and Tommy sometimes take your breaks together?"

"We have, but it's rare."

"Did you do that on Thursday?"

"No."

"Did you take two breaks last Thursday?"

"Yes, but it was slow. I wasn't the only one."

"What time did you take your breaks, Gene?"

"One around seven thirty, and the other at my usual time. That's ten o'clock. I like to take my break late in the shift. That way, worst case, I only have about ninety minutes to go, once I get back to the booth."

"What time did you return from the seven thirty break?"

"A few minutes after eight."

"So you were gone when Tommy took his seven thirty break?"

"I must have been. He was there when I left. I remember, because I almost didn't leave. He was on the phone. He got a lot of calls on Thursday. There were so many that our supervisor said something to him."

"Is that unusual?"

"Very."

"Was he back when you returned?"

"Barely. I saw him enter the booth ahead of me."

"I understand Tommy hasn't been himself lately."

"Yeah. It's all because his sister died. What a shame."

"What's different about him?" Pete asked.

"He seems a bit more irritable. I don't know. More nervous?"

"When did that start?"

"He was that way when the fair started."

"Did he look upset when you got back from your seven thirty break?"

"Yeah. He said he'd had a problem. Said his sugar got too low. I guess that can be pretty upsetting."

"When you returned, did he look disheveled?"

"He was all sweated up, but I guess that also happens if your sugar gets too low. Besides, it was the warmest day of the fair so far this year. Remember? On days like that, I always start sweating like a pig as soon as I walk out of the air-conditioned booth. I was soaking too when I returned, even though I left my fair T-shirt in the booth."

"Does Tommy sometimes fall when his sugar gets too low? Was there blood on his shirt?"

"I don't know if he fell. If he got bloody, his fair T-shirt hid it."

"Did he have his fair T-shirt on when you got back at eight o'clock?"

"Yeah, I guess. I don't really remember. But if he didn't get his uniform shirt on and there was blood, I'd have noticed. I'd have insisted he go to the first aid building. It isn't that far from our booth, you know."

"Did he take off his fair shirt before he left Thursday night?"

"I don't remember. He wouldn't have, if there was blood on the other shirt."

"What color was the other shirt?"

"I don't remember."

"If you left the booth at seven thirty and returned at eight o'clock, Tommy's first break must have been a brief one."

"First, I didn't leave the booth at exactly seven thirty, and I can't tell you the exact time I returned. We don't have a time clock in the booth, you know."

"Didn't mean to suggest there was a problem, Gene. When I was at the fair yesterday, I saw a woman in one of the Midway ticket booths. She wore a turquoise colored T-shirt. When I spoke with Gary Henderson yesterday, he had the same T-shirt. Does everyone who works in the booths wear that same shirt?"

"Yes, it's our official uniform."

"Does Tommy usually take the fair T-shirt off, before he goes on breaks?"

"I'm not sure. Some of us do. That way we stay cooler. More important, we don't get food on them. But some of us don't wear another shirt under the uniform shirt. What difference does it make?"

"You said Tommy got a lot of calls on Thursday. Do you know who called him?"

"Rachel for sure. I heard him mention her name. I mean like, 'Now Rachel . . .'"

"Anyone else?" Pete asked.

"I don't know. All of the calls might have been Rachel. I didn't hear him mention any other names, but I was busy and it was none of my business."

THIRTY

Driving to headquarters on Labor Day, Pete thought about his priorities. He and Martin must speak with Virginia Green's other two siblings, Tim Green and Caroline Campbell. He hoped to do that today. For now, however, thanks to his lies, the victim's uncle, Tommy Wells, took precedence.

As soon as Martin arrived, they left for Lauderdale. Martin's unmarked car knew the route by heart.

When Tommy's house came into view, Pete got a sinking feeling. On Saturday, there was a Chrysler 200 in the driveway, and Tommy was home. Did no car mean no Tommy?

Pete rang the doorbell.

Mary Ann answered. When she saw the two investigators, she retreated a step and narrowed the door's opening.

Her reaction to yesterday's meeting, Pete figured.

"We're looking for Tommy," Martin said.

"He left about a half hour ago. Was he expecting you?"

"Where did he go?" Martin asked. His tone was patient, not demanding.

"He's going to Menards and Cub, but he may go other places, too. It depends on what kind of luck he has, and what else occurs to him while he's out." She finished with a hands-up shrug.

"Any idea when he'll be back?" Martin asked.

"Noon at the latest. It depends on how much his list grows as he shops."

"Will he go to Menards or Cub first?" Martin asked.

"Menards. Otherwise the frozen stuff will thaw while he's at Menards."

"Which Menards and which Cub does he shop at?" Martin asked.

"Before the light rail construction made such a mess of things, he always went to the Menards on University Avenue. When he's in that vicinity, he goes to the Cub in Midway. Otherwise, he shops the Cub in Har Mar."

"Once the construction began, which Menards?" Martin asked.

"The one on Highways 36 and 61. I'm not sure if that's St. Paul or Maplewood or White Bear Lake. The boundaries are so erratic."

"Would you call his cell and find out where he is?" Martin asked.

"Just a minute." Leaving the investigators outside and the door open a crack, Mary Ann walked away.

Before long, Pete and Martin heard a melody playing somewhere in the house. "Great!" Martin said, suspecting he knew the source.

Mary Ann returned, smiling and carrying a cell phone. "He forgot it. Left it on the bed."

"Is Tommy driving his Chrysler 200?" Pete asked.

"Tommy isn't driving. Will picked him up."

"Was Will driving his Impala?" Pete asked.

"I assume so, but he might have his wife's car. It can haul more stuff."

"What does she drive?" Martin asked.

"A RAV4."

"Color?" Martin asked.

"Silver."

After they reached the unmarked car, Pete asked, "Do you believe her?"

"Yeah, I do. We aren't on her list of favorite people, but she looked me right in the eye while answering my questions. Based on our limited interactions, I don't think she's capable of doing that while lying."

"How would you peg our likelihood of success if we attempt to track him down?"

"All I know is, it's significantly better than if we don't try."

Martin drove to the parking lot of the Menards in Maplewood.

En route, Pete contacted dispatch and, after a brief wait, obtained the license plate numbers for the Impala and the RAV4.

As Martin drove up and down the aisles, he and Pete scanned both sides, looking for the cars Tommy and Will may have taken, assuming Martin was right about Mary Ann.

The lot was packed. There was one RAV4, but the color and license plate were wrong. There were also a couple of Impalas. Neither was the one they sought.

"Now what?" Martin asked.

"There's no guarantee they're in the Impala or the RAV4, and there's no guarantee they're here. Feeling lucky?"

"No, if luck was on my side, Tommy would have been home." Martin smiled.

"Hoping that isn't indicative of what we're up against, how about finding a parking place with a wide open view of the entrance and the exit?"

"Then?"

"One of us will sit there and meditate. The other will go inside and look for them."

It wasn't an easy task, but Martin waited patiently for a car parked in a coveted spot to back out. Then he made an enemy or two when he captured that space.

Pete thought about contacting dispatch, and getting a few squads to case the two Cub lots and the other Menards. He decided against it. It required too many resources, and Tommy and Will might not be at any of those locations.

Martin voted for waiting in the unmarked car, while Pete checked inside.

Pete was familiar with the layout of this Menards. He started with the checkout counters and worked his way through the rest of the store. It was too large and the layout too convoluted to aid with his mission. He knew success would be highly unlikely if Martin wasn't outside watching.

Pete struck out. Exiting the store, he saw Martin and the unmarked car where he'd left them.

Getting back in the car, Pete said, "Let's sit here for about fifteen minutes, just in case we got here first."

"Or should we forget about Tommy for now?" Martin asked.

"The thing is, I'd like to talk to him before we meet with Tim Green and Caroline Campbell. I want to know why he lied to us. Those answers could impact what we ask Tim and Caroline."

"Or eliminate the need to talk to them." Martin smiled.

"That would be good. Tim is in Rochester. The roundtrip alone will take almost three hours."

"Yeah. Let's ask Tim to drive up and meet us at Caroline's." Martin chuckled.

"Okay. Should we ask him to stop and pick up lunch on the way?"

While he and Martin watched the doors, Pete cautiously changed the subject. "Is Michelle feeling better today, Martin?"

"Sorry to say, no."

"Did she make an appointment with her doctor?"

"Yeah. Thankfully, the appointment line operates seven days a week. By some miracle, she's getting in late tomorrow afternoon."

"That's great, Martin. Are you going with her?"

"We haven't discussed it. What do you think?"

"I'm not in your position, so I can't really say. What are the benefits and drawbacks of each?"

"Well, she may be less forthcoming with her doctor, if I'm sitting there. But it also means she won't cancel at the last minute."

"Would she do that?"

"I don't know. With all that's happening, I wouldn't think so. Still, she might."

After sitting in front of Menards for almost twenty minutes, Pete said, "Let's go to the Har Mar Cub. If we don't find him there, we'll check his place again. If necessary, we'll camp outside his house and wait for him."

Once he reached the Cub parking lot, Martin again drove up and down the aisles. Failing to find the Impala or the RAV4, he looked for a parking spot near the entrance.

There were lots of perfectly positioned handicap spaces. He drove past them. He remembered the lecture once leveled at him, regarding the difficulties endured by the people who need those spots. The woman who lambasted him that day made a lasting impression, and cured him of the temptation.

Instead, he found a spot on the eastern edge of the lot. This placed them about thirty yards from the entrance. "You don't suppose they parked elsewhere and are entering through the mall, do you?" he asked.

"That's a distinct possibility. Do you want to wait here? Or would you rather check out the store, then observe the other entrance from one of the benches in the mall?"

"Out of deference for your age, Pete, I'll stay here. You can walk through the air-conditioned store, then rest on a bench in the air-conditioned mall."

"We'll hang tough for a half hour, Martin. If I don't hear from you, or vice versa, I'll be back in thirty minutes."

Pete got out of the unmarked. He scanned the parking lot as he walked to the grocery store. He made his way through the store, checking all of the aisles. Every step of the way, he looked and listened for any signs of Will and Tommy. With nothing to show for his efforts, he exited through the mall entrance. Instead of taking a seat on one of the benches, he leaned against the east wall. From there, he had an unobstructed view of the Cub entrance and another mall entrance leading to the grocery store.

The mall was nearly vacant. There was significantly more traffic through the Cub parking lot entrance. Pete started counting the people entering Cub from this location. When the designated time rolled around, he was all the way up to eight. He pushed himself away from the wall and headed back to Cub. As he neared the door, an elderly woman exited, struggling with two armloads of bags. "Where are you headed, ma'am?" he asked.

"I'm parked through those doors," she said. She pointed with her chin to the door at the end of the hallway that lay straight ahead.

"Looks like you could use some help."

"Yes, didn't plan on buying so much. Should have parked in front, where I could have taken the cart right up to my car. Wish they didn't have those stupid posts, keeping me from taking a cart out this way."

"Let me carry the stuff for you," Pete offered.

"You're a life saver." She smiled.

Five minutes later, after escorting the woman to her car and loading her groceries, Pete re-entered Cub through the mall entrance. Once again, he scanned for anyone resembling Will or Tommy. Approaching the entrance on the other side of the store, he scanned the checkout counters. Coming up empty-handed, again, he walked to the unmarked car.

Martin smiled when he spotted him.

Pete knew his partner felt relieved to conclude this tedious undertaking.

"Did you catch a few winks or suffer through the whole ordeal?" he asked Martin as he got in the unmarked.

"I stayed awake almost half of the time. Do I get some sort of award for that?"

"Absolutely! It's the Lost Cause Award."

"Back to Tommy's house?" Martin asked.

"You've got it."

"Should we place a bet on when he'll show?"

"I'll pass. After the last failed efforts, I'm not sure how much credence I'm willing to give his wife's estimate."

"Do you think he skipped, and she was buying him some time, Pete?"

"Believe me. It's occurred to me. Unfortunately, we won't know until he doesn't show up for the fair."

"We could put out a BOLO for the two cars he may be in," Martin suggested, ". . . get some other pros looking out for them."

"I have no reason to think it's necessary just yet, and he could be in a different vehicle."

"True."

Martin followed Highway 36 back toward Tommy's house.

Both men walked to the front door to check whether Tommy returned while they were gone.

Mary Ann looked surprised to see them. "I told you I didn't think he'd be back until noon. Do you want to come in and wait?"

They didn't. They didn't want to take a chance that Tommy would see the unmarked car, and keep going. "Thanks, Ms. Wells. We'll wait in the car," Pete said.

Martin repositioned the car so they'd see Tommy approach, before he saw them. Both men felt exhausted. It had already been a long day. There were few things worse than sitting, watching, and waiting, only to come up empty-handed.

"I'm working on believing that our morning has been a simple case of being in the wrong place at the wrong time," Pete said. "I don't want to jump to any conclusions about Wells—either him or her. At least for now, it would be counterproductive."

"Yeah, but after a morning like this, it's hard to be objective."

"What was your worst stakeout ever, Martin?"

"It had to be the time I spent a few hours watching a house. A guy walked up to the front door with a baseball cap pulled down low over his eyes. My partner and I jumped out of the squad, and started walking toward him. He took off through the yards, jumping fences, doing everything he could to evade us. A runner I'm not, but I kept pushing. I was dying. My partner and I split up and trapped him between a garage and a chain-link fence. Not only was he the wrong guy. He had no rap sheet."

"Why was he running?"

"Same reason a lot of young black men run. Not trusting cops comes easily to guys who've been profiled by the time they turned fourteen."

Pete nodded.

"And you don't have to tell me about your worst stakeout, Pete. Your reputation preceded you. Everyone in the department has heard about the time your first partner was shot when you were chasing a suspect."

Pete's face reflected the seriousness of that memory. "Yeah, I thought I was going to lose Keith."

"I heard you're the reason he lived to tell about it. You risked your life to drag him out of the line of fire. He would have bled out if you hadn't torn off your shirt and applied pressure to the hole in his chest. You're a hero, my man."

"Can't believe everything you hear, Martin." Pete smiled.

"True, Pete. If you try to convince me that story isn't true, I won't believe you."

Pete shrugged noncommittally.

At half past twelve, Tommy arrived. He drove a Taurus.

THIRTY-ONE

Martin followed Tommy onto the driveway and parked within an inch of his back bumper.

"Good afternoon," Tommy smiled, emerging with a great deal of effort from the Taurus. "It's Labor Day. One more shift at the fair. What a relief. I can't wait to watch the clock hands pass five tomorrow evening, then have a beer. And I can't wait to have dinner with Mary Ann, for a change."

If he's that exhausted, why did he spend all morning running errands? Pete wondered. "We've been looking for you," he said.

"Oh? I thought I answered all your questions?"

Pete tried to read the man. *Could he be that oblivious or was he that divorced from the events of Thursday?* "Where shall we talk?" he asked.

"Is the usual place okay?"

"Your call," Pete said.

He and Martin followed Tommy into the living room.

"Tommy, you're home," Mary Ann called from the kitchen. "Those two men . . ." Stepping into the living room doorway, she saw "those two men," raised an eyebrow, and went silent.

"What do you need to know?" Tommy asked.

Before he began, Pete Mirandized Tommy.

Tommy looked dumbfounded.

Mary Ann stared unbelieving at the proceedings.

Pete began with, "Where were you this morning, Tommy?"

"Shopping."

"Alone?"

"No, with Will."

"I told you that," Mary Ann said.

"You took the Taurus?" Pete asked.

"You already know that. You saw me drive in."

"I thought Will picked you up," Mary Ann said.

"Last minute change of plans."

"I did some checking," Pete said. "You had more than one break on Thursday, didn't you, Tommy?"

"I did?" Apparently Tommy had acting talent, was a sociopath, or couldn't remember Thursday.

"What time did you take your breaks that day?" Pete asked.

"I took a break at the usual time."

"And?" Pete asked.

Tommy stared at the ceiling for several seconds, then said, "Oh, yeah. I guess you're talking about when I didn't feel well. I needed something to eat, so I left just long enough to grab some food. It wasn't really a break."

"Coincidentally, Virginia was alive when you left the booth, and you returned after she was stabbed. Does that ring a bell?" Pete asked.

"How would I know that? You didn't tell me what time it happened. I already told you I didn't leave the fairgrounds. I wasn't gone long enough to get to and from the parking lot."

"Can anyone vouch for that?" Pete asked.

"Sure. Everyone who works with me can."

"That's not what they told me," Pete said.

"But it's true," Tommy drew out the last word.

"You spent a lot of time on the phone on Thursday, didn't you, Tommy?" Pete asked.

Tommy swallowed hard. "I had a few calls."

"From?"

"I can't remember. It couldn't have been that important."

"How about Rachel? Does that jog your memory?" Pete asked.

"She called looking for her dad. That's all."

"Who else called you? You had more than one call while in the booth," Pete said.

"I called him," Mary Ann said. "I couldn't find the keys to my car. I had yarn in the trunk, and wanted to start working on my new sweater."

"How about you, Tommy? Who did you call?" Pete asked.

Tommy stared at his clasped hands and didn't respond.

"You know, Tommy, we can get a warrant to check your phone. We can also check your records with your service provider. We're going to find out. You may as well tell us. If you don't, I'm going to have to haul you in on charges of obstruction."

Tommy remained tight-lipped.

"I hate to do this, Tommy, but you're going to have to come with us," Pete said as he stood and walked to the chair where Tommy sat.

Tommy refused to look at him.

Pete didn't relish the thought of carrying Tommy's mass out of his house. He reached for Tommy's arm.

Tommy drew it away.

"Either answer my question or stand up, Tommy," Pete instructed.

Tommy continued to sit, unmoving.

Mary Ann ran to his side. Tears flowed down her cheeks. She grabbed his hands and said, "Talk to them, Tommy. Please."

Tommy looked up at her. He wore a pained expression. He reached up and gently brushed a tear from her cheek. "Okay," he whispered.

Staring at his feet, Tommy said, "I called Will. He didn't answer. I couldn't reach him."

"Why were you so bent on reaching Will? Why couldn't it wait until your usual break time?"

Tommy retreated back to unresponsiveness.

"I'm not going to drop this line of questioning, Mr. Wells," Pete said. "You can answer my questions either here or at headquarters."

"Tommy, please, tell them what they want to know," Mary Ann sobbed.

"I was too upset to wait. I needed to talk to someone."

"Why didn't you call me, Tommy? I was here all night," Mary Ann said.

Tommy grasped her hand and said, "Because, sweetheart, I needed to talk to Will."

"Why did you need to talk to Will?" Pete asked.

"Because I was upset with Ginny, and he's her brother!"

"Why were you upset with Ginny?" Pete asked. He hated this line of questioning almost as much as Tommy.

Tommy sighed deeply and shook his head dejectedly.

"Tommy, why were you upset with Ginny?" Pete repeated.

Tommy started crying.

"Please, leave him alone!" Mary Ann wept. "Stop torturing him. He didn't do anything."

"By answering my questions, you can make this a lot easier on your wife, Tommy. What did Ginny do to upset you?" Pete asked.

"She was at the fair on Thursday. She was having a grand old time. We buried her mother on Monday. How could she be so callous? So uncaring? It tied my stomach in knots. Like I said, I had to talk to someone. I was a wreck. I had to get away from the ticket booth. I had to get some food and get my head screwed back on. I thought talking to Will would help. I thought he would calm me down. He didn't answer his phone."

Mary Ann sat on the arm of Tommy's chair and put an arm around him.

"So what did you do?" Pete asked.

"I was shaking. I started crying and couldn't stop."

"And?" Pete asked.

"I texted Ra . . . Rachel."

"Did she text back or call you?" Pete asked.

"She called."

"What did she say?"

"She couldn't believe it. She blew up and called Ginny every name in the book. She told me I couldn't let Ginny upset me that way. She said it wouldn't help my sister. She said Emma is in a better place, now that she's beyond Ginny's reach. I knew she was right. I calmed down. I was still upset, but I felt a little better."

"You also talked to Ginny that day, didn't you?" Pete continued.

"No. I didn't have a chance. Couldn't have anyway. I was way too angry."

"Then how did you know where she parked?" Pete asked.

"I didn't."

"So you had to follow her to her car," Pete said.

"Have you walked from my booth to the Como lot and back in thirty minutes? Maybe you can do it. I can't."

"So you tried, Tommy," Pete said.

"No! I'm speaking hypothetically!"

"Where were you when you texted Rachel?" Pete asked.

"In the booth."

"Where were you when she called?" Pete asked.

"In the booth. I walked out while I was talking to her. I went to get some food."

"Where was Rachel when you spoke with her?" Pete asked.

"I don't know. I didn't think to ask. She was probably at home, with her husband and her daughter, Emma."

"What time did you text Rachel?" Pete asked.

"A little after seven, maybe as late as half past."

"Did you leave a message for Will?" Martin asked.

"Yes."

"Did he return your call?" Martin asked.

"Yes."

"When?" Martin asked.

"Friday morning. He was pretty shaken up over what happened to Ginny."

"Did you ask where he was when you called on Thursday evening?" Martin asked.

"Yes."

"What did he say?" Martin asked.

"He was home. He forgot his phone in the car. Couldn't hear it ringing. Didn't realize he didn't have it until he wanted to call me on Friday."

"Where did you go after you spoke with Rachel?" Martin asked.

"I sat at a table near the Grandstand, trying to stop crying and calm down. Then I went back to the ticket booth."

"Did anyone you know see you sitting there?" Pete asked.

"I don't think so. I hope not!"

"That's all for now," Pete said. "Don't go anywhere. We may want to talk to you again."

"What about work? Can't I go to work? They're counting on me."

"Yes. You don't have to stay in the house. You do have to stay in the Twin Cities," Pete said.

THIRTY-TWO

A safe distance from the house, Martin said, "Guess you want to talk to Rachel, huh?"

"*Have* to talk to Rachel seems more accurate."

They talked about calling to make sure she was home. Doing so could prevent a futile trip. It would also give Rachel a heads-up. Then, if she wanted, she could confer with Will and Tommy before they arrived. Even so, they knew in all likelihood Tommy would alert her. They could have instructed him not to, but that would have been as useful as telling a gold finch not to sing.

The Lansings lived in Lake Elmo, a suburb on the east side of St. Paul, southwest of Stillwater. The large, two-story home hid behind walls of foliage. The color and the window and door placements made the house look like a jack-o'-lantern with eyebrows.

Martin leaned on the doorbell.

After a significant delay, a man answered.

"Mr. Lansing?" Martin asked.

"Yes. Why?"

Martin went through the usual routine, then asked to speak with Rachel.

"She and Emma are at her parents' house."

"As long as we're here," Martin said, "do you know where she was last Thursday evening, between six and nine?"

"She picked up Emma at her parents' home around six. Shortly after seven, she drove home. She got here around seven thirty or a short time later. She was here the rest of the night."

That's interesting, Pete thought. He saw her at Will's at ten o'clock Thursday night, when he and Martin were there to tell Will about Ginny's death.

"How sure are you about that?" Martin asked.

"I'm positive."

"You're positive because?" Martin asked.

"Because I was here with her."

"Rachel will vouch for that?" Martin asked.

"Definitely."

"Am I correct in assuming you know the consequences if you impede this investigation by lying to us?" Martin asked.

"Yes, of course. I'm telling the truth."

"Where's your money?" Martin asked Pete after they walked away from the Lansing home. "Here are your choices. Option one: Rachel is at Will's now and will be when we arrive. Option two: she's there now, but won't be when we get there. Option three: he thinks she's at Will's, but is wrong. Option four: he knows she's not at Will's."

"By all indications, lying is his native tongue. At this moment, we have no way of knowing if he is bilingual and switches regularly between truth and fiction. Hence, I won't hazard a guess. I will call her cell. She, too, may be bilingual. Assuming she picks up the phone, I'll do my best to corral her here, there, or wherever she happens to be."

Rachel didn't answer her cell. "Strike one," Pete said and dialed Will's home number. When Will answered, he asked to speak to Rachel.

"I think she just left."

"I suggest you catch her. I'm not in the mood for games."

Pete listened to dead air long enough to wonder if Will set the phone down, and walked away with no intention of returning. That would prime his competitive spirit.

THIRTY-THREE

By the time Rachel picked up the phone, Pete and Martin were en route back toward St. Paul.

"Stay right where you are," Pete told her.

"But I promised Emma I'd take her to McDonald's."

"She'll have to wait. We'll be there before you can get to McDonald's and back."

After Pete put his phone away, Martin said, "Do you think, as long as they're together, Will and Rachel are busy creating airtight alibis?"

"Martin, I'm shocked. Do they need alibis more than the other names on your matrix?"

"It's certainly possible."

"Fortunately, a lie does not a killer make. If it did, I'd build a safe room and lock myself away—permanently."

"Would you invite Katie in, before you sealed the entrance?"

"Only if she brought dinner." Pete laughed.

Returning via the same route they took to Lake Elmo, Martin looked at the gas gauge. "Glad I'm not buying the gas."

Rachel's Volkswagen Beetle sat in Will's driveway.

"Ready?" Martin asked.

"Yeah. Let's split up. We don't want to make it convenient for them to share information about what we're asking, before we get to all three of them. I'll start with Will, and you take Rachel. Whoever finishes first can either question Will's wife, or keep her apart from the others, until we both have a chance to interview her. I'll use the front yard as my office, in case anyone decides to cut out."

They walked to the front door, and Martin rang the bell.

Will answered. He stood behind the screen door and tried to stare them down. He failed.

"We want to talk to you and Rachel," Martin said.

"Fine. Come in." Will looked over his shoulder and hollered, "Rachel."

Rachel peered around the corner from the kitchen, then shuffled into the living room. She approached without looking at any of them. Emma rested on her left hip.

"Let's step outside and talk," Martin said. "Leave your daughter in here."

"She won't be a problem."

"Doesn't matter. Leave her here anyway."

A disgusted looked flashed across Rachel's face. "Okay, fine. Whatever." She handed Emma to her dad.

"Will, you come with me," Pete said. "Rachel will go with my partner."

Will handed the child to his wife.

Martin led Rachel toward the backyard, stopping a sufficient distance from the driveway, where Pete stood with Will.

"Did Tommy call you from the fair last Thursday?" Martin asked.

"No, he texted me."

"What time?"

"Around seven. I can't be more specific than that. If it was much later, I'd have been on my way home."

"Where were you at the time?"

"I was here, picking up Emma."

"Did you text back to him?"

"No, I called."

"What time did you call him?"

"Between seven and seven thirty. Want me to check my phone?"

"Yes."

"Then I have to go in the house and get my purse."

"You can verify it after we finish. Does Tommy frequently text you?"

"No, he usually calls."

"Why did he text on Thursday?"

"I don't know. Maybe he wanted to be sure to reach me."

"What did he want?"

"He was upset. He couldn't reach Dad, and he needed to talk to someone."

"What was he upset about?"

"Ginny." She spat the word out.

"Why was he upset with her?"

"You should ask him."

"I'd like your take on it."

"Ginny was being disrespectful of Grandma."

"What did you do after you spoke with Tommy?"

"I took Emma out to my car and drove home."

"Did you tell your mother what Tommy wanted?"

"Yes. I told her to have Dad call Tommy as soon as he got home. Dad came in the door just as Emma and I were leaving, so I told him myself."

"Where was your dad when you spoke with Tommy?"

"He must have been on his way home."

"You're certain?"

"Yes. I heard his car drive up and the door slam while I was saying good-bye to Mom."

"What were you doing while your mother watched Emma?"

"I had an appointment with my personal trainer."

"What's your personal trainer's name?"

"What difference does that make?"

"I may want to speak with her or him. I also need their location."

Rachel sighed and provided both.

Martin knew the location was approximately a mile and a half from the fairgrounds. "Was your husband home when you arrived?"

"Yes."

"What time was that?"

"Around seven forty-five."

"We saw you when we were here that night. What time did you leave home, when you came here that time?"

"Eight thirty or nine. Why?"

"Where did you go between the time you left home and arrived here?"

"I drove around, trying to put Emma to sleep. Sometimes riding in the car does the trick. It obviously didn't work that night. She was wide awake when we got here."

"Was your husband home when you left that time?"

"Yes. What difference does that make?"

"Did he see you leave?"

"I assume so."

"That's all, for now. Except, check your phone, and let me know what time you called Tommy on Thursday evening."

THIRTY-FOUR

Meanwhile, Pete and Will stood the width of the yard away from Martin and Rachel. Will anchored himself with feet wide apart and hands jammed deep in his pockets.

"Tommy called you from the fair last Thursday," Pete began. "What did you talk about?"

"I didn't talk to him. I didn't hear my phone ring. He left a message."

"When did you get the message?"

"Friday morning. When I got home on Thursday, Rachel told me to call him. I tried from my home phone. The call went right to voicemail. I left a message. I didn't realize until Friday morning that my cell slipped out of my pocket and was in my car. I wondered why Tommy didn't call back. He did. He called my cell and, like I said, it was in the car."

"What did the message say?"

"It said he saw Ginny at the fair."

"That was newsworthy?"

"No."

"Where was she when he called?"

"At the fair."

"It's a big place. Where at the fair?"

"The message didn't say."

"You're telling me Tommy stopped doing his job, stood in the booth, and called to tell you your sister was at the fair? Seems like a stretch."

"He was upset about seeing her."

"Seeing Ginny was upsetting?"

"No!"

"Yet he called just to tell you about it?"

"When we talked on Friday, he said he was upset that she was having such a good time."

"Why was he upset about that?"

Will crossed his arms and scowled. "Because she was having the time of her life, and it was only three days after Mom's funeral. Tommy, Rachel, and I, for starters, were still in mourning. Tommy thought Ginny should be, too."

"So Tommy lost it, lashed out, killed her. That's understandable."

"Tommy didn't kill her!" Will's voice dripped with disdain.

"And you know that because?"

"Because he'd tell me if he did. He couldn't keep something like that inside."

"You, on the other hand, are keeping it inside."

"I don't have anything to keep inside."

"That makes you unique."

"You know what I mean," Will snarled, pointing a finger at Pete's nose. "Stop with the games. I'm not in the mood."

"What time did you arrive at the fair on Thursday?"

"Around seven in the morning."

"You spoke with Ginny that day, didn't you?"

"No. I already told you, I talked to her on Wednesday. That was the last time."

"You like to be in the know. You knew where she parked at the fair, didn't you?"

"No. How would I?" Will shook his head emphatically.

"What time did you get home from the fair?"

"My best guess is around seven."

"Rachel called you, after she spoke with Tommy. What did she tell you?"

"She didn't call me. She didn't have to. I got home right after Tommy called her."

"Did Ginny have a boyfriend?" Pete asked.

"She had boyfriends off and on."

"Did she have a boyfriend during the last few months?"

"Yes, he came to Mom's funeral."

"What's his name?"

"Mark something. I don't remember his last name."

"Describe him."

"A few inches shorter than me. Black hair, sprinkled with gray."

"Did you and your friends meet somewhere and go to the fair together, or meet at the fair?"

"We met there."

"Who did you go with?"

Pete made notes as Will rattled off the three names and where they lived.

"Are you retired or do you have a job?"

"I'm retired, and I have a part time job."

"Doing?"

"Stocking shelves or whatever they need me for."

"Where?"

"Home Depot." Will looked at his watch, and kept staring at it.

"Did you see Tommy today?"

"Yes, I went shopping with him."

"Make sure you're available in the event that I want to speak with you again."

Will blew out a long breath, spun, and stomped back to the house.

THIRTY-FIVE

Pete strode to where Martin stood with Will's wife. Not knowing what Martin had covered, he held back several steps. He didn't want to interrupt the exchange.

Martin nodded at him, and continued. "Did Rachel get any phone calls while she was here, picking up her daughter last Thursday evening?"

"Tommy texted her. Does that count?" Her look said, *You know the answer. Why are you asking me?*

"How did Rachel react to that message?"

"She called Tommy."

"What did she say?"

"She tried to console him."

"Why did she need to console him?"

"He was upset with Ginny."

"Why was he upset with Ginny?"

"Something about the way she was acting at the fair."

"How did Rachel react to that conversation?"

"She seemed angry."

"Why was she angry?"

"I don't know. She didn't say."

"And you didn't ask?"

"I asked. She said she was too upset to talk about it."

"Did Rachel call Will after she spoke with Tommy?"

"Let me think." She closed her eyes and chewed on her lower lip. After a few seconds, her eyelids flew open. "Oh, no, she didn't. Will came home shortly after she hung up."

"Then?"

"She went home."

"Will told you what Tommy said to Rachel, didn't he?"

"No."

"Nonetheless, you saw Will's reaction, didn't you?"

"Yes, I saw it when Will called Tommy on Friday."

"How did he react?" Martin asked.

"Like someone let the air out of him."

"Yet he said nothing?"

"Not a word." Shrugging, she drew out the last syllable.

"What was Will's reaction?"

"He seemed upset."

"What time did Will leave for the fair that day?"

"I don't know. He was gone when I got up."

"What time did you get up?"

"About eight."

"What time did he return?" Martin asked.

She took a deep breath and put a hand over her mouth. "I'm not really sure. Did you ask Will? I'm sure he knows."

"I want to know what you remember."

"I don't remember."

"But you have a general idea, don't you?"

"Emma and I had eaten. It was probably six thirty, seven or seven thirty."

"What time does Rachel usually pick up Emma?"

"It all depends on when she drops her off, and what she needs to do while I watch Emma."

"Did you expect Will that early?"

"When he goes to the fair, I never know when to expect him. Sometimes he's home for supper, sometimes he isn't."

"Was Emma still here when Will returned?"

"I think so."

"You can't remember?"

"I can't be certain."

"I understand your brother-in-law, Tim Green, stayed with you when he was in town for the funeral. What day did he leave?"

"Thursday?"

"Are you asking me or telling me, Ms. Green?"

She looked away from Martin—and Pete. "Thursday. He left on Thursday."

"What time on Thursday?"

"We had an early lunch, and he left as soon as he finished. He had a lot of errands to run before he returned to Rochester."

"What kind of errands?"

"I don't know. He didn't say. All I know is he was anxious to get going. He was so antsy. He couldn't sit still while we ate, and he paced the whole time I fixed lunch."

Stepping forward, Pete said, "Based on what we've heard, neither Tim nor Caroline was as upset as the rest of you about Virginia's handling of Emma's affairs."

"I disagree! Didn't anyone tell you that Tim and Ginny almost came to blows before the wake? I don't remember who else was there. It was so upsetting. Honest, I thought Tim was going to hit her. He told her, 'It's too bad the funeral's for Mom, not for you.' It was so out of character for Tim. I've never seen him that way. I didn't mention it when we spoke on Thursday. It seemed disloyal and none of my business."

"Maybe one of the things Tim did on Thursday was meet Ginny and apologize," Pete said.

"I don't think so. When he left, he hadn't yet forgiven her. At least that's the impression I got during lunch."

"What did he say during lunch?" Martin asked.

"I don't know. It's just the impression I got."

After allowing enough time for her to expand on that, Martin said, "Thanks for your help, Ms. Green."

She hurried away from the two investigators. Then she slipped into the house, after glancing back over her shoulder at them.

THIRTY-SIX

The two investigators left, after Rachel told Martin she called Tommy at seven twenty on Thursday evening. They shared the results of their respective meetings, and Pete told Martin, "That's enough for today. Why don't you drop me off at headquarters and head home? It'll give you some extra time with your family."

On the way, Martin brought up a topic he'd considered for some time—a subject not unusual between two men who faced the possibility of death in the course of their work on a daily basis. "You believe in heaven, don't you, Pete?"

"You know I do."

"And you believe that it goes on and on and on for eternity?"

"You can't have one without the other, can you, Martin?"

"I guess not. So, here's my question. Does the thought of going on and on and on, for ever and ever bother you?"

"No, why would it?"

"Well, I can't wrap my mind around it. Sure, it would be hell if you went the other direction." Martin smiled. "Even if, by some miracle, I end up in heaven, I think I'd prefer that it ends at some point. I've never been to a party that was so fantastic I didn't eventually want to leave. I can't imagine heaven being so wonderful that I won't want, ultimately, to check out—lie down, close my eyes, and fade away, never to wake again. Do you know what I mean?"

"Is this what you do in your spare time?" Pete laughed. "Leave it to an introvert to anxiously await the end of any party."

"I'm serious, Pete."

"Okay, you're thirty-three. Are you so tired with your life that you want to lie down, go to sleep, and so she wrote?"

"No." Martin frowned.

"Exactly. Maybe heaven will be more like life. Maybe the souls there are always doing different things. Perhaps they're trying to earn their wings, like in *It's a Wonderful Life*. George's angel had his hands full. I don't think he grew tired of the eternal party. Look at it this way, Martin. We're incapable of comprehending eternity. Relax. Just think, maybe you'll spend eternity doing cold case investigations."

"You mean finding the culprits and redirecting them to hell? That's depressing."

"If you feel that way about it, it won't be your heaven. Maybe you'll have time to catch up with your loved ones who died. Do you want more than thirty minutes with the grandmother you lost a year ago?"

"Yes, of course." Martin looked thoughtful.

"How about the great grandparents you never met? Would you like to find out what your parents and grandparents were like as kids?"

"That would be interesting."

"For sure. Lots of elderly people are ready to die. If they could go back to the bodies they had when they were twenty or thirty, do you think they'd still feel that way?"

"Probably not," Martin agreed.

"Once you're in heaven and your body is no longer a consideration, age won't be a factor. Bottom line, we can't imagine what it's like. Have you ever heard 'Eye hath not seen, nor ear heard' . . .

something something . . . 'the things which God hath prepared for them that love Him'?"

"Sounds familiar."

"If you believe what it says, we can't begin to imagine how wonderful the afterlife will be. We can only decide that getting there is the goal. I imagine that an eternity in hell lasts much longer than one in heaven. We have to act accordingly." Pete paused and then asked, "Martin, are Michelle's health problems putting you in this frame of mind?"

"In part, perhaps, but it's also the regular reminders that life is fleeting."

THIRTY-SEVEN

When Martin scrambled into headquarters on Tuesday morning, trying to beat the clock, Pete greeted him with, "How's Michele?"

"No change. I'm glad her appointment's today."

"Me too, Martin. What time?"

"Four forty."

"Guess that means we should stop screwing around and wrap up this case. Then you won't have second thoughts about going with her."

"Don't worry. I won't, either way."

"I can't believe today's Marty's first day of middle school, Martin. Is he excited?"

"And how. Hope he still feels that way tomorrow—and next month. Sometimes the novelty wears off too quickly. Mom came over this morning. I called and asked if she'd mind. With Marty back in school, I didn't want Michelle to have to take care of Olivia all by herself."

"Good thinking, Martin."

"Where do we start today, Pete?"

"Thus far, we've drawn a blank when it comes to locating the man who checked Virginia Green's pulse in the State Fair parking lot. This is day five. With zero leads, it seems unlikely we'll ever find that man or determine his identity. Unless and until our other efforts fall flat, we may as well continue along the current lines. Thus far, we've spoken with only one of Virginia Green's three siblings, her brother Will. Will and his family steered us in a variety of directions. We can't exclude any of those leads, but we're up against the wall, at least for now, across the boards. Intentionally or not, Will's wife indicated we can't forget about Virginia's brother Tim. I think we've avoided the drive to Rochester long enough. If we leave now, we'll be back in plenty of time for you to make it to Michelle's appointment. What do you say?"

"Uh oh. Does this mean you want to clear our schedule for another heart-to-heart? So far, you've counseled me on heaven, and I've told you how to proceed with your relationship with Katie Benton. What's today's topic, the meaning of life?" Martin chuckled.

"Hell no, I already know that. Siri told me."

"Huh?"

"My cell phone."

"Oh yeah. You AT&T folks think it's the only game in town."

"Back on topic, when it comes to the meaning of life, if you want to benefit from my vast pools of knowledge . . ."

"Are they pools of wisdom or pools of something you don't like to get on your shoes? Anyway, thanks, but let's save that for next week." Martin smiled and shook his head.

Today's temperature was eighty-four, and the humidity was tropical. Not an ideal combination for a couple of men in suits. At least the low-hanging clouds blocked the sun, making the car's air conditioner more effective.

Martin went south on Highway 52. Best case, they'd reach Rochester in an hour and fifteen minutes. Once out of the Twin Cities, they saw farmland from horizon to horizon. Fields of corn and soybeans spread as far as the eye could see. The corn stalks were brown, and the soybeans yellow—a sure sign it was harvest time.

Soon the Pine Bend refinery's city of smoke stacks came into view. "I haven't been here in years," Pete said. "Do they still spew noxious fumes?"

"Not anymore. I'm not sure what they did, but you can't smell it, unless the wind's just right. Remember when you used to see the flames shooting out of the top of the stacks? Now there's only steam."

Prior to Cannon Falls, the landscape was as flat as a tabletop. Then it changed to rolling hills. Occasionally, an old church or farmhouse dotted the landscape.

Near Oronoco, they passed the site once scheduled to become a large biotech lab. It was to be the biotech version of Silicon Valley. The land was purchased, and the roads were adapted to accommodate the facilities and the required housing. It went no further.

The two investigators spent most of the trip discussing the case.

"We need to catch a break," Pete admitted. "Someone knows something. We're either not asking the right questions or not talking to the right people. I'm trying to determine the best way to approach Tim Green."

"Does he know we're coming?"

"Yeah, guess I didn't tell you. I called him this morning."

"Where was he?"

"At work. At IBM."

"Maybe he'll give us some free samples. Marty keeps telling me we need a new computer. I hate the fact my eleven-year-old kid knows more about computers than I do," Martin sighed.

"It will be even more difficult when he knows more about sex than you do." Pete laughed.

"I dread the day."

"Don't worry, Martin. I bet it'll be a year or two."

"Thanks for the encouragement. You're indispensable."

"Not to change the subject, but Tim drove home early Thursday afternoon. Do you suppose he left via the State Fair?"

"You're so suspicious."

"Martin, they're paying me the big bucks to be suspicious."

"True. If Tim stopped at the fair, no doubt he'll tell us. And no doubt he'll also tell us that he parked in the east Como lot, and left a little before eight that evening."

"You are such an optimist. Maybe his wife will tell us he didn't get home until ten o'clock. Never mind. He isn't married. Maybe he has a roommate he didn't want to take to his mother's funeral."

"And maybe the price of gas will soon be under two dollars per gallon."

"Right."

Reaching the outskirts of Rochester, Assisi Heights came into view. The one-hundred-acre complex contained the home convent for the Rochester sisters of St. Francis.

Seeing the gray stones and red tile roof, high on a hill overlooking Rochester, Pete said, "Did you know Assisi Heights dates back to the 1870s, and they modeled it after the Basilica of St. Francis of Assisi?"

"No, but I've never been a tour guide. Have you ever been inside?"

"Yeah, I attended a conference there."

"No kidding? What kind of conference?"

"A recruitment for the seminary."

"Really?" Martin sounded shocked.

"No. They refused to consider me. Said I wasn't obedient enough."

"How many nanoseconds did it take to determine that?"

"Approximately negative one-hundred-twelve."

Pete called Tim and obtained directions to his location. After disconnecting, he said, "He's in the Development Laboratory. It's located in a large industrial complex on the west side of Rochester."

When they reached the parking lot, Pete called again.

Tim arrived a few minutes later. He stood a little over six feet, an inch or so shorter than Pete. He looked like the stereotypical nerd, but his shirt pocket lacked the mandatory plastic pen-holder.

"I've always wondered how IBM ended up in Rochester. Do you know?" Pete asked.

"Yes. I understand Watson, IBM's president, used to travel here from Armonk, New York, for medical care. Rochester has a reputation for the foremost medical care in the country. There are now several Mayo clinics around the country, but people still travel here from around the world. Watson emphasized family and health, so he decided to construct a facility here, giving his employees access to world-class medical care. They broke ground in 1956, and opened the doors in 1958. All of the IBM supercomputers are constructed here. Did you hear about Blue Gene, the IBM supercomputer that competed against a top contestant on Jeopardy? Blue Gene was built right here." Tim grinned with pride. "IBM's corporate finance is also located here."

"Interesting," Pete said. "Now, I'd better get down to business. First, I want to tell you I'm sorry about the loss of your mother and your sister."

"Yeah, it's been a rough year. I didn't make it up to see Mom as often as I should have. I really regret that. Now I also wish I'd been nicer to Ginny."

"What do you mean?" Pete asked.

"I sort of unloaded on her."

"When did you do that?" Pete asked.

"Almost every time I saw her after Mom died."

"When was the last time?" Pete asked.

"Before I left town on Thursday."

"You saw Virginia on Thursday?" Pete asked.

"Yeah."

"What time did you leave her on Thursday?" Martin asked.

"About eight that morning."

"Who contacted you to tell you what happened to Ginny?" Martin asked.

"Will. He was pretty choked up. But he was only the first one. I also heard from Mom's brother, and Will's daughter Rachel."

"You stayed at Will's house while you were in the Twin Cities for the funeral?" Martin asked.

"Yeah, ever since Rachel moved out, he has plenty of room."

"After the funeral, when did you return to Rochester?" Martin asked.

"Thursday. I stuck around a few extra days to bicker with Ginny and help her with some of Mom's things."

"Ginny was handling your mother's estate?" Martin asked.

"Yeah, she's the mathematician in the family. Dad named her as the administrator of their estate. After he died, Mom didn't want to change anything. I think she thought if that was the way Bill, my dad, wanted it, that's the way it should stay."

"What time did you leave the Twin Cities on Thursday?" Martin asked.

"Around six. I stayed and had lunch with Will's wife Patty. She's a prize! Don't know how Will managed to capture her."

"Did you spend that afternoon at Will's?" Pete asked.

"No. I don't get to the Twin Cities very often. I spent the afternoon with friends."

"What time did you get back to Rochester?" Pete asked.

"Around seven thirty."

"Can anyone vouch for that?" Pete asked.

"On my way out of town, I filled the gas tank in Inver Grove Heights. I have a receipt. Does that count?"

"What time?" Pete asked.

"A little after six."

"In that case, no, it doesn't count," Pete said. "Did anyone see you in the Rochester area between seven thirty and nine?"

"Not that I'm aware of."

"Talking to Will, I got the impression he blames Ginny for your mother's death," Pete said.

"True, but Will wouldn't hurt Ginny, if that's what you're asking. There were a lot of family arguments the last few months. It was a stressful time for all of us. Our emotions were near the surface. Even so, not one of us is capable of flipping out and murdering any of the rest of us."

"I understand you and Ginny went toe to toe prior to the wake," Pete said.

Tim sighed and looked away.

"Well?" Pete asked.

"Yeah, it's true. I regretted it later that day, and even more when I heard what happened to her. I lost my cool. I apologized before I left on Thursday. So glad I had the chance."

"Any idea who might have been angry enough to attack her?" Pete asked.

"Will and I talked about it. We both think her ex-husband. He's a real SOB. He doesn't bother masking his hatred for her."

"Yet he went to your mother's funeral?" Pete asked.

"Everyone in my family was shocked. He must have seen the obituary. I don't think he said a word to Ginny—to any of us."

THIRTY-EIGHT

"I have plenty of time," Martin said as he started the car. "Want to meet with the victim's sister, Caroline Campbell?"

"Sure do, even though she's the only one of the siblings no one has pointed a finger at."

Martin drove, and Pete called Caroline.

She gave him directions to her location at Dakota County's Western Service Center.

The service center, located in Apple Valley, sat in an area dominated by commercial and retail establishments. Strip malls, big box stores, restaurants, banks, and the Apple Valley City Hall staked their claims to pieces of the nearby turf.

The Apple Valley Police Department was housed in city hall. Out of courtesy, Pete called the PD and notified an officer of their meeting with Caroline. With the PD across the street from the service center, it should be convenient if an Apple Valley officer wanted to join them.

The officer with whom Pete spoke asked someone in the vicinity, then came back and said, "No, thanks. Just let us know if you're going to take it further than questioning. At that point, of course, we'll get involved."

A holding pond occupied a portion of the median situated between the service center's entrance and exit lanes. Rock, perfectly trimmed bushes, and prairie grasses adorned the remainder of the median.

As soon as Martin turned into the entrance, Pete noticed the mammoth clock on the face of the building. It stood directly above the main entrance. He wondered if the huge display announced the arrival of each employee, motivating them to get there on time.

The cement and rust-colored brick exterior represented 1990's construction. A sign listed the agencies located here. In addition to Community Corrections, where Caroline worked, the building housed Courts, Children's Services, Public Health, the County Treasurer, Physical Development, and a branch of the Dakota County Library.

Martin parked in a lot that provided ample parking plus some, and the two investigators hurried to the entrance. Passing through the automatic doors, they found themselves in a large atrium lit primarily by the natural light, flowing through huge windows. The ceramic tile floor was a rust color. A freestanding stairway accessing all three floors drew Pete's attention, by virtue of its teal color. Immediately inside the door, and on the right, stood a reception desk.

Pete called Caroline from the atrium.

She met them there and introduced herself. She had masses of light-brown hair, which she repeatedly brushed away from her forehead and eyeglasses. A scowl marred her looks.

All business, Pete thought.

Both men said they were sorry to hear about her mother and her sister.

Caroline nodded solemnly. Her eyes grew moist, and her grimace relaxed a few degrees.

"Can you tell me about that sculpture?" Pete asked, pointing at a wood-and-metal artwork in the atrium.

"It's a relief created to commemorate the county's sesquicentennial in 1999. It depicts the county's history and beginnings, including a log cabin and a teepee."

"The teepee represents the Mdewakanton Band of the Dacotah, correct?" Pete asked.

"Yes, and the flag represents the US flag in 1849."

"Isn't the county name derived from the Dacotah Band?" Pete asked.

Caroline nodded.

After getting them past security, she led the two investigators to a cube in a large bullpen area. On the way, she borrowed a chair from a neighboring cube. Her cube measured six by eight—at best.

Pete felt claustrophobic. He was glad he reached the rank of commander, entitling him to an office, before headquarters converted to cubes. "Is there a place that offers a bit more privacy?" he asked.

"Let me see if one of the conference rooms is open."

Caroline returned a minute later. "I found something. Follow me."

She led them through the maze to a large room on the opposite side of the bullpen. A massive oval table and upholstered office chairs, complete with wheels, filled the room. The far wall consisted of a panel of windows, looking out on the parking lot.

"Have a seat. Can I get you some coffee? I already checked. There's still some in the pot."

Pete declined.

Martin accepted.

After she got the coffee, Caroline said, "Okay, what can I do for you?"

"Did you commute back and forth when you went to your mother's wake and funeral?" Pete asked.

"Yes. It's only forty-five or fifty minutes, and commuting is easier than packing a suitcase. Besides, if we stayed, we'd have had to make arrangements for our dogs."

"What kind of dogs?" Pete asked.

"Shih Tzus. My husband's retired. They keep him company while I'm at work."

"I hear they're often lap dogs. Are yours?" Pete asked.

"For sure. As soon as I sit down, one or both of them is on my lap. But I know you didn't come to talk about my dogs." She clasped her hands on the table in front of her, looking impatiently from one man to the other.

I was right. She is all business, Pete thought. "As with most of us, it sounds like there were a lot of machinations going on within your family," he said.

"Yes, but like you said, it's a fact of life."

"I understand the problems escalated recently," Pete said.

Caroline studied the two investigators, seeming to decide how much to share. After several moments, she said, "Mom's death seems to have brought things to a head."

"We're investigating your sister's case. That's why we're here," Pete said. "In order to do that, we need to understand the dynamics in your family."

"Look, Ginny had her detractors. At times, my brothers and I grew exasperated with her. In case you're drawing the wrong conclusions, not one of us would attack or murder her! If you think that needs looking into, I can assure you that you're wasting your time."

"Who in your family was closest to Ginny?" Pete asked.

"Will. They're also the closest in age. Will is two years older than Ginny. Tim and I came along much later—sort of a second family."

"Who notified you of Ginny's death?" Pete asked.

"Will. If you'd heard him break down when he told me, you'd know he didn't do it."

"Apparently you think you need to steer us away from him. Why's that?" Pete asked.

"Because you keep bothering him."

"When did Will notify you?" Pete asked.

"Thursday night. He called me right after he spoke with Tim."

"Did he notify Tommy before he called you?" Pete asked.

"I don't think so, but I don't know for sure."

"Tim was in the Twin Cities until Thursday. How was his relationship with your sister?" Pete asked.

"Tim isn't the physical type. He might have bored her to death with his nonstop talk about IBM and computers. He wouldn't attack his worst enemy."

"Who is Tim's worst enemy?" Pete asked.

"I have no idea. He's in Rochester. I'm up here. We talk regularly, but other than that, he has his life and I have mine. The one thing I do know is that no one in our family is Tim's enemy."

"I understand your Uncle Tommy and your mother were close," Martin said.

"Yes, for sure." Caroline nodded briskly. "Tommy spent a lot of time with Mom, both before and after she moved into the apartment. He took her to lunch and shopping. He was the first one in the family to notice she was slipping."

"What caused her to fail?" Pete asked.

"I think it was a matter of advancing years." Caroline sighed. "I'm not sure about Tim. Will and Tommy blamed it on the move to assisted living."

"How did your mother react to the move?" Pete asked.

"Leaving the home she and my dad had for so long made her sad. I think that's the natural course of events." Caroline shrugged.

"Any idea who might have wanted to harm Ginny?" Pete asked.

"The only person I can think of is her ex-husband."

"How many children do you have?" Pete asked.

"Two daughters."

"What are their names?" Pete asked, verifying the information he got from Will.

"My oldest daughter, Heather, is married. Her married name is Bingham. My other daughter is Brittany."

"Where do your daughters live?" Martin asked.

"Heather lives in south Minneapolis. Brittany recently moved back home with my husband and me. She quit a job she hated and returned to school. She decided accounting wasn't for her. She decided medicine is a better fit. She wants to become a nurse practitioner."

"I'd like the work and home phone numbers for both of your daughters," Martin said.

After Caroline recited them, Pete asked, "Did Will and Tommy gang up against Ginny because of the move?"

"I wouldn't say they ganged up. They did make nasty remarks, often when Ginny was within hearing distance. I felt so sorry for her. She was their whipping post. They took all of their frustrations over Mom's deterioration out on her. It was awful! I told Ginny to ignore them. I don't think she succeeded. I think it hurt her deeply. It's a crime. She did everything she could for Mom. She did everything in her power to make Mom comfortable. I'm sure Dad, may he rest in peace, is furious with Will and Tommy." Caroline shook her head mournfully. "I think they should both have been shot, figuratively speaking, of course."

"Does your brother Tim agree with you about your mother and Ginny?" Pete asked.

"It all depends upon with whom he's speaking. If he's talking to me, he agrees with me. If he's talking to Will or Tommy, he agrees with them. I have no idea what he really thinks—about that or almost anything else. He's a curious guy."

"Where were you Thursday evening, between six and nine, Caroline?" Pete asked.

"You think I did it?" The scowl returned.

"It's something I have to ask everyone," Pete said.

"I was home with Brittany and my husband."

"The whole time?" Pete asked.

"Not the *whole* time. I got home a few minutes after six."

Pete and Martin thanked an obviously irritated Caroline for her time. They gave her business cards, and asked her to call if anything that might help occurred to her.

THIRTY-NINE

"Interesting how radically different viewpoints can be in a single family, isn't it, Martin? I'm going to call Brittany. Someone separated by a generation might have a different perspective on family dynamics. I want hers."

From the unmarked, Pete called the phone number Caroline provided. He smiled when a woman answered.

Brittany gave him directions to Caroline's home. It was less than ten minutes south of the service center, in a middle class neighborhood. The development was too new for the trees to catch up with the height of the houses. The homes here were built so close to the street, any vehicle passing at night must illuminate the interiors.

Brittany answered the door. Her black hair hung in ringlets around her face and past her shoulders. She had delicate features and a broad smile.

After the two investigators showed their badges and IDs, she invited them in. They followed her from the foyer to the living room.

Pete gave her his condolences, then asked, "How would you describe the relationship between your uncle Tommy and Virginia?"

"Over the last few years, I rarely saw the two of them together. I understand, from listening to Mom and Dad, that things haven't been good. Sounded like it started after Grandma was forced out of her home."

"Is that the way your parents referred to it? That she was forced out?" Pete asked.

"Oh no. Quite the opposite. Mom and Dad thought it was the right thing to do, and as long as Ginny took the lead, the task didn't fall in their laps. They were happy to let her take the blame."

"But they agreed with the move?" Pete asked.

"If they didn't, I never heard about it."

"You didn't agree?" Pete asked.

"No. I agreed with Tommy and Will. Grandma didn't need to be shuffled off to a place where she didn't want to be. It was at least a few years too soon. Ginny took Grandma's car away at the same time. I heard Will tell Tommy it was like a one-two punch."

"Will and Tommy were angry with Ginny?" Pete asked.

"Furious."

"I heard Tommy was, but I thought Will went along with Ginny," Pete said.

"Who told you that?"

"I don't recall," Pete fibbed.

"Well, whoever it was, they lied."

"Some men are capable of striking a woman, some are not," Pete said. "Which group would you place Tommy in?"

"The latter. Definitely not capable. He's like a big teddy bear. When Heather and I were little, he often got down on the floor and played with us. I've seen him angry. I heard he's gotten into fist fights with a few men, but I can't imagine him hitting a woman. He treats his wife Mary Ann like a princess. He still opens the car door for her. He's that way with the rest of us, too. He's very protective of women. I'm sure he was that way with Ginny, also."

"Was he that way with Ginny the day of your grandmother's funeral?" Pete asked.

"Actually, yes. It surprised me, because I know he blamed Grandma's death on her."

"Do you blame your grandma's death on Ginny?" Pete asked.

"Yes," Brittany whispered, and nodded. Her lower lip quivered.

"Why do you blame her?" Pete asked.

"Because I too saw Grandma give up after Ginny moved her. She died because she gave up. Mom and Dad are wrong. It had nothing to do with her age." Brittany brushed a tear away. "Sorry, I can't help it."

Pete nodded. "Will believed that also?" he asked.

"He sure did!"

"How do you know that?" Pete asked.

"He was very vocal about it."

"Did Will and Tommy convince you it was Ginny's fault?" Pete asked.

"No, I saw it myself. I saw the change between the last time I saw Grandma at home, and the first time I saw her at the new place. It was less than a month. You wouldn't believe the difference. I don't know how anyone could miss it."

"Would Will ever strike a woman?" Pete asked.

"No way," Brittany shook her head. "Like Tommy, Will holds women on a pedestal. When I was a kid, there were a few times when he should have swatted me. He never did. He just took my hands, looked into my eyes, and said, 'You have no right to hurt another person, B.J. You have to think before you act.' I've never forgotten it. Uncle Will is a good, good person. He would never hurt Ginny. That would fly in the face of everything that makes Will the person he is."

"Can you think of anyone who was angry with Ginny, or who might have a reason to hurt her?" Martin asked.

"Her ex-husband. He came to Grandma's funeral. I didn't recognize him. When I pointed him out, that's who Mom said he was. This guy was in Ginny's face. I don't know what he said, but I could tell from his face and the way his arms flew that he was irate. I can't think of anyone else, but I don't think I'm the person to ask."

"How about you, Brittany? Sounds like you were angry enough," Pete said.

Brittany smiled. "You're right. I was, but I was here with Mom and Dad. Want to call them?"

FORTY

"Kind of her to corroborate her mother's alibi," Pete said.

"Yeah. Did you accomplish what you'd hoped?"

"In a very limited sort of way."

"After that speech, are you eliminating Tommy and Will from consideration?"

"Definitely not. I regret to inform you that you're going to have to entertain yourself on the way back to St. Paul. I want to talk to the people who worked at the fair with Tommy, again. He told us he broke down during his first break. I want to see if anyone can or will corroborate that."

"Don't worry, I'll turn on the radio and sing all the way back."

"Sorry, Martin, you can't do that. When I wear earplugs, I can't hear the person I'm talking to."

This time, the order of the calls wasn't random. Pete started with Gene, the one who shared the most the last time around.

After identifying himself, Pete said, "Gene, I have a few more questions. Did Tommy look like he'd been crying when you returned from your first break last Thursday?"

"Crying? Really? Why was he crying?"

"That's what I'm trying to find out. I thought you might know."

"No. I didn't even know he was crying. He should have said something."

Pete thanked him and called the woman who thought Tommy was a doll. He asked her if Tommy looked like he'd been crying, when he returned after his first break last Thursday.

"No. I'm sure I would have noticed. Maybe he was wearing sunglasses. He wears them a lot. I'll bet that's it."

"I hear he was pretty upset when he got back. Did you notice that, or did he say anything about it?"

"Why was he upset? He didn't say anything. Why didn't he tell me?"

"He may have been too choked up to talk. So you had no idea something happened?"

"No. I feel like such a heel! What happened?"

Pete thanked her for her time and hung up.

"Two down, two to go," he told Martin.

"Sounds like you're making excellent progress." Martin snickered.

"Just keep driving. I'll tell you when to talk." Pete smiled.

Martin saluted.

Pete called the second man—the least helpful co-worker the last time around. "I don't understand why you think I should be his babysitter. We work in the same booth. That's all! He does his thing. I do mine. If you have all these questions about Tommy, why don't you ask him?"

Martin heard most of that. The guy talked so loud, Pete had to hold the phone a foot away from his head.

Pete tried another approach with the last co-worker. He told her, "I heard you asked Tommy Wells why he'd been crying, when he returned to the ticket booth at around eight on Thursday."

"No. I wanted to, but I didn't want to be nosy. He tried to cover it up with sunglasses, but I sat kitty corner from him, and could see that his eyes were red. Besides, I didn't want to interrupt. He was on the phone."

"Do you know with whom he was speaking?"

"I heard him say 'Will.' He could have been speaking to him or talking about him. I also heard him mutter something about Ginny. I don't know what, and it didn't sound like he was talking to her. Know what I mean?"

"Other than hearing those names, did you understand any of the conversation?" Pete asked.

"No, I only saw him sigh and shake his head. Then he blew his nose and wiped away a tear."

While Pete carried on that conversation, Martin's phone rang.

Pete saw Martin's reaction. Whatever the news, his partner wasn't happy about it.

FORTY-ONE

After hanging up, Pete asked Martin, "What's the word?"

"You mean the call I just got?"

"Yes."

"Michelle's appointment was rescheduled. Her doctor was called away on a family emergency. I think *we* have a family emergency. How dare they?"

"When's the new appointment?"

"Tomorrow morning. I can't believe someone else couldn't see her."

"Do you want to call and see if you can arrange something?"

"No. I suggested it. Michelle wants to stick with this doctor. She's comfortable with her." Martin sighed, and shook his head.

"Sorry to hear it, Martin. I know you're anxious to get some answers."

"Yeah, but thinking about it won't help. Sounded like the last person you contacted was more helpful. What did you find out?"

Pete shared the information.

"Pete, do you think Will lied to us? Do you think he talked to Tommy on Thursday night?"

"I was surprised he waited until Friday. Tommy was at work, so it seems possible. Why would he lie about it?"

"I could give you several good reasons. Bottom line, I don't know. Guess I know where we're going next."

"While you drive, I'll call the guys who went to the fair with Will. Planned to get to it before now, but . . ."

"That's not a very convincing excuse." Martin smiled. "Maybe we're finally making some progress."

"Did I hear a note of sarcasm?"

"No, it's a note of impatience."

"Well, now that you're free, let's see what we can accomplish in the next eighteen or twenty hours."

Martin rolled his eyes.

Pete used the browser on his cell to search for a phone number for Charlie Kasson, the first name Will gave him. He drew a blank. Apparently the guy didn't have a home phone. How inconsiderate. He sighed and searched for Ron Hopkins. God bless the Internet. He found an address and a phone number for a man residing in Roseville, the location Will gave him.

Pete dialed, and connected with the answering machine. He left a message, explaining who he was and asking for a return call ASAP.

"One to go, then you can start singing," Pete said as he searched for a Brian Ellsworth in Roseville. A smile crept across his face when he found Brian's contact information.

"Okay, Martin, I need your help. Cross your fingers—on both hands. We need a break."

Martin's fingers didn't do the trick. Once again, an answering machine greeted Pete. Again he left a message. Again he requested a return call ASAP.

"Okay, Martin, we're going to change our line of attack. Let's find out what Will Green's neighbors saw last Thursday. Since I can't reach his friends, this may be the best way of verifying what time he got home."

Martin parked on the western end of Will's block. The two men started there. They split up and worked their way along both sides of the street. Most of Will's neighbors proved to be in his age group. That was unfortunate. People in their seventies and eighties spent more time observing the day-to-day events in their neighborhoods. Investigation after investigation proved that.

The first three people with whom Pete spoke had no idea what time Will arrived home on Thursday. Will always parked in the garage, cutting down on the possibilities.

While they were speaking with these people, the two investigators also sought information on Will Green's psychological state over the last several days. That line of questioning was more productive. Several neighbors told Pete that Will was testy and impatient these days.

Pete was between houses when a school bus pulled around the corner and stopped several houses beyond Will's.

"Martin, I'm going to catch those kids. They could be our best bet."

Pete took off running. Kids tended to be as observant as the elderly. He reached the side of the bus as two boys emerged. "Hey, guys, first day of school, huh?"

The two boys shrugged, noncommittally.

Undaunted, Pete said, "Got a few minutes? I have a couple of questions."

Both boys shrugged, again.

"Do you know the Greens?"

"Yeah. They live right there." The boy who answered pointed at Will's house. "Why?"

"Guess there were a lot of cars hanging around there last week, huh?" Pete asked.

"Yeah, his mom died," the vocal one said.

"Right, but there were also several cars parked there last Thursday. I know it's been a while, but do you remember that?"

Martin joined Pete and the boys, panting from running to catch up.

The spokesman's face lit up. "Wasn't that the day his brother left? We talked to him before he left. He's awesome! He knows everything about computers. I wish he lived around here."

"You saw him leave?" Pete asked.

"Yeah."

"What time was that?" Pete asked.

"Two or three?"

"There were still several other cars parked there after he left, weren't there?" Pete continued.

This time the quiet one spoke up. "Yeah, Tim said those cars belonged to the guys who went to the fair with Will."

"Did you notice what time those cars arrived?" Pete asked.

"All I know is, they were there when I got up."

"What time was that?" Pete asked.

"I don't know. Eleven?"

"Do you know when they left?" Pete asked.

"Not sure about the time. It was after dark," the first kid said, perhaps wanting to regain the limelight.

"Do you have any idea what time it was?" Pete asked the other boy.

"I only know it was a while after dark. Not right after it got dark."

"One more thing, guys. Did you notice if the men who went to the fair with Will hung around a while before they left?" Pete asked.

The two boys glanced at each other. Then both shook their heads.

FORTY-TWO

"Let's talk to Will," Pete said. He turned and headed toward Will's home. "We'll refresh his memory on the details of his trip to the fair last Thursday. Let's see how much he wants to change, in addition to the fact he didn't get home at seven or even seven thirty."

"It's possible he got home that early, but his buddies hung around until after dark."

"That's the first thing I plan to ask him about."

Martin jogged to keep up with Pete's long and rapid stride. "Pete, for the sake of novelty, can you walk at a normal pace? I've barely caught my breath after my last stroll."

"Sorry, Martin. Didn't mean to tax your heart."

"Heart nothing. My lungs are about to explode. Don't you think it would be better if we talked to the guys Will went to the fair with before we question him, again?"

"There'd definitely be some benefit to that. Since I don't know how long we'll have to wait, thought we should proceed without their help. Don't worry, I think Will still has several openings on his dance card. We can talk to him now and later."

"Do you track the number of times you speak to each person for each case, Pete?"

"No. Why would I?"

"I'm wondering if you might set a new record."

Martin didn't need to worry about talking to Will now *and* later.

Will's wife Patty came to the door. She flashed a smile when she saw the two men. "More questions?" she asked jovially.

"Yes," Pete said. "Is Will home?"

"No. I ran some errands. He was gone when I got home." She looked apologetic. "I'm not sure where he is or when he'll be back. Want me to call his cell and find out?"

"Please." Pete nodded.

Patty invited them in. After depositing them in the living room, she walked into the kitchen.

In less time than Pete thought it took to speed dial, she returned. He wondered if she faked the call.

"His battery must be dead. My call went right to voicemail."

"Did you leave a message?" Pete asked.

"No, it never occurred to me. Should I call again?"

"No, thanks anyway," Pete said. "But I have a question for you. How long did Will's friends hang around after they returned from the fair on Thursday?"

"They didn't. They didn't even come in the house. I asked Will about it. He said they were exhausted, thanks to the heat."

"What do you think?" Martin asked as he and Pete walked toward the unmarked car. "Did she call her husband, or was she pretending?"

"I have the same question. If she was pretending, why? Is Will getting nervous? Did he take off?"

"Getting nervous for himself or for Tommy?"

"Maybe for both of them."

"Maybe the friends who went to the fair with Will called him, not you."

"Sounds a little paranoid, Martin, unless you think that many people had a hand in it."

FORTY-THREE

The two investigators walked up to Tommy's front door, and Pete rang the bell.

Mary Ann answered. She stood silently inside the door and stared wordlessly at them.

Pete knew he shouldn't be surprised. He hoped to be wrong about what would follow. "We're looking for Tommy," he said.

"He isn't here. He's with Will."

It took a measure of self-control for Pete to keep his eyes from rolling. "When do you expect him?" This time, he didn't bother asking where they went. He and Martin wouldn't go looking for them.

"Any time now, I suspect." The way she lifted and dropped her shoulders, indicated she had no idea. "They've been gone for quite some time," she added.

"Which car did they take?" Pete asked.

"Will's."

"Will's Impala?" Pete clarified.

"Yes, and this time I'm sure it's the car they took. Why?"

"Please tell him we were here. We have more questions," Pete said.

Mary Ann nodded curtly and closed the door.

Walking away from the house, Martin said, "Ask me if I'm surprised."

"No need. I know the answer."

Several steps from the unmarked car, Pete saw something red out of the corner of his eye. He turned his head for a better look.

A block and a half down the road, a red car sped through an illegal U-turn. Was it Will? With such a fleeting glimpse, he didn't know. Couldn't identify the make or model. It was the right size. So few midsized red cars these days. What are the chances?

"Martin, quick! Did you hear the squealing tires? It was a red car. I think it's Will's." Pete moved in fast forward as he spoke. Reaching for the door with one hand, he pointed down the street with the other. The car was gone. "I know either Tommy or Will is our killer. We're going to arrest one or both, as soon as we get our hands on them. Let's haul ass!"

Martin started the car. It faced the wrong direction. He wanted to kick himself. He shifted into gear, and sped through a U-turn of his own. "Which way do you think he'll go, Pete?"

"I hope he doesn't stay on city streets. That would be crazy. The closest highways are 36 and I-35W. Unfortunately, there's a lot of residential between here and both."

"Yeah, I don't need to be reminded."

"He could take 36 east or west," Pete continued. His words oozed adrenaline. "It's still pre-rush hour. East might be preferable. Going west, he's in Minneapolis before long. North on I-35W means less traffic, and lots of exits. What do you think, Martin?"

"I think it's fortunate you're in shape. Otherwise, I'd worry about a heart attack." After that, Martin shut up. His hands, and mind, were wrapped up in the driving.

Now pointed in the right direction, he turned onto and tore down Walnut, toward Roselawn.

While Martin did this, Pete reached over and turned on the lights and siren.

Martin knew Roselawn dead-ended at a large wooden wall, just west of the intersection with Walnut. That limited the threat of tangling with another car, if he did as planned and blew the stop sign that lay ahead.

As they approached the intersection, a Dodge Durango pulled out in front of them.

Martin slammed on the brakes. They screeched to a sliding stop.

"He pulled in so close, he almost clipped your bumper." Pete shook his head.

"Yeah. Now he's barely moving. Maybe he saw us at the last second, and now he's petrified. Dammit!"

Walnut was a single lane in each direction. Pulling into the other lane to pass the Durango was a gamble. A car turning onto Walnut from Roselawn might not see them until it was too late.

Martin's grip on the wheel tightened and relaxed. Tightened. Relaxed.

The driver of the Durango didn't pull over or speed up.

Martin flipped the siren off and on, striving to get the driver's attention.

The Durango stopped dead—in the middle of the road.

"Got his license in a box of corn flakes," Martin muttered and sped around the Durango. He didn't slow for the stop sign at Roselawn. Jaw clenched, he peered unblinking through the windshield.

Pete observed all of this in silence. He knew how Martin felt. He experienced his own version. His heart pounded. His mind raced. He worked to formulate a plan. There were so many unknowns. Was the killer Will or Tommy? Did Will take off to protect one or both of them? Did they have a plan? Were they desperate? If it was Will, would he endanger Tommy—or anyone else?

Taking the corner wide and scrambling back into his lane on Roselawn, Martin saw the red car. He saw it too briefly to be positive it was Will. A couple of blocks and a Ford F150 separated them. The Ford blocked his view of the red car. Relying on occasional glimpses, Martin felt the distance between them grow. He considered his options. The streets were narrow. The danger of hitting a kid—a kid like Marty? Too great. He kept his speed in check. His eyes darted from side to side, taking it all in. He had to catch up with that car!

"I'll contact dispatch and get backup," Pete said. "This is Lauderdale. They contract with St. Anthony for their law enforcement. We need to get St. Anthony Village out here."

"Glad you thought of it. I didn't. Can you see the red car? The truck's blocking my view."

"Ditto, Martin."

The red car and the truck seemed oblivious to the lights and siren blasts. Both continued east on Roselawn. The red car sped. The Ford approximated the speed limit.

Exercising caution, Martin closed the distance between him and the F150. The houses and yards along his path concerned him. The thought of a kid chasing a ball, or stepping in the street to see what was happening, scared him. That made his foot lighter. "Wish I was driving a semi about now," he said. "Then the truck wouldn't block my view."

"You should make that recommendation, Martin. Think of it, unmarked semis instead of unmarked cars. Has a certain appeal, doesn't it?"

"What are the chances that isn't Will? Would another red car make an illegal U-turn at Walnut, then take off at these speeds?"

"The chances are pretty good, if the driver didn't know Roselawn dead-ended there, and the detour means he or she is now deadlining it."

"Yeah, thanks for the optimism."

"However, Martin, despite those qualifications, I'm convinced that red car is Will's Impala."

FORTY-FOUR

Glancing at Pete, Martin said, "In response to your earlier question, I have no idea which way he'll head. I don't know if Will is thinking or simply reacting. So, I haven't a clue. I do know I don't like a chase through a residential neighborhood. It's far too dangerous for the residents . . . and for us."

"Agreed."

Martin silently cursed the F150 and added more siren blasts.

Miraculously, moments later, the driver reacted. The truck pulled over to the right and stopped.

Finally, they had an unobstructed view of the red car. It was several blocks ahead, but Pete knew it was an Impala. He couldn't read the license plate. "What do you think?" he asked.

"I think it's them, but not willing to bet my life on it."

The quiet residential neighborhood through which they passed continued serving as a deterrent. Martin was chomping at the bit. Even so, he couldn't or wouldn't swiftly close the distance.

"See how he's pulling away from us. He's got to be going at least sixty," Martin said.

"I think you're right. Brilliant move in this area."

After glancing in both directions, Martin blew through the four-way stop at Eustis. All the while, his grip on the steering wheel tightened, loosened, tightened, loosened. Finding it difficult to cover both fronts simultaneously, his focus shifted second by second from the neighborhood through which he drove to the road and car ahead of them.

Where are the squads? Pete wondered. *Shouldn't they be here by now? Shouldn't I hear a siren or two?* It was hard to be patient at a time like this. Tearing his eyes away from the windshield for a half second, he reached around to the back seat and grabbed a tissue from the box Martin kept there.

Martin saw Pete wipe his forehead and said, "Sorry I'm doing the driving?"

Pete knew the worst thing you could do to a guy behind the wheel in a chase was criticize his driving. "You're doing fine, Martin. Keep it up. Should be getting some help soon. Just stay the course."

When he and Martin were together, Martin usually drove. Typically, Pete liked that arrangement. Not now. Right now, he hated it! He wanted to push Martin out the driver's side door and take the wheel. Sitting on the sidelines at a time like this was nerve wracking. His feet were braced against the floorboards. He clenched and un-clenched his fists and bit his lip, trying to deal with the adrenaline rush. By now, he would have closed the distance between them and the Chevy Impala. He knew he would have. Even so, he kept his mouth shut. Where was their backup? Someone had to be in the vicinity. Someone had to be close enough to be here any second, didn't they?

"Where in God's name are the squads?" Martin asked.

Pete thought Martin sounded as exasperated as he felt.

The thin layer of calm in the unmarked threatened to dissolve, as the levels of anticipation and anxiety escalated.

In this neighborhood, homes and garages crowded the street. Pete worried about a kid. He worried about a car backing onto Roselawn, oblivious to the chase. He worried about the driver ahead losing focus and running into a kid, a house, a garage. He contemplated the sparse knowledge of this area he'd gathered during their visits to Tommy's house. This was Tommy's neighborhood. Pete wondered if Tommy was coaching Will.

Switching gears, he thought about what to do, once backup arrived. If Will stayed on Roselawn, Cleveland Avenue seemed like the best place to set a trap. They should have another minute or two to stage some squads there—if the squads showed in the next thirty seconds or less. Where were the squads?

They needed an assist from the St. Anthony PD. Was a St. Anthony squad en route?

"We're nearing the end of the residential area on the right," Martin said, as they approached Pleasant Street. His hands continued massaging the wheel. His head bent forward as he fixated on the road.

Suddenly, several short siren blasts broke the uncomfortable silence. Until that point, the only interruptions were from their siren and the radio traffic. Four squads made radio contact with Pete. All responding vehicles got on the MINSEF channel and worked to plan a strategy, as Pete read off the streets they passed.

For the first time since the pursuit began, Martin relaxed a bit.

Per the radio traffic, two Ramsey County Sheriffs' squads approached Roselawn and Cleveland Avenue from the north. A St. Anthony squad moved north on Cleveland, approaching Roselawn. A second St. Anthony squad moved west on Roselawn, toward their unmarked.

Both Pete and Martin noted that for a short distance, trees replaced the houses that had been on both sides of the street. It was a welcome change. "Coming up on Lake Street and more houses on the left," Martin said. "We now have some of the 'haves' on the left. Look at the size of those houses. Here comes an apartment complex."

While residential resumed on the left, undeveloped land sprouted on the right.

Pete shared their reasons for the pursuit with everyone on the MINSEF channel.

"I'll try to get a visual," the St. Anthony officer heading toward them on Roselawn announced.

Seconds later, there was another transmission from that squad. "I see it! I see two large men in a red Impala. Can't yet read the license plate. They're approaching Fulham. Hang on. He's moving left. I think he's going to turn onto Fulham. Watching, watching. He just took a wide right onto Fulham. He's going south. I'm turning onto Fulham. Hang on. Okay, I'm behind him. There's no one between us. He's speeding up. I'm going sixty. He's pulling away from me."

Pete and Martin saw the Impala turn south on Fulham.

Without slowing, Martin yanked the wheel hard to the right. Tires squealing, they skidded around the corner. Martin made that turn with enough trouble for Pete to semi-seriously contemplate bailing out. There were a lot of things he still wanted to accomplish, not the least of which was getting married and having kids.

He used a hand to wipe the sweat off his forehead. This time, he refused to take his eyes off the road long enough to grab a tissue. The one snatched previously was now a moist ball in his fist.

Once Martin had the car under control and on a straight path, he sped up. There was a squad car between them and the Impala.

Pete looked surreptitiously at the speedometer.

Martin was going sixty-five miles per hour on this city street. Granted, with a park on the right and the University of Minnesota golf course on the left, there was clear sailing—for a bit. However, in no time at all, they'd be in the trunk of the St. Anthony squad that followed the Impala onto Fulham.

All too soon, residential resumed on the right, as the golf course continued on the left. Again, Pete worried about an unknowing driver pulling out into their path, despite the lights and sirens. A car radio, operating at full volume and maximum bass, could drown out the sirens. So could impaired hearing. Once again, he allocated his attention between the road ahead and the yards and driveways to the right. He saw a few golfers on the university golf course pause to observe and point at the activity on Fulham.

Pete carefully evaluated the area through which they passed. As they went, he planned how he'd respond if this was where the chase ended. He looked for places that could serve to his advantage, and places that could benefit Will and Tommy. He wanted to be prepared. His feet were on another mission. They pressed so hard against the floorboard, he expected they'd soon be scraping the street.

Wiping his forehead with a damp hand, Pete glanced over his left shoulder. He saw a Ramsey County Sherriff's squad take the corner. It rapidly closed the distance between them.

FORTY-FIVE

"We need a plan," Pete announced over MINSEF. "Who's familiar with these streets?"

"Ione Street is next, then Larpenteur," a voice answered. "Anyone near Larpenteur or Ione, in the vicinity of Fulham?"

"Yeah, I'm on Larpenteur, approaching Fulham," another voice answered.

"Me, too."

"We'll reach Larpenteur in about thirty seconds," Martin said.

Pete repeated that to everyone on the channel, adding, "The few cars ahead of us are getting out of the Impala's way. They're pulling off on the grass. Does anyone have stop sticks?"

"How about the PIT maneuver?" Martin asked. "If you get the St. Anthony squad out of the way, I can bump the Impala."

"I wouldn't risk it, Martin. We're almost to Larpenteur. There's an apartment complex ahead on the right. It has too many driveways emptying onto Fulham. Let's check out the other options."

"Ramsey County, here," a voice came over the radio. "Fulham ends at Larpenteur. Think they'll get out and run? There's a large stand of trees south of Larpenteur. It's part of the U of M Golf Course. They may try to get lost in there. I have the westbound traffic on Larpenteur blocked, just before Fulham. Another squad is in the process of blocking the eastbound lanes. I see you coming. I have stop sticks. I set them out on Larpenteur, heading west from Fulham. I'll try to get them out on Fulham, too."

"Too risky," Pete said, almost before the other man's words were out. "It isn't worth your life. We'll get these guys." He wished he felt as confident as his statement implied. "How about Larpenteur? Do we have stop sticks out on Larpenteur, east of Fulham?"

"Got it covered," a voice answered.

"Anyone out there with a K-9?" another voice asked.

"Yup, I'll be to Larpenteur and Fulham in less than a minute. I'm traveling south on Fulham. I see your unmarked."

Bearing down on Larpenteur, Pete reached up and grasped the handle mounted above the door. He studied the area they approached, and what lay ahead. He saw the Impala about thirty yards out front. He saw a St. Anthony squad ahead and Ramsey County behind. He saw the squads on Larpenteur, east and west of Fulham. He saw a stockade-design fence on the far side of Larpenteur and to the right. The height and points on the upright posts made scaling it impossible for Will—and him. That ruled out the south side of Larpenteur as an escape route—at least for a few hundred feet.

Will too must see all of this. What would he do when he reached the T at Larpenteur? There were trees dead ahead—literally dead ahead. Green would crash into a tree, if he didn't stop before crossing Larpenteur. Would he slam on the brakes at the last second? Could he slide across and off Larpenteur and into the trees? Could he pull off a miracle? Could he skid around the corner and head either east or west on Larpenteur?

What Pete wouldn't give to know Will's thoughts. Did he think the trees would provide an escape route? Tommy couldn't escape on foot. Neither could Will, for that matter. If the trees weren't part of Will's plan, he must intend to turn onto Larpenteur. Traffic was blocked in both directions. That meant no oncoming traffic. That would benefit Will.

Pete saw the condos on the north side of Larpenteur. Less threatening. Houses lay beyond the condos. Was there something drawing Will in that direction? Did he know one of the residents? Had he called? Were they expecting him? Would they defend him? With gunfire?

Will maintained his speed. Only a highly skilled driver could hope to go east on Larpenteur at these speeds. Taking a right and going west on Larpenteur would also require skill—but a bit less. With all these squads, did Will think he could escape? How could he? Was he crazy?

If Will saw the squads blocking traffic, he must have missed the stop sticks. He went wide, taking a right onto Larpenteur on two wheels. He regained control as the passenger side tires rolled over the stop sticks. They deflated, too slowly to please Martin.

That didn't stop Will.

The St. Anthony officer who'd positioned the sticks yanked on the cord, clearing the path for the St. Anthony squad and Martin.

The St. Anthony squad held back.

Martin went around him and headed west on Larpenteur. Gaining on the Impala, he wondered how long Will would or could drive on two flat tires. The Impala listed to the right. Steering had to be a challenge. How far could Will go? Martin didn't have to wonder for long.

Will slammed on the brakes. His door flew open.

Martin and the St. Anthony squad skidded and stopped.

Will took off. He ran across all four lanes of Larpenteur. He didn't pause to check for traffic.

An approaching driver saw him and floored the brake pedal. His car swerved, sliding out of control and off the road.

Will kept going, seemingly oblivious to it. Without breaking stride, he made a beeline for the apartment complex that lay ahead.

Pete took off after Will. Common sense and an approaching vehicle forced him to pause on the median. Standing there, he continued scanning the area, trying to predict Will's next move—and his options.

One building in the apartment complex they approached stood dead ahead. Another was off to the left.

It looked like Will's target was dead ahead. Why? Did he have a way to get inside? If not, Pete knew he'd catch Will before anyone could buzz him in. Will had to know that, too. For the second time in minutes, Pete wondered if Will was crazy. If he was, that added another dimension to the chase.

Pete saw a driveway that ran from the parking lot to the back of the building on the left. A dense stand of trees lay beyond that driveway. Did Will hope to get lost in there? That would be naive. He had to know about K9s. What was beyond those trees? Did Will know? Pete was confident of one thing. Will knew the area at least as well as he did.

Pete yelled, "Stop, Will! Give up! You won't get away. Stop and put your hands in the air, NOW!" He gained on Will, but he was amazed at how fast the sixty plus man ran. He knew the benefits of adrenaline. This was an excellent demonstration. It was also a demonstration of the benefits of running in track shoes rather than dress shoes. It wasn't the first time he regretted wearing dress shoes on the job.

Pete's heart pounded from the adrenaline rush, and the exertion. He thought about drawing his Smith & Wesson. He decided against it. He didn't believe Will had a weapon. He couldn't see anything in either of Will's hands. He didn't believe he had a concealed weapon. He ran faster with the pistol holstered. If something happened to change his mind, his gun was handy. He'd have it out of the holster in a second. As Pete ran, he studied and evaluated Will's path.

Twice, Will looked to the left, took a step in that direction, and returned to the current path.

Pete wondered if Will feigned those moves or couldn't decide which way to go. Did the stand of trees lure Will?

* * *

Meanwhile, with a uniformed St. Anthony officer at his side, Martin dealt with Tommy. Using the unmarked as a shield, Martin yelled,

"Stay facing forward, Tommy. Put your hands up, where I can see them."

Tommy remained facing forward, but otherwise ignored Martin.

"Put your hands in the air, and do it now!" Martin repeated.

Tommy hesitated, briefly, then did as instructed.

For the first time since exiting the unmarked, Martin breathed.

Continuing to utilize the shield offered by the unmarked car, Martin yelled, "Open the car door and get out with your hands in the air, Tommy. Leave the door open. Continue facing the direction you now face. Do NOT turn around. Do NOT face me. I only want to see your back."

Tommy didn't move.

"Did you hear me, Tommy? We don't want to hurt you. Do as I say, and you won't get hurt. Open the car door, Tommy. Do it NOW!"

Tommy's head began turning to the left.

Martin wondered if Tommy wanted to see what was happening with Will. He wanted to know the same thing. Pete should have caught Will by now. Will couldn't be that fast. Pete was a runner. Was there a problem? Did Will have a weapon? He pushed all that out of his head. He had to concentrate on Tommy. He had to keep his eyes on Tommy.

He yelled, "Stop turning, Tommy! Don't test me. Keep your face and eyes pointed straight ahead. Don't do anything you'll regret. Don't do anything Mary Ann will regret. Stop turning. Don't force my hand. I don't want to hurt you. Do exactly as I say. Nothing else! Open the door. Get out. Keep your hands in the air. Stay facing forward. Leave the car door open."

This time, Tommy did as ordered, at a frustratingly slow pace.

Martin could see that his hands were empty.

Another St. Anthony squad pulled up behind him.

The officer hurried, cautiously, to his side.

"What's happening with my partner?" Martin asked.

"He's still chasing the other guy. I'll go help." The St. Anthony officer took off, crossing Larpenteur.

Watching for any sudden moves, Martin and the other uniformed officer approached Tommy. When they were within arm's reach, the uniformed officer grabbed Tommy's arms, one at a time. Jerking each arm around behind Tommy's back, the officer hand cuffed him.

As he escorted Tommy to the St. Anthony squad, Martin tried repeatedly to get a glimpse of Pete. He wondered why it took so long. He wanted to assist his partner.

FORTY-SIX

Pete's attempts to decipher Will's intent continued. Suddenly, he heard someone running behind him. "That you, Martin?" he called out, certain it couldn't be.

"St. Anthony PD," a voice called back. "Here to assist."

Pete made a large semicircle with his right hand. The motion ended with his index finger pointing to Will's right. Using this signal, he attempted to direct the officer to move to his and Will's right.

Will continued running full throttle toward the apartment building in front of them. Suddenly, he swerved left, taking the road that lead toward the trees.

Within forty feet of Will and preparing to dive and tackle him, Pete kicked it up a few notches, closing the distance more rapidly.

Will must have heard the nearness of Pete's footfalls. He glanced back over his shoulder. He looked Pete straight in the eye. His eyes painted a picture of fear. Unadulterated fear.

Pete saw no trace of malice, anger, or revenge. "Stop, Will," he yelled. "Can you hear the other man? A St. Anthony officer is also closing in on you. You don't have a chance. Don't make us hurt you.

We don't want to hurt you. There's no place to go. Just put your hands in the air and stop."

Will slowed down. He didn't stop.

Pete didn't know if Will was tired or giving up. At this inopportune moment, his cell phone vibrated. Curiosity distracted him for a heartbeat. He couldn't allow an interruption at a time like this.

Will continued ignoring his commands. Although he moved more slowly, he kept running. His hands remained in front of him, pumping. He headed for the trees.

Pete narrowed the distance. He placed his right hand on the butt of his Smith & Wesson. He saw the uniformed officer, roughly an equal distance, on Will's right.

The St. Anthony officer had his pistol in hand.

The turf dropped off between the parking lot and the trees. Either Will didn't notice that or a dip in the surface tripped him. He went sprawling, arms outstretched. When he hit the ground, he rolled a couple of times. He came to rest sitting with his back to Pete.

"Stay right there! Put your hands in the air!" Pete breathed deeply. He heard Will gasping for air. He slowed and walked toward Will. Soon, he had to abandon that plan.

The St. Anthony officer reached the slope. His luck wasn't any better than Will's. It looked like he caught a toe in the turf. He too went flying. He did a belly flop on the grass. When his gun hand slammed on the ground, the pistol somersaulted through the air.

Pete saw the pistol's trajectory.

It followed the worst possible path.

Taking a flying leap, Pete attempted to grab the pistol in midair.

Turning his head to watch the uniformed officer's plight, Will saw the gun and Pete. He dove to his right to block Pete's attempted save. He succeeded.

Pete crashed head first into Will's back.

Will's weight advantage prevailed. He grunted, stretched, and grabbed the pistol off the ground.

The collision rang Pete's bell. He tried to shake it off. Then he saw the pistol—in Will's hand. That did it. Instantly, his head cleared.

Will sat there, back to Pete.

The St. Anthony officer sat off to Pete's right.

Will didn't point the gun at either of them. He just sat there, hunched over, gasping for air.

Pete spun backward, away from Will. He had to put distance between them. He couldn't risk Will rolling back on top of him or grabbing him. After adding to the distance, he sat on both knees, facing Will. Then, scrambling to his feet, he drew his Smith & Wesson. The whole time, he watched Will. He looked for the slightest movement or twitch. He had to anticipate Will's actions.

He didn't know Will's state of mind. Did Will intend to remain in the current position, hoping for an opportunity to use the gun? Would he choose suicide by cop? Pete wanted to avoid both scenarios. He had to talk Will into putting the gun down.

"My gun is pointed at your back, Will," he said. "You gave me no choice. Put the gun down. Think about what you're doing. You don't want to paint yourself into a corner. Just set the gun down. Then stand, and put your hands in the air. Once you do, we can talk."

The St. Anthony officer hustled to get out of Will's field of vision. Reaching Pete's side, he shook his head apologetically.

Pete smiled, glad to see the officer out of imminent danger. "Final chance, Will," he said. "I'm not going to ask you again. That gun won't buy you a ticket out of here. You have nothing to gain. Don't be stupid. Give yourself a break. Think of your family. Think of the granddaughter who adores you. Think of your mother. Put the gun down, Will. Do it NOW!"

Will's head dropped even lower. His shoulders heaved. He sighed deeply.

Pete's grip on his pistol tightened.

Will's right hand moved slowly from his lap and to the right.

Pete scrutinized every inch Will's hand traveled, preparing for the worst.

When Will's arm was fully extended, he laid the gun on the grass.

"Now stand up, Will," Pete said.

After several seconds, Will slowly rose to his feet. He remained bent forward, gasping.

Pete exhaled.

The St. Anthony officer scrambled and snatched his gun off the ground. Mission accomplished, he looked back at Pete.

Pete nodded.

After holstering his pistol, the officer closed the distance between him and Will. Then, yanking Will's arms around behind him, he slapped on the cuffs.

Will moved compliantly, as Pete and the St. Anthony officer walked him to the officer's squad.

Once there, Pete put a hand on the top of Will's head and guided him into the backseat.

After wiping the sweat from his face with the brush of a hand, Pete thanked the St. Anthony officer and said, "See you at headquarters. Please record the trip. I want a record of anything he says."

"Yes, sir. Commander Culnane, right?"

Pete nodded.

"You did a fantastic job of talking him down, sir. I didn't think we'd get out of this with no shots fired. Mentioning his family did it. You knew his Achilles heel, didn't you."

FORTY-SEVEN

Pete walked to the unmarked car and placed a hand on Martin's shoulder. "How are you doing?"

"A little hyper. Otherwise fine." Martin smiled. "And you?"

"Ditto—on both counts."

While Martin drove, Pete radioed in with their status. Then he checked to see who tried to reach him, while he was busy with Will.

He smiled. The caller was Brian Ellsworth, one of the guys who went to the fair with Will.

Pete was glad they talked to the kids in Will's neighborhood before reaching this friend. The boys gave him a yardstick against which to judge Ellsworth's answers. He might not need it, but just in case . . .

When Ellsworth answered, Pete got right to the meat of it. "What kind of mood was Will in on Thursday?"

"He was pretty quiet and withdrawn. That's not normal for him, but hell, he'd just buried his mother."

"Why didn't he cancel?"

"He tried. This is an annual event. We thought getting away would be good for him."

"Did he lighten up as the day progressed?"

"Initially, but then he sank back down."

"What caused that to happen?"

"Nothing that I know of."

"Were you together the entire time?" Pete asked.

"No, he took off for a while."

"When he took off, did he go alone?"

"No, Charlie Kasson went with him."

"Where did they go?"

"To see the horses."

"The rest of you didn't?"

"The only horses I care about are found beneath the hood of a car." Brian laughed.

"What time did Will and Charlie take off?"

"After we bulked up at the food building, and after we hung out at the Bandshell for a while. Don't know about you, but I don't see any sense in paying for a Grandstand show, when the free entertainment is that good."

"What time did you go to the Bandshell?"

"Don't know. Heard the music from the Food Building and wandered over. It's just across the street, you know. Didn't know about the talent show until we got there. This year, Will was too preoccupied to do the usual research."

"Did Will get any phone calls before he took off to see the horses?"

"He got a couple of calls. Don't ask who from. He didn't say."

"Did he get angry or perturbed after any of the calls?"

"All I can tell you is, after the second one, he walked away from the rest of us and made a call. Don't ask who he called. I don't know. What's with all the questions? Why don't you ask Will?"

"How long after that call did he leave to see the horses?"

"Several minutes? I don't know. What difference does it make?"

"You made it to the Food Building. How about the Beer Garden? Did you spend some time there?"

"Of course. It's a great place to tip a few, and watch people."

"How many did you tip?"

"Not that many. We weren't drunk!"

"I'm not suggesting you were. How much time did you spend there?"

"An hour or so."

"Did you buy beer by the pitcher?"

"Of course. It's the only way to go."

"How many pitchers did you buy?"

"Who knows? Two? Maybe three?"

"Did each of you buy a pitcher?"

"No, I don't think so. I know I did, and Ron did. Not sure about Charlie or Will."

Pete did some calculations. "Were they gallon pitchers? If so, that meant a half to three quarters of a gallon per man. A half gallon could affect Will's judgment. Were you at the Beer Garden just before you went to the Food Building?"

"Hell no. We went to the Beer Garden around two or three."

"Does Will check out the horses every year?"

"No, but he wanted to see the Clydesdales. Annheuser-Busch brought their Budweiser team up from St. Louis."

"Aren't they at the fair every year?"

"Got me. Are they?"

"Did you hang around the fair after Will and Charlie returned?"

"Not for long."

"How long?"

"I don't know. Maybe a half hour."

"Was Will different when he returned, Brian?"

"Well . . ."

Pete waited, silently.

"I guess," Brian said after the silence grew uncomfortable.

"What was different about him?"

"He was off in another world. He acted like a robot. He didn't talk, answer questions, or react to anything. He just went through the motions."

"Did you guys run into his uncle, Tommy Wells, on Thursday?"

"No."

"But Will talked to Tommy while at the fair, didn't he?"

"Got me."

"Did the four of you ride together to the fair?"

"Yeah. Will drove."

"Where did you park?"

"About a mile from the Snelling gate."

"Be more specific."

"Walk out the Snelling gate. Go straight ahead down Midway Parkway, almost as far as Hamline. Then go right a block or two."

"Did it take long to get back to Will's house?"

"Yeah. The traffic crawled. I kept telling Will to take the back streets. I don't think he even heard me. He was so distracted."

"What time did you leave the fair?"

"I don't know."

"Had the sun set?"

"It was setting when Will and Charlie returned."

"What time did you reach Will's?"

"All I know is it was after dark."

"Did you hang around Will's, before going home?"

"No. He wasn't in the mood for company."

FORTY-EIGHT

Pete wrapped up the conversation with Ellsworth, as Martin pulled into the headquarters parking lot. Walking toward the St. Anthony squads, Pete shared the highlights of his conversation with Ellsworth. He concluded with, "I hate giving either Tommy or Will enough time to concoct a story, but here's what I think. Either or both might point the finger at the other. Also, what each tells us could help when we question the other. So, instead of splitting up, let's start with Tommy. Once they're both situated, how about entertaining Tommy while I make one more call?"

"No problem. He likes me better anyway."

They spoke with the St. Anthony officers. The one transporting Will said he didn't utter a word during the trip. Tommy was more conversant. He kept saying they had no right to put him in cuffs, and they had to let him go.

Pete and Martin escorted Tommy and Will to Homicide. They talked to the watch commander and placed Will in a locked room.

Once they had Tommy in the interview room, Martin removed the handcuffs.

Pete stepped outside the room and called Charlie Kasson. Charlie was the friend who, according to Ellsworth, accompanied Will when he went to see the horses. This second attempt to reach Charlie also failed. Pete was disappointed. Did Charlie possess critical information? He left a message, again asking Charlie to call ASAP. Then he returned to the interview room.

With audio and video equipment recording everything, Pete said, "State your name, date of birth, address, and phone number."

"I'm Thomas Patrick Wells." Tommy rattled off his date of birth, address, and phone number, then added, "This is *crazy*. I didn't do anything!" He squirmed the whole time. First he pulled one pant leg down, then the other. He rearranged his shirt, repeatedly. He fidgeted with his watch, and his wedding ring.

"Relax, Tommy. We just want to ask some questions," Pete said.

"Then why did you drag me here in handcuffs?"

"Family is important to me, Tommy. I get the impression it's important to you, also. Am I right?"

Tommy nodded.

"Please verbalize your answers, Tommy."

"Yes, family is very important to me."

"I know you and your sister were close, Tommy. Emma's friends said you were wonderful to her."

Tommy stared silently at his hands.

"I get the impression you and Will are also close."

Tommy nodded, then said, "Yes."

"It looks like you and Will spend a lot of time together. Do you?"

"Yes."

"That gives you plenty of time to talk, doesn't it?"

"Of course."

"You probably share a lot of things, don't you?"

"Yeah."

"Did Will agree that the move to assisted living was the worst possible thing for Emma?"

"Yes, because it was."

"Will's wife told us he wouldn't listen when she tried to talk to him about it. Did she tell you that, too?"

"No." Tommy shook his head.

"She said for that reason she thought he agreed with Ginny. Did you think that?"

"Hell no! He agreed with *me*." Tommy pointed his thumb at his chest.

"So both of you were furious with Ginny."

"I'd say angry. I wouldn't say furious." Tommy's biceps tightened.

"After what happened, I could understand being furious," Pete continued.

Tommy shrugged. "I was angry. Furious is too strong."

"I also understand being angry enough to lash out without thinking. Is that what happened, Tommy?"

"I didn't hurt Ginny! I would *never* lift a hand against a woman!"

"Come on, Tommy. She killed your sister."

"But I didn't kill her! That wouldn't bring Emma back!"

"Will would do anything for you, wouldn't he, Tommy."

"Yes." Tommy nodded.

"Why did you ask him to run, when you saw us at your house?"

"I didn't. I *begged* him to stop. I was afraid he was going to kill one or both of us." Tommy sighed.

"Why didn't he listen? Why wouldn't he stop?"

"I don't know." Tommy shook his head, emphatically.

"You didn't ask him?"

"I asked. He said he couldn't talk. He said he had to concentrate on driving."

"How many hours were you together today?" Pete asked.

"I don't know. Five, maybe six?"

"How many hours have you spent together since Thursday?"

"Ten? Twelve?"

"With all that time together, Will must have told you what was on his mind."

"I talked about what I was thinking. So did he, if that's what you mean."

"And one of those things was that he might have to run, wasn't it?"

"No, I don't think he planned to take off."

"He must have had a reason. Don't you agree?"

"I already answered that question. If he had a reason, I don't know what it was."

Now Martin took the lead. "When you were together, you talked about Thursday, didn't you?"

"Yes, we talked about what happened to Ginny on Thursday."

"What did Will say about it?"

"He couldn't believe it happened. He was so sorry that Ginny was gone. What else could he say? He didn't do it! Neither of us hurt her!" Tommy said, slamming his fist on the table.

The table jumped several inches off the floor.

"You'd do anything for Will, wouldn't you, Tommy?"

"Pretty much." Tommy nodded.

"Is that why you're lying to us, Tommy? Are you trying to protect Will?"

"I'm *not lying*!"

"Do you really expect me to believe you don't know why Will ran?"

"You don't have to believe it, but it's true."

"Why are you trying to protect him, Tommy?"

"I'm *not*. I'm telling the truth. You're barking up the wrong tree. Will and I are innocent."

Pete jumped back in the driver's seat. "Innocent? He ran. He took off down Roselawn, trying to escape. Does an innocent man do that, Tommy?"

"I don't understand why he did it. I do know he didn't hurt Ginny. He swore he didn't hurt her."

"When did he swear that, Tommy?"

"When he called on Friday and told me what happened to her. He was crushed."

"But he knew you'd think he did it, huh? Is that why he thought he had to swear he was innocent?"

Tommy sighed deeply. He looked exasperated. "I don't know. Ask him."

"You talked to Will on Friday. You also talked to him on Thursday, didn't you, Tommy?"

"No! How many times do I have to tell you that?" Tommy's face turned beet red.

"You know we'll get access to your cell phone records, don't you?" Pete asked. "Any idea what will happen when they show you're lying, Tommy?"

Tommy stared silently at his hands.

"Answer my question, Tommy."

"Thing is, I'm not lying. I didn't talk to Will on Thursday. I'm tired of telling you that."

"You saw Ginny at the fair on Thursday, correct?"

"I already told you I did."

"You and Will talked to her, didn't you?"

"I didn't. Will said he talked to her Wednesday morning, but not after that."

"How did you know where she parked, Tommy?"

"I didn't know where she parked, until it was on the news." Tommy sounded annoyed.

"You met Will at the Como exit, didn't you?"

"No!"

"You wanted to punish Ginny for hastening your sister's death, didn't you? I can understand feeling that way, Tommy."

"No!" Tommy glared at Pete.

"What then, Tommy? She came to your ticket window and taunted you?"

"No. No. No!" A tear formed slowly in the corner of Tommy's eye.

"Explain it to me, Tommy," Pete said. "You're a logical guy. I want to understand what happened."

Tommy closed his eyes, and squeezed his head between his bear-paw-sized hands. He sat that way for a long time. Then he said, "For the hundredth time, I don't know what happened. How can I tell you, when I don't know?"

"Okay, Tommy, have it your way," Pete said. "As long as you're not going to talk, we're going to book you."

"I didn't hurt Ginny!"

"How did Will know where to find her?"

"I don't know," Tommy moaned.

"Take him to a holding cell," Pete told Martin.

"I swear, I didn't lay a hand on Ginny. I was angry with her, but I didn't touch her. You have to believe me."

"We can't believe you, if you don't give us something to go on. Tell us what happened, Tommy," Pete said.

"I don't know. I'm telling the truth. I swear I don't know what happened to her." Tommy stared pleadingly at Pete, then at Martin.

FORTY-NINE

Pete and Martin did a swap. They moved Tommy to the locked room occupied by Will, and took Will to the interview room where they'd questioned Tommy.

Pete removed Will's cuffs and told him to have a seat. With everything being recorded, he stated the date and time. He told Will to give his name, date of birth, address, and phone number.

Will did as instructed.

Pete Mirandized Will. Then he handled the first round of questioning. He started with, "What time did you speak with your uncle Tommy on Thursday?"

"On Thursday?"

"Yes." Pete nodded.

"I didn't talk to Tommy on Thursday. I didn't talk to him until Friday."

"Tell me how you spent your day at the fair."

"I already told you." Will glared at Pete.

"Tell me again, Will. I want to make sure I have it right."

"I saw Machinery Hill, and the Merchandise Mart. I spent time in the Grandstand."

"That's it?" Pete asked.

"Yup." Will nodded.

"How about the Beer Garden? Lots of us spend time there. You said you like to people watch. That has to be the best place for it."

"Yeah. I forgot about that." Will shrugged.

"How many beers did you drink that day?"

"I don't remember. Not many."

"What else did you forget to mention?"

"We stopped at food booths, stuff like that. Nothing special."

"What time did you get home?"

"I already told you." Will glowered. "Why are you asking me all the same questions?"

"Refresh my memory," Pete said.

"Around seven. Definitely before dark."

"You said you met your friends at the fair. Correct?" Pete asked.

Will nodded.

"Does that nod mean yes?"

"Yes."

"Care to change that story?"

"No." Will shook his head decisively.

"Do you think Charlie Kasson, Ron Hopkins, and Brian Ellsworth will be surprised to hear that?"

Will closed his eyes and shook his head.

"According to the three of them, they left their cars at your place, and you drove to the fair."

Will's face reddened.

"Remember leaving Ron and Brian at the Bandshell, when you and Charlie went to see the Clydesdales? We've been busy, Will. We know you've been lying. We have the goods on you. Give yourself a break. Start telling the truth. This is your last chance to cooperate and catch a break."

Will examined his hands.

"The trip from the Bandshell to the horse barn put you on the path to the Como gate, didn't it, Will?"

Still looking at his hands, Will's only answer was to raise and drop his shoulders.

"Couldn't be much more convenient, could it, Will? It put you there at the same time as your sister, didn't it?"

Again Will raised and dropped his shoulders without looking at Pete.

"We've spoken with a lot of people. You'd be surprised how much we know. You may want to consider your answers more carefully. For starters, we know you didn't get home until after dark."

"The traffic was bad. We left the fair way before dark."

Martin took over the questioning. "According to your friends, you left after dark. The sun was setting when you and Charlie rejoined the other two."

"We left before dark. I know we did. I don't know which of the guys told you it was after dark. They're wrong!"

"You lied about meeting your friends at the fair, not at your house. Why would we believe you now, Will?"

Will's attention again fixated on his clasped hands.

"We spoke with Ginny's friends. They gave us the story, regarding your mom and Ginny. They said Ginny was the only one who did anything to help your mother. They said you and Tommy just sat on the sidelines and criticized Ginny's efforts."

"We didn't sit on the sidelines. We did everything we could for Mom. Ginny was in the driver's seat. She made sure we knew that. If you want to know the truth, talk to Mom's friends." Will bit his lip, and shook his head.

"It seems believing those things puts you in the minority, Will."

"Everyone with a brain knows it's true!" Will stared through Martin.

"That's not what Ginny's friends told us."

"Of course not. Ginny dictated their opinions. All they knew was what she told them. It doesn't mean a thing."

"Why the change of heart, Will? Per your wife and daughter, you were solidly in Ginny's corner."

Will closed his eyes and propped his head on a hand.

"Answer my question, Will."

"I can't. I don't know the answer," Will mumbled.

Pete took the reins, again. "On Thursday, you told us you loved Ginny. That was a blatant lie, wasn't it?"

"No," Will moaned. "I did love her. We had our problems, but I always loved her." Will's eyes grew moist.

"Despite your love for her, things have been tense for months, haven't they, Will?"

Will shrugged.

"Is that a yes?"

"Yes," Will whispered. He avoided Pete's eyes, fixating instead on Pete's tie.

"Why did things change, Will?"

Will bit his lip so hard, it turned white.

"It was because of your mother, wasn't it?"

"Mom didn't do anything." Will's attention returned to his hands.

"It was because of what happened to your mother, wasn't it, Will?"

Will's fists clasped tight.

"Ginny killed your mother, didn't she, Will?"

"Yes!" The word shot from Will's mouth.

"It's hard to forgive someone, even someone you love, for something like that, isn't it?"

Will nodded.

"Did your mother love Ginny, even near the end of her life?"

Will nodded.

"I'll be right back," Pete said, exiting the interview room.

He returned a minute later, carrying several photographs. He set the crime scene photos on the table in front of Will and resumed the questioning, "How would your mother react to this, Will? How would she feel about what happened to her daughter?"

Will looked at the photos and broke down. Between sobs, he said, "She'd hate it! I hate it!"

"But your mother is in a better place. She understands the full picture, doesn't she, Will?" Pete asked.

"I hope so."

"Help us understand it, too. Did it start with Ginny having such a good time at the fair so soon after your mother's funeral?"

Will nodded, then said, "Yes."

"That's understandable, Will. I'd probably react the same way if Emma was my mother, and Ginny was my sister."

Will closed his eyes and hung his head.

"Tell me what happened, Will. What brought it to a head?"

"Tommy tried to call me. I didn't hear my phone. You already know that. He called Rachel, and she tried to reach me. Didn't get that call, either."

"Then how did Tommy connect with you?"

"He decided to text. I heard the notification. I read the message and called him."

"And?"

"He was crying. He saw Ginny, and it was more than he could handle. He couldn't stop crying. It broke my heart. I told him I'd talk to her. I didn't know what else to do."

"Then?" Pete asked.

"He said that would help. He said someone had to tell her it wasn't right. I told him I'd take care of it. He told me she went toward the Dairy Building. That's when I told the guys I wanted to see the Clydesdales. I figured I'd walk in that direction. Didn't think I'd see her. What were the chances? Charlie made it more difficult. He said he wanted to see the Clydesdales, too."

"What happened next?" Martin asked.

"Charlie started walking toward Cannes. It was the logical route to the Horse Barn, but kept us a block away from the Dairy Building. I had to do something, so I suggested we get a malt in the Dairy Building. It was the only way I could think of to change our route." Will clenched his fists and started sweating profusely.

After several seconds, Martin asked, "Did Charlie agree?"

"Yeah. When we got close, I saw Ginny and her friends exiting the Dairy Building. I wanted to talk to her, so I could tell Tommy I did as I'd promised." Will bit his lower lip, and closed his eyes.

"Then?" Martin asked.

"I told Charlie I needed to go to the head. Said I'd meet him near the malt window. He went into the Dairy Building, and I followed Ginny and her friends." Will sighed.

"And?" Martin probed.

"I wanted to get Ginny alone. I wanted to talk to her. I didn't want her friends butting in. She and her friends went down Judson, then took a left on Clough Street. I figured they must be heading for the Como exit. I was right. I decided to follow Ginny to her car. I knew she drove separately. She told me she was going to when I talked to her on Wednesday morning." Will wiped a hand across his face and on his pant leg.

"You followed them out the Como gate?"

"Yes. I got my hand stamped at the Como exit, so I could get back in. Ginny wore a bright pink shirt. She was easy to pick out. I hung back, so she and her friends wouldn't see me. Like I said, I wanted her to be alone when I talked to her. Ginny dropped her friends off at a bus, and walked to her car. All I wanted to do was talk. I wanted to tell her how mad I was at her. I wanted to tell her that Mom was barely in the ground, and she was carrying on with her friends. I wanted to tell her how much her actions hurt Tommy." Will sighed and stopped, as if the story ended there.

Pete nodded. "What happened next, Will?" he asked.

"As she approached her car, I hurried to catch her. I told her all of the things I already mentioned. She laughed. Ginny laughed at me. She said she was the only one who gave a damn about Mom. She said she knew it, and Mom knew it, too. She said Mom felt bad that I forced her to take full responsibility for everything." The tears pooled in Will's eyes began running down his cheeks. The last revelation dragged down the corners of his mouth.

"The more she talked, the angrier I got. She told me to live my life, and let her live hers. She turned her back on me. I was fuming. I grabbed her shoulder and spun her around. She laughed in my face. I don't know what came over me. While following her through the parking lot, I finished eating the corndog Charlie bought me on the way to the horse barn. Told him I didn't want one, but that never stopped Charlie." Will closed his eyes and shook his head.

"I should have thrown the damned thing in a trash bin. Just think, if I hadn't had that stick in my hand." Will's eyes closed, again, and his head dropped.

A minute later, he looked up and continued, "I didn't follow Ginny with the thought of killing or even hurting her. Ginny and I were close, until all of this stuff happened with our mom. When she laughed, I blew up. I raised my fist, and stabbed her with that stick. It was a knee-jerk reaction. I wanted to hurt her—until the stick went in. I couldn't believe it broke the skin. I couldn't believe it went in that deep. When it did, I gasped, 'Oh my God! What have I done?' All I wanted was to undo what I'd done."

Will took a deep breath and continued, "Ginny spun away from me, and the stick broke. She gasped. She looked astonished. Then her face went blank. She slid down the car behind her, and landed on the ground. I wanted to help her." Will's voice cracked. "I wanted to pull the stick out, but I couldn't see it. I knew it must have broken right at the surface of her stomach. The way she collapsed, blew out a long breath, and stopped breathing, I knew she was dead." Will broke down. Tears flowed silently, and his shoulders shook.

After a protracted pause, Martin asked, "What did you do next, Will?"

"At first I stood there, petrified. Then I ran. I was glad there were hardly any people in the parking lot. Even so, I figured I must look scared to death. I realized I had to compose myself. If I didn't, someone would see me and know what I'd done. I stopped running and got a grip. It took all of the strength I could muster, but I relaxed and put on a calm face. I walked back to the Como gate. I showed the stamp to the woman there, smiled and nodded. I knew I'd succeeded when she smiled and didn't say anything about the way I looked." Will sighed.

"Didn't Charlie wonder where you'd been?" Martin asked.

"Yeah. I told him I ran into a couple of friends. I said we started talking, and I couldn't get away from them. Said I was sorry for keeping him waiting so long. I said the other guys would wonder about us, and we'd better skip the horses. He agreed. We walked back to the Bandshell."

"How about the other guys?" Martin asked.

"I had to continue acting for them. My life depended on it. They knew I was rattled. I said it was because I was depressed about Mom. Guess they bought it. We left a short time later. That's the long and the short of it."

"Did you call 911?" Pete asked.

"No," Will moaned. "Like I said, I knew she died right away, because of the way her face went blank, and because I heard her final breath." Tears streamed down his cheeks with renewed vigor. "I bent over her and kissed her on the forehead. I told her I was sorry, and I loved her. Then I took off."

Pete knew from the reports that Will's sister survived long enough to reach Regions Hospital. Still, he saw no sense in making Will feel worse.

As the two investigators led Will out of the interview room, he locked his legs and said, "You didn't arrest Tommy, did you? The only thing he did was tell me he saw Ginny and how upset he was with her. You have to let him go. Please, don't arrest Tommy."

After Will was booked, Pete and Martin spoke with the district attorney.

It took some time and persuasion, but Tommy was released.

FIFTY

Pete pulled into his garage and walked through the backdoor. He hung the keys on the designated peg, went to the bedroom, and changed from his suit into jeans and a T-shirt. All the while, he thought about Martin's wife. He hoped Martin got some answers at Michelle's doctor appointment tomorrow morning. He hoped it was nothing serious. He knew how much Martin loved and depended on Michelle.

After several minutes, he put that aside and called Katie Benton.

When she answered, he announced, "Finished, except for the mountains of paperwork."

"You sound pleased."

"Major understatement."

"You also sound like you're feeling down."

"Right, again."

"Why, Pete? What happened?"

"I see so many cases that demonstrate anyone can become a murderer. Put the average person in the right set of circumstances, push the right buttons, and wham. These are people who'd never in their wildest dreams believe they could murder anyone. These are people who would never do it again. These are people whose lives are destroyed. It's depressing. Sometimes I wish I could wave a hand, and make it go away—let them walk."

"You just arrested a mass murderer, huh?"

Pete laughed and shook his head. "You're so understanding, Katie."

"Yes, that's probably my finest trait."

"Speaking of fine traits, have you seen any of the ads about the movie *Lincoln*? It looks really good. I just heard Lincoln delayed the end of the Civil War to gain passage of the Thirteenth Amendment."

"No kidding?"

"No, for real. The amount of arm-twisting and bargaining that went into passing the amendment is phenomenal. What amazes me is how Lincoln resorted to seemingly immoral tactics to achieve a moral goal. Do you want to see it?"

"Sure, if I get to sit next to you."

"I don't know. I'm happy to buy your ticket, but I hate it when you eat all my popcorn."

"There's a solution to that, you know, Pete."

"Oh? Lay it on me."

"Drown the popcorn in butter. Well, second thought, that may not work. As long as you're sitting next to me, I can wipe my greasy hands on your pant leg."

"Sounds like grounds for divorce." As soon as the words were out, Pete regretted the remark. Now it was too late to turn and run.

"Pete, are you serious about house hunting?"

"Yeah. I guess it's a chicken's way of asking the question."

"What question?"

"Do you enjoy torturing me, Katie?"

"Occasionally, but it goes both ways. Since Friday, I've wondered what you meant."

"I think it's a bad thing to say over the phone. Are you willing to put the crocheting away for a few minutes?"

"Oh, I don't know, Pete. I have to finish this before his first birthday."

"Sure, I understand."

"You understand I have to keep crocheting? Or you understand I'm giving you a hard time?"

"Which are you doing?"

"Both, I'm multitasking."

"Okay. I'll be there in about twenty minutes."

He wondered if he should change so he'd look more presentable. He decided against it. This was how he looked when he wasn't working. Love him or leave him.

Katie must have heard his car. She came down the front steps to meet him.

Pete bent down and kissed her.

"Did you have anything with that salad?" she asked.

"Guess I should have brushed my teeth."

"That wasn't a complaint. Come on in."

Pete reached down and grasped Katie's hand as they walked to the house.

He towered over her. In the living room, he put his hands on both sides of her face and said, "I want to ask you a question. I want you to think about it before you answer. I don't want you to regret your answer."

Katie peered into his eyes and held her breath.

"Katie, you know what my life is like. Can you cope with it—and me? Will you marry me, Katie? I love you. I want to spend the rest of my life with you."

A tear welled up on Katie's eyelashes, then rolled down her cheek.

Pete used a thumb to brush it away. "Does that mean no?"

"It means I thought you'd never ask. Yes, Pete, I'll marry you."

Pete took her in his arms, and sealed it with a kiss. Then a second . . . and a third.

Acknowledgments

My thanks to Don Gorrie, retired chief investigator, Ramsey County Medical Examiner's Office; Shane Clifton, paramedic, St. Paul Fire Department; Randy Villarreal, FEO, St. Paul Fire Department; Bob Pitts, EMS coordinator, St. Paul Fire Department; Jill Oliveira, Public Information Officer, Minnesota Bureau of Criminal Apprehension; Dr. Marc Conterato, emergency medical physician; Bill Martinez, assistant chief, St. Paul Police Department; Keith Mortenson, retired investigator, St. Paul Police Department; and Troy Peek, St. Louis Park Police Department. Errors in any of these areas are the result of my misinterpretation or misapplication of the information these people so generously shared.

Thanks to Beverly Summerbell, State Fair Information Booth volunteer who provided the trivia included herein; Deb Harper, Rick Winter, Gale Hawkinson, Ruth Krueger, Tara Kennedy and Marly Cornell for their proofreading and editorial expertise; Christopher Smith for being quick to share his computer and photographic expertise; and Matt Gorrie for designing the front cover.

Items Found on a Stick at the 2013 Minnesota State Fair

- Spaghetti and meatball dinner on a stick
- Deep fried Twinkies on a stick
- Deep fried candy bars on a stick (Snickers, Milky Way, Three Musketeers, Reese's peanut butter cups, Nut Goodie)
- Corndogs
- Double bacon corndogs
- Jalapeño cheese corndog
- Sweet corn corndog
- Pronto pups
- Pickle on a stick
- Grilled pork chop on a stick
- Chicken on a stick
- Chicken breast on a stick
- Hot dish on a stick
- Macaroni and cheese on a stick
- Breakfast lollypop (sausage in corn muffin batter, deep fried, served with maple syrup)
- Walleye on a stick
- Puff Daddy on a stick (Thai sausage wrapped in puff pastry)
- Lamb chop on a stick
- Salmon on a stick
- Chocolate-covered marshmallows on a stick
- S'mores on a stick
- Frozen fruit on a stick
- Buffalo on a stick
- Sirloin steak on a stick
- Belgian waffle on a stick
- Slice of key lime pie on a stick dipped in chocolate
- Deep fried olives on a stick
- Grilled shrimp on a stick
- Bacon-wrapped grilled shrimp on a stick

- Hawaiian dog (pineapple wrapped in ham and baked in pretzel dough) on a stick
- Pitchfork sausage on a stick
- Wine glazed deep fried meatloaf on a stick
- Cheese on a stick
- Granny's cheesecake on a stick
- Teriyaki chicken on a stick
- Chocolate covered cheesecake on a stick
- Tino's pizza on a stick
- Cheddar mashed potatoes on a stick
- Sweeties Delight (mashed sweet potatoes) on a stick
- Porcupine meatballs on a stick

Northwoods salad (mozzarella cheese, grape tomatoes, dressing chilled wild rice) on a stick

- Nut rolls (peanut, pecan, cashew) dipped in chocolate and served on a stick
- Taffy pop on a stick
- Hot dog wrap (hot dog in a wrap, deep fried) on a stick
- Poncho dog on a stick
- Caramel apples on a stick
- Cajun seasoned alligator sausage on a stick
- Tater tot hot dish on a stick with cream of mushroom dipping sauce
- Ice cream on a stick
- Hot dago on a stick
- Stick in the mud (white, milk, dark chocolate covered pretzel)
- Pancake battered maple sausage on a stick
- Cajun steak and chicken on a stick
- Fudge on a stick
- Bacon on a stick
- Cotton candy on a stick
- Whole dill pickle on a stick
- Espresso on a stick cookies and biscottis

- Vegetable kabob style on a stick
- Mango on a stick
- Italian sausage on a stick
- Batter dipped deep fried fruit on a stick
- Chicken nachos on a stick
- Bacon wrapped turkey tenderloin on a stick
- Fried Swiss cheese on a stick
- Fried jalapeno pepper cheese on a stick
- Catfish on a stick
- Frozen bananas on a stick dipped in chocolate and rolled in nuts
- Strawberries on a stick dipped in chocolate
- Strawberries and bananas on a stick dipped in chocolate
- Sliced ice cream on a stick dipped in chocolate and rolled in nuts
- Lo mein and chicken on a stick
- Scotch eggs on a stick (hardboiled egg wrapped in sausage, rolled in bread crumbs, deep fried)
- Scotch meatball on a stick
- Lobster on a stick
- Scallops on a stick
- Italian style chicken on a stick
- Pepperoni and cheese super stick dipped in a garlic batter and deep fried on a stick
- Lamb kabob on a stick
- Beef kabob on a stick
- Gyro on a stick
- Stuffed grape leaves on a stick
- Twisted Sister on a stick (Italian Sausage wrapped in bread stick dough)
- Pappa Pup on a stick (flour-battered, deep-fried hot dog)
- Steak dinner on a stick
- Texas tater twister and sweet potato (spiral cut potato on a stick)
- Foot long pizza on a stick
- Cheeseburger on a stick

- Sausage on a stick
- Pretzel dog on a stick
- Cookies & cream wonder bars—hand cut ice cream bars dipped in chocolate on a stick
- Frozen bananas and cheesecake dipped in chocolate on a stick
- Frozen grapes on a stick
- Pineapple on a stick
- Oranges on a stick
- Cherries on a stick
- Ostrich on a stick
- Pork and cabbage egg roll on a stick
- Tornado potato (spiral cut potato on a stick)
- Deep fried chocolate chip cookie dough on a stick
- Fudge puppies (a Belgium waffle on a stick dipped in Swiss chocolate)
- Super Dogs batter-dipped, deep-fried hot dogs on a stick (6", 12", 18")
- Baby potatoes on a stick
- Virginia Green

89424448R00143

Made in the USA
Lexington, KY
28 May 2018